NEPTNE'S
CHILDREN

Bonnie Dobkin

Walker & Company

New York

Thank you to Erin Murphy, my wonderful agent, and to all of the fantastic folks at Walker Books for Young Readers who made this book a reality. Particular thanks to Emily Easton, who knew just what the story needed, and to Mary Kate Castellani, who watched over the manuscript every step of the way.

First published in the United States of America in 2008 by Walker Publishing Company, Inc.
Distributed to the trade by Macmillan

For information about permission to reproduce selections from this book, write to Permissions, Walker & Company, 175 Fifth Avenue, New York, New York 10010

Library of Congress Cataloging-in-Publication Data
available upon request
ISBN-13: 978-0-8027-9734-6 • ISBN-10: 0-8027-9734-2

Visit Walker & Company's Web site at www.walkeryoungreaders.com

Book design by Nicole Gastonguay
Typeset by Westchester Book Composition
Printed in the U.S.A. by Quebecor World Fairfield
2   4   6   8   10   9   7   5   3   1

For Jeff,
my husband and best friend

For the real O'Bannion Boys:
Bryan, Mike, and Kevin

And for Allen Bierman (my Acie),
my brother and my hero

ISLES OF WONDER
THEME PARK
Selected Attractions

PROLOGUE

The plague struck like a snake, silent and deadly.

Its designers had been patient, planning their attack with meticulous care. First, their scientists developed a virus that, once unleashed, would work within hours, giving its victims no time to respond. The virus was stored in small canisters, each with a timing mechanism programmed to open the container on a given date, at an exact hour. The canisters themselves were then hidden in the ventilation systems of buildings, on the undersides of airplanes, inside the walls of water towers.

At the same time, the leaders of this invisible war inoculated their own people, shielding them from the plague that soon would sweep over their enemies. When the end of the world came, they told each other solemnly, only the righteous would remain.

So on the day the virus was released—from tens of thousands of locations, all at the same moment—the war was over before anyone was even aware it had begun. People dropped in the streets, collapsed behind the wheels of cars, fell unconscious in the fields, and slumped forward in desks and cubicles. They died while cooking dinner, while watching TV.

But those who had engineered the plague hadn't truly understood what they had created. It spread so fast, and was so deadly, that it crept across oceans and continents with the speed of nightfall. And it mutated so frequently that even the safeguards and vaccines didn't work. The architects of the plague fell as quickly as their enemies.

And the third thing no one had counted on: the plague killed all of the adults. But it left the children.

CHILDHOOD ENDS

Isles of Wonder had been envisioned as the ultimate theme park: the biggest, best, and most awe-inspiring of them all. The crown jewel of the Wonder World Resort, its thousand acres rose from the middle of a huge, picture-perfect lagoon, which was connected to the nearby ocean by a wide meandering channel.

The park itself was actually a cluster of five islands, each its own distinct world. The central island, Atlantis, was a glittering kingdom of sand and shells that looked as though it had risen from the depths of the ocean. It had been built higher than the rest, so that its magnificent Palace, one of the most photographed buildings in the world, would be visible from everywhere in the park. The Palace had the shape and brilliant colors of living coral, its glittering spires tapering to thin, impossibly delicate points.

Near the top of the Palace, from a balcony molded to resemble a chariot pulled by sea horses, the animatronic figure of King Neptune emerged four times a day to thrust his trident out over his empire and greet the cheering crowds who gathered in the Palace courtyard. Then, to the delight of the spectators, the reflecting pool across from the Palace erupted in flames, and from the fiery waters would rise a serpent, or a chorus of singing sea nymphs, or the twisting, tentacled Kraken, each paying homage to their King.

The other four worlds—linked to Atlantis by wide, arced bridges—were no less magical. The one to the southwest, Enchanted Island, was a favorite of younger guests, a land of sweet whimsy and mild wicked-witch frights. There, visitors could stroll down Animation Alley or travel in jeeps, in miniature boats, or on flying carpets through scenes from their favorite fairy tales, TV shows, and movies. Just to the north was Timescape Island, where disparate lands and time periods flowed together seamlessly. The Lost World—a lush, prehistoric jungle inhabited by huge dinosaurs and giant apes—was just a short walk from the Ancient Cities and Roman Coliseum. Those, in turn, morphed into the Heart of Africa and the Barbary Coast, with its six-times-daily pirate battles.

Guests with an eye to the future took the southeast bridge to Inspiration Island and its incredible, visionary attractions. At every intersection, genial robots greeted visitors and ushered them to SkyTown, where "flying" cars zipped by cluster homes in layer-cake neighborhoods, or toward the Exploratorium, where the latest in technology was always on display. Guests could also visit the huge, working BioPods, which replicated what self-sustaining space colonies might look like, climb the moving sculptures in the Kinetic Playground, or talk to holographs of fictional and historical figures in the silver-paneled Holodome.

The final world was Nightmare Island, where it was permanently Halloween. Visitors who had overdosed on the bright colors and wholesome entertainment on the rest of the Islands could wander past an ominous, iron-fanged gate to visit the central city of Necropolis, or venture up the Haunted Hill to where Dracula's Castle peered down from just beyond the Howling Forest. Not surprisingly, this Island was most popular with teenagers.

Despite its size and complexity, the huge park ran flawlessly. Its atomic power station was actually a government-subsidized prototype for cities not yet built—it could generate electricity for years using a minimum of resources, including the waste that visitors were always providing in abundant supplies. And an elaborate computer management system controlled everything on the Islands, from the lights to the rides to the recycling plant. The minimal human staff liked to joke that people were almost unnecessary.

With its perfectly imagined attractions and state-of-the art engineering, nothing would ever stop Isles of Wonder from being, in the words of its founders and the prayers of its stockholders, "the most magical place on earth."

And nothing ever did. Until the plague.

The horror began quietly, almost imperceptibly. As children laughed on the rides, wandered through souvenir shops, or stared at the audio-animatronic figures, parents and older siblings began stumbling as they walked, or collapsed beside them on the rides, or slumped on the park benches where they waited patiently for family members who had more energy than they. And then the panic started, the screaming, the mad rush for the exits. People swarmed onto the ferries, stormed the monorails. Some even leaped into the lagoon, trying desperately to leave the insanity behind them.

But it all happened too fast. The four ferries, which for years had tirelessly transported passengers between the mainland and Atlantis, now crashed into the far shore, the nightmares on board no different than the ones taking place on the Islands. The monorails managed to make one last circuit on the double tracks and reach the final exit, but when their doors slid open, only a few people staggered off, some collapsing before they cleared the opening. And since the doors wouldn't close on the bodies of the fallen, the monorail remained where it was, its gentle mechanized voice asking passengers to please clear the doorways.

Within an hour, no one was running. Within three more, the

only sounds on the Isles of Wonder were the moans and sobs of those who remained. And the soft hum of rides that waited patiently for passengers who would never board.

The sun set, rose again, and set. The survivors began to move, forced by hunger and thirst to roam the Islands, searching out the restaurants and concession stands that held the previous day's supplies of food. A few, some animal instinct kicking in, guarded the supplies they found like starving dogs, refusing to let others come near.

Slowly, small groups began to form. Older children automatically took charge of younger ones, and weaker kids attached themselves to those who seemed stronger. Everyone tried to figure out what to do next. Some climbed to the top of the coaster mountains, using them like crow's nests to see as far into the distance as possible. Others gathered on the beaches of the lagoons, staring across the water for the rescuers who were sure to be coming for them.

But no help materialized. All anyone could see were the tall poles that marked the parking lots, or, at night, the now-empty shells of the resort hotels that ringed the lagoon, or glowing halos from distant towns where electric lights blinked on at preprogrammed times. But there was no movement—not a car, not a plane, not a person. And what made it all even eerier was that everything looked so utterly peaceful, so completely unchanged. Except for the bodies lying on the ground around them.

Josh sat motionless near the edge of the lagoon, his mind empty. His eyes were wide open, but he didn't see anything. Sun warmed his skin, but he couldn't stop shivering. And when a thought tried to enter his head, his mind skittered away like a terrified rabbit.

Like the others, he had been wandering around the Islands in a near-trance, his body forcing him to do the minimum he needed to stay alive. Find a bite of food. Take a sip of water. He probably couldn't have done even that, except for his little sister, Madeleine.

The trip to the park had been the family's special present to her. Maddie had been battling leukemia since she was four, enduring endless treatments, from chemo to radiation to bone marrow replacement. Josh, six years older than his sister, had changed overnight from the eternally annoyed older brother to her special friend and fiercest protector. He played games with her when she couldn't get out of bed, put on puppet shows with her stuffed animals, helped feed her when she was too tired to lift a fork. Somehow he felt that if he stayed near her, nothing could ever steal her away.

And then, one day, about three years after the treatments began, a beaming doctor announced that the cancer was officially in remission. As soon as the laughing and weeping and hugs had subsided, the whole family—his mom, his dad, and his sixteen-year-old sister, Caitlyn—decided to celebrate Maddie's return to health with a special trip.

"Where do you want to go, Maddie?" their mom had asked, though all of them already knew the answer.

"Isles of Wonder," Maddie shrieked, bouncing with excitement. "Isles of Wonder!"

"Yeah!" said Caitlyn, jumping up and down next to her sister and calling on her experience as the high school's loopiest cheerleader to support Maddie's cause:

Isles of Wonder!
Isles of Wonder!
We want to go
To Isles of Wonder!
Ya-a-a-a-ay, team!

Josh and his dad looked at each other, shrugged, and joined in, the four of them creating a small earthquake in the family room.

Isles of Wonder!
Isles of Wonder!
We want to go
To Isles of Wonder!

Maddie stopped bouncing and stomped over to their mother. "And we want to go *right now!*"

Their mom had stretched out her arms and bowed low before Maddie. "Yes, Princess Anemone," she said, referring to one of the more popular Island characters. "Your wish is my command."

They'd all laughed, and Josh's mom had jumped online and made reservations. Luckily, since it was early February and the off-season, the hotels were wide open; just two weeks later the whole family was getting off the monorail and running up to the gates of Atlantis.

Their first two days at the park had been truly magical. They all reveled in Maddie's excitement, hugging each other as she danced ahead of them from shop to shop and ride to ride. And since the lines were almost nonexistent at this time of year, they happily indulged her compulsion to visit every attraction at least three times.

In Atlantis, they explored the Living Ocean, laughing at the Peanut Butter and Jellyfish show, then gliding on a moving side-walk through an acrylic tube and into the huge undersea bubble where rainbows of fish and solemn sea turtles swam around and above them. In the Ancient Cities, they sailed on a barge through an Egyptian pyramid, shrieking as they were stalked by lurching mummies and vicious tomb raiders.

But Maddie loved the thrill rides best, the ones she'd never been strong enough to go on before. Josh himself had proudly been the one to accompany her on her first roller coaster, the Tsunami, his arms wrapped tightly around her as she screamed her way through its loops and tunnels and sea-spray archways. But then he'd stood contentedly outside the loading area as she went on again and again, first with their mom, then with their older sister, and finally with their father, who dared her to ride with her arms raised in the air.

Now Josh and Maddie were the only ones left.

At first, like thousands of others, Josh had crouched next to his family, screaming for help as he watched each of them twitch and shudder where they lay, then grow more and more still. When it was over, he had simply run, stumbling aimlessly around the park, dragging Maddie roughly by the hand and searching for an escape from the madhouse.

Finally, he returned to stare at the ones he had loved most in the world. His mom lay next to Caitlyn, one hand resting on the girl's cheek as though still trying to comfort her. His dad had collapsed just a few steps away, looking like a bad wax replica of the big man who had cheered on Josh and Caitlyn at a hundred sporting events and school shows, never allowing Maddie's illness to compromise his attention to his other two children.

This isn't real, Josh thought. It can't be. He continued to stare, waiting for the flicker of an eyelid, the twitch of a finger.

There was nothing. And so, still not really believing, he gently moved his family to a protected, shady spot under a beautiful old fiberglass cypress tree. He covered them with blankets from one of the souvenir shops, picked some nearby flowers and laid them on top. Then he sat next to them, Maddie shivering by his side, and they cried.

Eventually, they slept, terror and grief overwhelming them. Around them, the rides and attractions shut down section by section, responding to some automatic timer that had been designed to conserve energy as each area was vacated by the departing crowds. They slept long past sunrise, their eyes refusing to open to the world that was waiting for them.

But finally they did wake, and soon melted into the silent, shambling stream of survivors looking for food and drink at the concession stands. After a bite or two, they lost their appetites again and made their way to the lagoon. There they waited, looking dully out over the water, astonished that there was still sunshine and birdsong and gently lapping waves.

Maddie curled up on the sand next to her brother and went to sleep. Josh retreated to a dark place in his mind. Hours melted past.

An electric shriek split the air. Josh jerked upright, looking frantically around him. All he saw were other survivors blinking in shock, faces tight with terror. There was a crackle of static and a low, steady hum. And finally, from the top of the Coral Palace and thundering from every loudspeaker, came a voice.

"EVERYONE ON THE ISLANDS. IF YOU CAN HEAR ME, COME TO THE PALACE."

It was the voice of King Neptune.

KING NEPTUNE

"Maddie. Wake up."

The little girl moaned softly, pulling one arm up over her head. Josh shook her gently, and then more roughly.

"C'mon, Maddie. I need you to wake up."

This time she didn't respond at all, other than to draw her knees up to her chest.

"EVERYONE ON THE ISLANDS. IF YOU CAN HEAR MY VOICE, COME TO THE PALACE."

Maddie twitched awake, and she sat up, wild-eyed.

"Daddy?"

Josh put a hand on her shoulder.

"No, Maddie. It's not Dad. It's ..." He looked toward the Palace. "It's King Neptune."

All around them, other children were slowly rising from the ground, pulling younger ones up by the hand, looking at one another in bewilderment. Then, a few small groups stepped tentatively onto the painted brick paths that led to the Coral Palace. The rest soon followed, not speaking, eyes glued to the spires that sparkled against cloudless blue skies.

Josh fell into step next to a thin, brown-haired girl around his own age who had been sitting nearby for the past day. She didn't look like someone who would willingly come to the Islands. She was wearing a short black top and ripped jeans, and her bloodshot eyes were rimmed with the streaked remains of thick black eyeliner. She also had maybe ten ear piercings and a navel ring. But, like Josh, she was watching over a younger child, a boy around five years old.

Suddenly he realized she was looking at him. Looking at him looking at her.

"Got a problem?" she asked. Josh felt like she'd caught him peeping at her through a window.

"No," he said, flushing. "No problem." He immediately felt ridiculous. Right. There was no problem at all. Except that everyone was dead.

Neptune's voice thundered again from the Palace, and the girl's attitude dropped away.

"Who do you think it is?" she whispered. "Think there are some adults left?"

Josh shook his head. Given what lay all around, it didn't seem likely.

A kid behind them, a chunky, dark-skinned boy, added his opinion. "At least it is not a recording," he said, a slight accent coloring his perfect English. "A recording would not know what to say." He glanced up at the towers, then moved a little closer to Josh and the girl.

"Is it all right if I walk with you?"

They nodded.

"I am Hamim," he said.

"Josh."

The girl hesitated, as though afraid of giving something away. Then she shrugged. "Zoe." They walked on for a moment before Josh took a breath and asked the necessary question.

"Anyone with you, Hamim?"

"No," the other boy said softly. "Not anymore."

It didn't take long for them to reach the exquisitely manicured courtyard that stretched out from the Coral Palace and surrounded the reflecting pool. Thick green bushes in sunken planters had been sculpted to look like dolphins and sea serpents rising from the waves, and the stone and glass pathways sparkled with swirling mosaics of green and blue—except where the hideous heaps and still forms spoiled the perfect design.

Josh looked around, noticing things clearly for the first time in days. A sea of kids, maybe three or four thousand, stood silently on the pavement, staring up at the Palace. Even that large number didn't seem like much, not in a park that on a peak day could hold sixty thousand visitors, as well as all the staff.

Josh got a hollow feeling inside, looking at them. None of the kids appeared to be much older than he, maybe thirteen or fourteen at most. A lot of the others were merely toddlers, and he could see whimpering babies being cradled in Snuglies by exhausted brothers and sisters, or sleeping in the whale-shaped strollers that were supplied by the park. Some of the younger kids were fidgeting; others stood unmoving, sucking on their thumbs and staring at nothing.

They all looked so helpless.

The speakers shrieked again, and everyone jumped.

"Jeez!" said Zoe. "Where's that coming from?"

Josh scanned the side of the Palace, and a flicker of movement caught his attention. He pointed.

"There," he said.

About three quarters of the way up, on the balcony from which King Neptune normally addressed the park visitors, a slim, dark-haired boy had appeared. He looked like one of the older ones—maybe around thirteen. He was fidgeting with the mouth-piece of a headset. At each touch, static crackled through the air.

Finally, he stood still, looking out over the crowd.

"Hi."

The simple greeting was at odds with the voice, which some device in the sound equipment was altering to create the regal timbre of the ocean king. The boy himself suddenly seemed to realize how unsettling the sound was, and he disappeared inside the Palace. When he returned a few minutes later, his voice was still amplified, but the tone now matched his appearance.

"I'm Milo. My dad works . . . used to work in engineering. He was in charge of the sound systems here." He stopped, and even at this distance Josh could see him struggle to keep speaking. "I don't know what happened. I guess none of us do. But I think maybe it's time we got organized."

Josh heard a collective sigh come from the kids around him, then realized that he, too, had slumped in relief. Someone was taking charge. Finally.

"Anyone who wants to help—maybe all of us who are a little older, or who know how to do stuff—come meet in Neptune's Theatre. Just make sure all the little kids have someone to watch them, okay?"

The boy pulled something from his pocket and flipped it open with a twitch of his wrist. "My cell has 2:20. Let's meet . . . I don't know, around 3:00." The eyes of the assembled children stayed fixed on him. He stared back for a moment, then shrugged. "I guess that's it."

He stepped away from the balcony, pulling the headset off as he did, and disappeared into the Palace.

Josh continued to look up at the balcony for a several seconds, unutterably grateful to the unknown boy. For the first time since . . . since *it* happened, he felt a rush of energy. At least now there was something he could do.

He looked over at the brown-haired girl. "Zoe, would you watch Maddie? My sister? I want to go to that meeting, help figure out what to do."

She hesitated, looking off in the direction of the theatre. "I was going to ask you to take care of Sam. I want to go, too."

They eyed each other, neither willing to be the good guy. A few feet away, Josh saw the boy Hamim watching them. He gave Josh a sympathetic smile.

"I'll tell you everything," said Josh, returning his attention to Zoe. "I promise."

"Guys suck at listening. You stay with the kids, and I'll go."

But the little boy next to her began shaking violently. He grabbed at her shirt, eyes wild with terror, a cry erupting from him and building into a frenzied howl. Zoe's expression changed, mirroring her brother's terror. She dropped to her knees and threw her arms around him.

"Okay, Sam, okay, baby! Shh. I won't go anywhere."

The odd noise subsided, but Sam didn't let go of her. Zoe looked up at Josh, her face white. "Guess you've got a sitter."

Josh felt a little awkward, like he'd won something on a cheat. But Zoe clearly couldn't leave. He crouched next to his sister, taking both of her hands in his.

"You okay, Maddie?"

She nodded.

"Good. 'Cause I'm going to take care of you. Just like I always have. All right?"

She gave him a small smile, and the trust in her eyes ripped at his heart. She was such a brave little kid. He swallowed past a thick knot in his throat.

"The first thing I'm going to do is, I'm going to go talk to King Neptune. See if he can help us. All right?"

Her eyes widened. "You're going to talk to the King?"

"Yeah."

Her mouth opened slightly. Without another word, she nodded. Josh glanced again at Zoe. She'd been watching them, he realized, and her expression had softened, just a little. Josh turned Maddie around, gesturing toward the older girl.

"This is Zoe. She'll take care of you 'til I get back."

"Hi, Maddie," said Zoe, her voice suddenly gentle. She put her hand on her brother, who was again staring blankly ahead of him. "This is Sam. Sam, say hi." But the boy remained silent. Zoe stroked his head, her brow furrowed. Then she sighed, and got to her feet.

"Okay," she said to Josh. "I'll take them to find some food. We'll meet you back on the beach, where we were before."

"Thanks." But he still felt uncomfortable leaving.

"What are you waiting for?" asked Zoe, the flinty tone returning. "This offer has a time limit."

"Okay, okay. I'm going."

"Yeah, you are. But remember—you're going to tell me everything."

MILO'S VISION

Josh arrived at Neptune's Theatre, hurrying down one of five meandering walkways that funneled visitors toward the entrances. Sparkling jets of water leaped from side to side over the pavement, and at each of the entrances, liquid curtains rippled down towering, blue-tiled walls that curved up and away from the concrete path, giving the impression that the ocean had just divided in order to allow humans to enter.

Inside, the theatre was a huge half-circle stadium with dozens of long rows of seats stretching across its length and facing a deep pool. Behind the pool was a massive glass-brick wall that could project hundreds of background images and videos. Normally, the theatre was packed, every tier filled with families waiting to see the Seven Seas Spectacular, the park's hallmark musical production that combined human performers with dolphins and whales, dancing waters, and, at night, a laser show.

Today, though, the stadium was empty, except for the bodies slumped on the floor in front of some of the seats, and others lying in tangled heaps in the aisles and near the exits. Josh picked his way around them, refusing to look at the faces, staying focused on the dark shadows of dolphins gliding back and forth in the pool. Pretty, he thought, watching their smooth, shining backs breaking the water.

Toward the bottom of the arena, Josh could see the boy who had spoken from the balcony. Milo. He sat cross-legged on a small square of blue concrete that extended out over the pool, the platform from which the show's trainers usually signaled to the dolphins and whales. His head was bowed.

Josh moved down the stairs and stood in front of the platform, waiting for Milo to notice him. But the boy seemed deep in thought, sealed off from the world around him.

Josh cleared his throat.

"Hey," he said.

Milo's head jerked up, and he stared down at Josh. He was very thin, almost frail, and his long black hair flopped low on his forehead. But the eyes peering through the dark mop were startling, the pupils no more than pinpricks in pale blue irises.

"Hey," he replied.

"I'm Josh."

The boy nodded, but didn't say anything else for a few seconds. Then . . .

"So what do you think happened?"

Josh hesitated. "Some kind of gas?" he said. "Poison gas in the air?"

Milo shook his head. "Then we'd all be dead."

Josh thought a moment, pulling together scattered fragments of TV news reports and his parents' dinnertime conversations.

"Then some other kind of terror thing. Remember after the attacks a few years ago? When people were finding white powder in envelopes and shutting down buildings?"

"Biological warfare," murmured Milo.

"Yeah. Some kind of germ or something. A disease."

"Why didn't it get us?"

"I don't know."

They fell silent. Soon others began entering through the arena doors, glancing at each other warily before spotting Josh and Milo and heading toward them. Josh flicked open his cell. Almost 3:00. Not nearly as many had come as he would have thought—a couple hundred at most. Of course, a lot of them, like Zoe, had little guys to take care of. And the rest were probably still too shell-shocked to respond.

Those who did come filed down to the bottom of the stadium, settling in the first couple dozen rows. With few exceptions, no one sat too close to anyone else. It was as though everyone feared that whatever had struck down their families might still be hiding in the bloodstreams of those who remained.

Milo stood up on the platform. All eyes locked on him.

"Okay," he said. "Thanks for coming, everyone."

He scanned the crowd slowly, as though deciding how to begin.

"I know we've all been waiting to be rescued. But it's been a couple days, and no one's come for us. And it's not like there's bombed buildings or torn-up roads stopping them. So I figure that means the same thing's happened all over. No adults left."

Josh looked around to see a few heads nodding. A boy raised his hand.

"What about kids? There's gotta be tons of 'em out there, just like we're all here."

Milo nodded. "You're right. There must be. But has anyone been able to get in touch with anyone? Or maybe gotten a call?"

Josh looked around. No hands. He thought about his own frantic attempts to make contact. He'd hit every number on his speed dial, over and over. No one had answered. Shortly after that, the screen had begun flashing *Service Unavailable*. It had given Josh a sick feeling, like the world had disappeared.

"What about computers?" said another kid, a short, lumpy boy whose eyes popped wider when he spoke. "There must be a bunch in the offices here, or those, whaddya call 'em, those Guest Relations places. We could go online and find people that way."

"Good idea," said Milo. "What's your name?"

The boy hesitated, shooting a nervous glance at the small girl next to him. "Ted."

"But we call him Toad," said the girl immediately. "On accounta his eyes." The boy's face burned red.

"Hi, Ted," Milo said, emphasizing the name. The boy looked up gratefully. "Like I said, it's a good idea. Only I already tried it. All the big networking sites have already gone down. There's no IMs, no MySpace or Facebook—nothing. Everyone must've jumped on at once, crashed the system."

"Or," said a girl in the second row, absently thumbing the buttons on her cell phone, "maybe whoever did this wrecked the communication systems, too. That could've been part of the plan."

"What do you mean—?" He stopped, waiting for her name.

"Moira." She looked up from her phone, and Josh's jaw dropped. She was one of the prettiest girls he'd ever seen, with greenish-blue eyes and thick auburn hair that fell nearly to her waist. Milo looked equally impressed.

The girl continued.

"In every movie like this I ever saw, and in books, too, the first thing the enemies do is get control of the phones and news sites and broadcast systems. So no one can talk to each other. And so they can control what people hear."

Everyone digested this possibility. It makes sense, Josh thought, looking again at the girl. So . . . she was pretty *and* smart.

Milo scanned the crowd again, waiting for more ideas, but no one else spoke.

"All right. So we can't count on help from outside. Anyone out there is in the same shape we are. So whatever's going to happen next, it's up to us. Any ideas? I mean, what are our choices?"

One girl tentatively raised her hand.

"It's not school," said Milo. "Just talk. Maybe stand up and say your name first."

The girl's hand dropped, and she stood, looking around uncomfortably.

"I was thinking—"

"What's your name?"

"Oh. Sara." She took a breath. "I was thinking. Some of the rides in Atlantis have passenger cars that look like boats. And there are canoes and things like that on Timescape. We could try them out, see if they work, then maybe take turns going across the lagoon."

Josh pictured the colorful sailing ships on the Argonaut Adventure, thinking that each of the fiberglass boats probably weighed a few hundred pounds. Put them in the lagoon and they'd sail, all right. Straight to the bottom.

Milo responded quickly.

"Terrific," he said. "Great idea, Sara." Josh looked at Milo in surprise. But Sara was flushing with pride, and Josh kept his mouth shut. Milo knew exactly what he was doing.

Someone else didn't think so. Josh heard a loud snort, turned, and saw a group of boys clumped together a few tiers up. Two were unremarkable, sitting like slugs on either side of a bigger kid with short blond hair. The fourth, a skinny string bean with a faux-hawk and a pinched expression, sat just below them. Josh remembered seeing the four of them guarding one of the Snack Spots, crouched there like snarling pit bulls.

It must've been the bigger one who'd made the noise. The kid still had a smirk on his face, revealing big, crooked teeth that were at odds with his surfer-boy looks.

Josh looked up at Milo, who shook his head almost impercep-tibly. Ignore them, was the silent message.

"Okay," he said. "What else?"

A boy stood up, a muscular kid with an open, honest face who looked like he spent most of his time outdoors. Still, he flashed a nervous glance at the Clump before turning back toward Milo.

"I'm Greg. What if we just walked along the monorail tracks and got to shore that way? I think it's probably only a couple of miles."

"Three and a half miles," someone said.

Josh looked toward the voice. A girl with a shaggy mop of multicolored hair was standing. "I'm Micki. My dad worked on the monorail. It had a seven-mile circuit. So half of that in each direction."

"Okay," said Greg. "So that would work, right? I mean, it's a long walk, but we could do it."

But Milo was still looking at Micki. Josh, just a couple of yards away, could almost see gears shifting behind those odd blue eyes. Finally, Milo refocused. But something had changed in his expression.

"Listen. I was just thinking. I was here today because the park always gave passes to employee families to use on low-attendance days. Micki, same with you?"

The rainbow-haired girl nodded.

"So how many of us had parents or something who worked at the park?"

A couple dozen hands went up.

"What'd they do?"

A dark-skinned girl stood. "I'm Paravi. My uncle was in trans-portation, like hers." She pointed at Micki. "But he did the trams and Segways inside the parks."

Now others were getting to their feet.

"I'm Alex," said a boy with an English accent. "My mom was on the theatre crew. She helped with the big production numbers."

"My dad worked in food service," announced another kid, who said his name was Eli. "Ordered stuff for all of the Snack Spots."

More and more kids jumped to their feet, shouting out their parents' jobs and status in the park. One boy, wearing a Choppa Brotha T-shirt, scrambled up on one of the seats, waving his arms and shouting.

"Yo! Check it out! I got all you losers beat!"

"Yeah?" grinned Milo. "Who're you?"

"Evan. My mom's one of the Visioneers." From a collector's book at home, Josh knew that this was the trademarked name for the engineer-visionaries who designed the rides and other attractions. The boy's face glowed with pride. "She's worked here for nine years, so I always know about stuff that's coming. Like, she was just telling me that they're working with Hiro Omati—you know, that movie director?—to design this new Teleport ride—" He stopped, reality clawing through his excitement. His face crumbled, and tears began flowing down his cheeks. Slowly, he sat down again.

"It's okay, man," said Milo softly. "It's okay."

There was an awful silence. The excitement that had temporarily animated the others seemed to vanish. They shrank into themselves, staring at the concrete. Josh felt his own enthusiasm drain from him and leave him shivering.

Milo's voice pushed through the sludge of grief.

"Hey," he said. "This isn't going to do us any good." He paused. "Besides, I have an idea." A few at a time, the others looked up.

"Okay. Here it is. We don't know what's out there. But we can probably guess. And it's going to get bad, and then a lot worse."

"Why?" someone asked. "Why's it any different out there?"

"Think about it," said Milo. "People who came here came with families, or on school trips or something. Good people. But out there, it's everyone. Like maybe kids who'll beat the crap out of you just for the fun of it."

Josh shot a glance at the Clump. I think we've got a few of those in here, he thought. But Milo had a point. Outside, it could already be like one of those end-of-the-world movies: packs of kids roaming like wolves, preying on anything weaker.

"Plus, the Visioneers built the Islands to work without any power or anything from the outside. So for a while, at least, things here are going to keep running." Milo's words were coming faster and faster. "And there are probably enough supplies to support us for a long time. All the restaurants, the concession stands—"

"And all the food prep facilities," said Eli. "I know there are big kitchens somewhere, and warehouses where they store the food—"

"There's the gardens and stuff, too."

Josh looked behind him. One of the kids who had been standing was still on her feet. She was almost as pretty as Moira, but tiny, like a doll, with short raven hair and almond-shaped eyes.

"I'm Aiko," she said, her voice light and happy-squeaky. "In the BioPods, there are the hydroponic gardens—gardens that grow with just air and water. All kinds of fruits and vegetables and stuff. My dad was one of the horticulturalists. Things are always being planted and harvested. There are some animals, too. Chickens and geese, some goats for milk. A lot of the stuff for the Inspiration restaurants came straight from there."

"And we've got fish," said someone else. "All the stuff in the Living Oceans, and I think the lagoon is stocked. Plus, they need little fish to feed some of the big fish, right? There must be tanks full of them."

Milo kept nodding, energy radiating from him. "See? Everything we need, if we can just get things organized."

Possibilities crackled through the audience. Josh felt his own heart racing. Milo was right. They could build their own world here. A perfect one, maybe better than the old one, with everyone getting along.

The big blond kid from the Clump suddenly stood, arms folded, and glared at Milo. One by one, his companions got to their feet, and their combined menace drew all eyes to them.

The happy buzz died, and Josh's insides turned to water. But Milo looked steadily at the other boy, his expression unchanged.

"Something wrong?" he asked.

"Yeah, something's wrong. I don't think I like you telling everyone what to do."

Milo nodded. "Okay. So what's your name?"

The question seemed to take the big kid off guard.

"Huh?"

"I just asked what your name is. So we can talk."

The boy frowned. "Caleb."

"Hi, Caleb. And your boys?"

Caleb hesitated, then poked a thumb at the skinny kid. "This is Farrel. And those're Kurt and Willard." Milo smiled, but the smile didn't travel above his lips. His unblinking eyes remained fixed on Caleb, who shifted uncomfortably.

"Okay, Caleb. Here's the thing. I think we're all just trying to figure out what to do here. But we'll decide together, and no one'll have to do anything they don't want to. Unless you've got a better idea?"

He waited. Caleb didn't say anything.

"Maybe later," said Milo. He stared at Caleb a moment longer, then switched his attention back to the larger group. Caleb stood awkwardly for a few seconds, then spat on the ground and lowered himself back into his seat. The rest of his Clump looked confused but followed his lead.

"So," Milo continued. "Let's get started. Everyone who had someone who worked in the park, come down front so we can find out what we know about this place. And then we need some volunteers to go through the different Islands and find out what kinds of supplies we have. Food, clothes, that kind of thing. And maybe—"

"Wait." Josh stood, images from the last two days seeping into his mind. He walked over to Milo, motioning him closer. The other boy leaned down, and Josh's voice dropped to a whisper. "There's something else we have to do first."

NIGHT CREW

As Milo listened intently, Josh finally put into words what, until that moment, he hadn't let himself think about. Something had to be done with those who had died. Like him, most of the survivors had tended to their families as best they could. But he had read enough books and seen enough movies to know what would happen if nothing more was done.

Milo's pale face went even whiter as he listened. But he nodded. "Okay," he said, his voice as quiet as Josh's. "You're right. But we can't just—we can't just start digging holes or something. Everyone'll go crazy. We've got to find just a few people who can handle it and figure something out."

The crowd was beginning to murmur nervously. Milo raised a cautionary finger to Josh, then stood again.

"Okay. Like I was saying. We've got to get control of the supplies before everyone just goes in and starts wasting stuff or stealing it all for themselves. We're gonna have to . . . what's the word, when you make sure no one takes too much at one time?"

"Ration?" said Eli.

"Yeah. We're gonna have to ration things until we figure out how to get our own food."

"I been thinking about that," said Evan, the son of the Visioneer.

He'd gotten his emotions under control and looked eager to erase the impression he'd made earlier. "What if we organize different groups to go to each Island, find all the food? Then we can use the guide maps to find what the biggest restaurant is and store it all there. Maybe set up guards."

"Good idea," said Milo. "Everyone who wants to look for food with Evan, join him over at the first entrance, up there." He pointed to the tunnel at the far right of the theatre. "Especially anyone like Eli who knows the concessions a little and can help figure out how to store things."

"I'll go, too," said Paravi. "They'll need to know where the trams and stuff are, so they can collect what they find."

"Right," said Milo, glancing briefly at Josh. "But then come back, okay? I need you for something else." Paravi's brow furrowed, but she nodded. Then she scurried after Evan, who was already heading up the stairway.

Milo looked back at the waiting crowd. "Okay. Now, what else do we have to do?"

Over the next couple of hours, everyone threw out suggestions. Moira, the pretty girl with the theory about the communication systems, recorded everything in a souvenir autograph book she'd retrieved from under one of the seats.

Moira had said, "I'm good with words and I'm seriously anal," as Milo and Josh noticed when the meeting first began. "Which means I'm a great note taker. I'll try to keep things organized."

"That'd be great," said Milo. He'd stared at her a moment, then glanced at Josh, raising an eyebrow. Josh grinned, returning appreciative eyes to Moira. As he watched, though, she ripped the first few pages out of the autograph book, and the glitter-ink signatures of Princess Anemone and Gilly Gollywog fluttered to the ground.

For just a moment, Josh imagined some little kid collecting the autographs, parents smiling nearby.

Under Milo's direction, the meeting was enormously productive. Together, they determined what the most critical jobs were. Then Milo began asking for volunteers to work on each task, his eyes automatically picking out those who had said they knew the Islands.

Some formed additional food teams. Others offered to look for clothes and blankets. A third group, headed by a tough, wiry girl named Chelsea who had come to the park with a troop of Canadian Girl Guides, agreed to search all the first-aid stations and collect bandages, ointments, and other medical supplies.

"What about the babies?" The voice was soft, scared, almost a whisper.

Everyone turned to look. The girl who had spoken was very plain and more than a little overweight. She wore a cheap, tropical-patterned shirt, and her dirty-blond hair was pulled back with a thick blue rubber band. But her eyes were gentle, and her plump arms were wrapped around a tiny boy who was sleeping on her lap. She ducked her head as attention shifted to her, as though speaking had used up whatever courage she had.

Milo smiled encouragingly. "Don't be scared. What's your name?"

"Lana," she said.

"Hi, Lana. Please tell us what you were going to say. It sounded important."

The girl took a breath. "The babies and toddlers. They could get sick real easy if we don't take care of them. And a lot of them don't even have brothers or sisters left. Like this one. I found him crying by . . . by his parents."

Josh stared at the boy, thinking about all the little ones he'd seen wandering through the park. It hadn't really dawned on him that they might be alone. And there would be babies, too, like Lana said. Who would watch over them?

Milo was nodding. "You're right, Lana. We've got to figure something out. It's good you were looking out for them." He smiled at her again, and she blushed, her face and neck going blotchy. Josh was impressed by the exchange; Milo must've realized Lana was not the type of girl who was used to getting smiles from a boy. Or being noticed at all.

"So what do we do?" asked Milo, addressing the larger crowd. "Does anyone know how to take care of babies?"

A boy waved for Milo's attention. He had soft curly hair and dark eyes under heavy black eyebrows.

"I'm Ari," he said, before Milo could ask his name. "Maybe we could set things up like on the kibbutz where my aunt lives."

"What's that?"

"A kibbutz? They're like these little villages in Israel where everyone lives and works together and helps everyone else out. Anyhow, on my aunt's kibbutz, all of the little kids spend a few hours a day with parents, like at dinner and in the evenings. But the rest of the time, caregivers watch over them in nurseries. Even at night. What if we did something like that?"

"Makes sense," said Milo. "Maybe over on Enchanted Island. It's already aimed at the littler kids."

Ari offered to organize a group to locate the babies and toddlers, as well as to find some volunteers to take care of them. He'd even be one of them, he said. He'd always been a favorite with his little cousins. Milo thanked him, and Ari turned to Lana.

"You wanta help me?" he asked. Lana's skin went blotchy

again, and her eyes dropped. But then she nodded. What a good guy, Josh thought, as Ari sat down next to her.

As the minutes swept by, different work groups began to cluster, making plans. Milo whispered to Josh that now they could start picking out people to help with the last, most important job. Kids who appeared strong enough—both emotionally and physically—to deal with the unthinkable.

Josh immediately started looking for the kids who had spoken up during the meeting, or who showed some kind of leadership. Neon-haired Micki, for example, and the muscled kid, Greg, and even Ted the Toad, who seemed especially eager to help.

"Least I can do after you guys ignored my nickname," he said, eyes popping with gratitude.

Josh thanked him, wondering how long it would be until the nickname returned, and continued to search the crowd. He spotted Hamim walking toward him, one hand raised in a shy greeting.

"Hey," said Josh. "Didn't see you here."

"I came a bit later," the boy said softly. "I helped your friend Zoe with the little ones. The boy was causing problems for her."

Josh felt a stab of guilt.

"They are all right," Hamim reassured him. "And now, perhaps, I can help here?" It was a question, not a statement.

"You sure? You know what we're doing?"

"Yes." Hamim's solemn face grew even more serious. "That is why I want to help. I am Muslim. We believe in *akhriah*—in life after death—so it is important to me that those who have died are treated with honor." He swallowed. "Including my parents."

Josh tried to think of something to say. He simply nodded.

Nearby, Milo was talking quietly to the Clump, his expression earnest. Josh half expected Caleb to laugh in Milo's face, but to his surprise, he saw the big kid nod. Gesturing to his posse, he slouched over to a group of Milo's other recruits. Josh noticed that in addition to some obvious choices, like Moira, Milo had approached the kids who had been the most sullen or resistant during the earlier meeting.

"Why them?" Josh asked. "They're like my worst nightmares back at school."

"Exactly," said Milo. "So better to get them on our side."

The other work teams finally went off on their tasks, leaving the selected ones behind. They huddled together silently, no one really wanting to begin the discussion.

"So what do we do?" Milo asked finally. "Josh is right. If we don't figure something out, we won't be able to stay on the Islands."

"Couldn't we just . . . have funerals?" said Greg, his voice unexpectedly soft for a kid his size. "And maybe say prayers or something?"

Josh shook his head. "It'd be good if we could. But there aren't enough of us to do all the work. And on TV, it always shows them doing special things before the burial. We don't have whatever it is we need." There was a murmur of agreement, although several of the volunteers looked less certain. Then Caleb spoke.

"Why don't we just dump 'em in the lagoon?"

Josh stared. "What?"

"Dump 'em in the lagoon. I mean, they're dead. What's it matter?" Farrel snickered, his faux-hawk jiggling.

"No," said Hamim. "We can't do that."

"Why not?" Caleb glared at him, and Hamim flinched. A new voice interrupted.

"Because even the dead deserve respect." They all turned. The speaker, a tall, rail-thin boy named Seth, sat somewhat apart from the others. He had an unnerving stillness about him, as though he were tapped into something dark and secret. He stared hard at Caleb, his eyes black pools. Caleb tried to return the stare, but failed.

"Seth is right," said Milo, though he quickly turned away when the other boy's gaze shifted to him. "Besides, they'd just . . . float back. Eventually. And poison the water."

Silence followed his statement.

"What about funeral pyres?" said Moira, tapping her pen thoughtfully against her chin.

"You mean . . . fire?"

"People do it in other countries. It's a whole religious ceremony. So it's respectful. And then there's no disease."

"Maybe," said Milo, looking a little uncomfortable. "It's the best idea we've had so far, anyhow."

Hamim took a deep breath, and Josh could see he needed all of his courage to speak again. "I am sorry, but I must say this. Muslims do not believe in cremation. We believe the body is holy and must not be harmed, even in death."

"Buddhists, too," said Aiko. "We feel the same way."

Milo ran his hand back through his hair, thinking. "I wonder, though," he said. "Would anyone's religion think it was good to risk everyone getting sick instead?"

One by one, the others shook their heads.

"So maybe what Moira said is still our best choice."

No one disagreed this time. But Greg still looked troubled.

"What about the little kids?" he asked.

"What about them?" asked Milo. "Ari and Lana are going to take care of them."

"I don't mean that. I mean, what they're going to see and remember. Everything they've been through has been awful enough. We can't add another bad thing."

He's right, Josh thought, surprised again by the big kid's

gentleness. And not just because of the little guys. A lot of the older ones were hanging on to sanity by the thinnest of threads.

"Maybe I have an idea," came a girl's voice.

It was Sara, the girl who'd talked about sailing boats across the lagoon. She'd been one of Josh's picks. An unlikely choice, but he'd figured they could use her sweetness to offset some of the harder personalities.

"What we have to do," Sara continued, her eyes going soft, unfocused, "is make this into something . . . beautiful."

And then she told them what she'd been imagining—an almost poetically beautiful solution to a hideous problem, based on a movie she'd once seen. At first, there was only nervous laughter in response to what she said. But then, one by one, everyone agreed. Best of all, they had the right people to put the plan into action.

Paravi would handle the transport. Evan thought he could figure out the control board for the attraction they needed. And Moira, who said she'd probably read half the books in the world and always got A's in English, offered to write the speech.

That evening, Neptune gently told the Islanders that he would be taking care of their loved ones, that they no longer had to worry about what to do. Then the volunteers all set themselves to their tasks, most of which took place at night. In fact, they began to call themselves the Night Crew.

Josh was forced to ask Zoe to keep watching Sam and Maddie. Her face went red with irritation until she heard the reason; then she quietly agreed.

LAST FAREWELL

Three days later, just as the sun was setting, the voice of King Neptune once again floated over the Islands. It was quieter than on the first day. Warm and compassionate.

"My loyal subjects," it called. "Please come to Pirate's Cove. Wait for me on the shores of the harbor."

From a tower window in the Coral Palace, Josh watched as all but a few of the survivors once again obeyed the comforting voice of the King and made their way toward the Barbary Coast on Timescape Island. As he followed their progress, Josh noted with deep satisfaction how clean the grounds of the park were, the close-cropped grass and meticulously tended gardens empty of the victims of the plague, the makeshift graves smoothed over.

Surprisingly, hardly anyone had commented on the changes as section after section was attended to. Maybe, Josh thought, they'd all gotten so good at blocking out the horrors that they barely noticed when they vanished.

But he also knew that he and the rest of the Night Crew had done a good job, managing to do most of the work while the rest of the Islands slept. Paravi had led them to camouflaged storage sheds that housed the battery-powered passenger trams used in the park. Cheerful and efficient, she explained the controls, proving that the trams were no more difficult to drive than electric golf carts. So a handful of drivers, accompanied by the rest of the Night Crew, had been able to travel silently through the parks, gently gathering, loading, transporting.

Josh turned away from the window and called to Milo through a narrow doorway that led to the nearby control room.

"It's working," he said. "Almost everyone's going."

There was no answer.

Concerned, Josh peered into the room. Milo was staring sightlessly at the soundboard, his fingers wandering over the slides and dials.

"Milo?"

The other boy started, then looked over at Josh.

"You okay?" Josh asked.

Milo took a moment to focus, but then he smiled briefly.

"Yeah. Yeah, I'm okay. I was just thinking . . . I remember when my dad brought me here for the first time. Let me help him work the controls."

Josh had had similar thoughts the last few days, every time he looked at the digital camera his dad had ceremoniously bequeathed to him just before they left home. They'd spent a happy hour together, his dad explaining buttons and settings Josh knew he'd never use, the two of them taking pictures of everything from the inside of the refrigerator to his dad's left nostril.

"You guys were close, huh?"

Milo didn't answer. Then he seemed to flick off his emotions and went back to the business at hand.

"So you said they look ready at the Cove?"

Josh blinked at the shift in mood, but then he nodded.

"And we've seen flares from the other four locations, right?"

"Right. They're all ready. Just waiting for the signal."

"Okay," said Milo. "We'll just wait until it gets a little darker, so the lights have more of an effect." He smiled. "Moira's idea."

Josh wasn't surprised. She'd orchestrated most of what was about to happen.

"Anything else we need to do?" he asked.

"Not here. Why don't you head over to the Cove and see if Moira or any of the others need help. Then go be with Maddie."

"Thanks." Josh headed back through the door and toward the stairwell. Just before he reached it, Milo swung around the control room entrance.

"Hey, Josh?"

"Yeah?"

"You've been a big help. I just want to say thank you."

Josh beamed, feeling the same pride as when his parents used to praise his report cards. Then he hurried down the spiral staircase of the Palace tower, across the grounds of Atlantis, and over the arced bridge that led to the Barbary Coast. Once there, he ran toward the shores of Pirate's Cove. The beach and piers were completely filled with children, all peering curiously toward the center of the lake. There, two tall ships with billowing sails moved slowly away from the town, their course determined by tracks hidden under the water.

Normally, the ships confronted each other in fearsome mock battles, their two pirate crews fighting for the right to pillage the nearby town. They fired fake cannons, swung from ropes to their enemies' decks, and called out bloodthirsty threats, their ferocity underscored by thrilling background music.

Toward the end of the battle, plumes of fire shot from the hulls as each took a fatal hit. Then, to the comical moans of tubas and bassoons, both ships slowly sank into the cove, pirates leaping frantically from the decks. (The best part actually occurred a few minutes after the end of the show, when the boats rose again from the water and the pirates clambered back on board, waving happily at the remaining audience.)

What few of tonight's watchers knew, though, was what new purpose the ships would now fulfill. Nor did they know that the decks had been splashed with gasoline, and that fuel-soaked rags and ropes had been tied near the jets from which the flames erupted. And only the Night Crew knew that from a building near the pier, unseen by anyone, Evan worked the controls with painstaking care.

Josh spotted Zoe, who was waiting near the water with Maddie and Sam. Not too far from her were Moira and Paravi. He hurried over to the two girls first. Paravi greeted him with a quick hug, but Moira was shifting nervously from foot to foot, unable to stand still.

"They ready at the sheds?" she asked.

Josh nodded. "We saw the flares."

"And Milo's set, too?"

"Yeah. He was just waiting for it to get a little darker, like you said. Everything okay here?"

"Seems to be. But he'd better start soon, before—"

She was interrupted by a loud hum from the speakers, followed by a fanfare of trumpets. It grew in power, the notes climbing higher and higher, then holding the crowd spellbound with one long, thrilling chord. The chord ended, its sound echoing off the distant walls of the Coral Palace. A soft melody began, introduced by flutes and oboes and picked up by a chorus of strings. It was both haunting and beautiful, sad and uplifting.

Josh smiled slightly. The music was from the soundtrack of *Neptune's Promise*, the Atlantis fireworks show that closed the park every night. Milo had made the perfect choice. Josh whispered goodbye to Moira and Paravi, then left to join Zoe, Maddie, and Sam. Zoe relaxed visibly as he approached.

"I was afraid you wouldn't make it," she whispered, then released Maddie's hand so that Josh could draw his sister to him.

The music became quieter, and the deep, now-familiar voice of King Neptune flowed over the melody. Josh looked back toward the Coral Palace, where he knew one of the Night Crew was handling the soundboard as Milo once again brought Neptune to life, voicing words that Moira had written.

"Hello, my friends. I thank you for coming." There was a pause, as though the King himself barely knew what to say. "The last few days have been terrible ones. Nightmares from which no one can wake up. As I've watched, I've grieved along with you." Impressed, Josh shot a glance toward Moira and saw her mouthing the speech along with Neptune. "We all know, too, that more difficult days are still ahead. But it's time to move forward. To do what needs to be done.

"The world that you lived in is gone. No one knows what happened, or who caused it. And no one knows what's happening outside the Islands. But here, at least, you're all safe. Here, no one can hurt you."

Josh looked around to gauge the listeners' reaction. Some of the older ones looked confused, others even seemed angry at the theatrics. But the little ones, including Sam and Maddie, were wide-eyed and quiet, and appeared to be taking comfort in what the "King" was saying.

Night had fallen. Colored lights danced on the surface of the lake, glowed softly from the harbor town behind them, sparkled on the spires of the Coral Palace. Neptune's voice continued.

"I'm inviting you all to stay in my kingdom. I have everything that you need. And we will all become a new family and build a new world. Maybe even a better world. Here. With each other."

Now even the older children were falling under the spell.

"But first, we have a solemn duty to perform. We have to say good-bye to the ones we lost. They're out there now, waiting to take their final journey."

All faces turned toward the water, understanding slowly dawning, and all eyes locked on the ships.

"I am the King of the Sea," said Neptune, his voice growing stronger and his words more eloquent. "And I have seen many great warriors, and many kings and queens, leave this world by sailing into the next one. Fire, the gift of the gods, lifted the tall ships and the ones they carried up into the heavens."

As Neptune spoke those words, tongues of flame leaped from vents in the sides of the ships, igniting the long cloth wicks. The music grew louder, more glorious. And only a few knew that at that same moment, members of the Night Crew—Hamim and Greg among them, and the silent boy Seth—were lighting other pyres in back lots at the most distant point on each island, hidden behind tall groves of trees, far from the eyes of the grieving families.

"Picture those you've lost. Tell them that you love them. And then . . . say good-bye."

The watchers grew utterly still, silent except for the soft sound of weeping. Josh saw Zoe sink down behind Sam, pulling him close. In front of them, the sails of the ships caught the flames, and orange light began to flicker on the masts and race up and down the decks.

"Good-bye!" someone cried, the voice trembling with pain and love. "Bye, Mom! I love you."

The sound shattered the emotional dams that all the survivors had built, and hundreds more voices joined the first, desperately calling out final farewells. Josh knelt next to his sister.

"Say good-bye, Maddie," he whispered, and the little girl waved at the ships, saying the names of their mom, their dad, their sister.

They held each other tightly. Josh could feel Maddie's body shaking and tears streaming down his own face.

They watched as the flames grew higher and higher, sending plumes of smoke toward the heavens, just as Neptune had promised. And then, just as the masts began to fall and the hulls became little more than glowing shells, the machinery hummed a final time and the ships slipped beneath the dark waters, silent and beautiful.

EXODUS

For the next day or two, very little was done. Most of the survivors huddled in comforting little clusters, sifting through memories, sharing their stories, dealing with sudden aftershocks of pain and loss. A few went off on their own, like wounded animals, searching for a quiet place to heal.

Josh sat again with Zoe on the beach outside the Coral Palace. Maddie was building a sand castle with little Sam, who still hadn't spoken. But after several hours of listening to the girl's nonstop chatter, the empty expression had left his face, and he was now following her progress with interest, occasionally offering a pebble or leaf for decoration. At the moment, though, she was trying to dig a tunnel through a shape that vaguely resembled the Coral Palace.

"Josh," Maddie commanded. "Come here and help! It keeps falling."

"In a minute," he said. "I'm talking to Zoe."

"No. NOW!"

"I said, in a minute! Just keep building, Bratty."

Maddie made a face and stuck out her tongue. Zoe laughed.

"It's amazing," she said. "You'd never know she'd been sick. Or through everything else that's just happened."

"I know." Josh looked at his sister affectionately. "She's a tough kid. A pain in the ass, sometimes, but tough." He glanced at Zoe, thinking that someone had probably described her the same way when she was Maddie's age. "So, you were here with your dad?"

"Yeah. He'd just gotten home from a tour of duty in the Middle East. His third one. He'd been there for over a year. And it was kind of weird—like having a stranger in the house."

"Well, yeah, if he hadn't been around for so long."

"Right. So Mom had this idea that just the three of us would come here, and Dad would have us all to himself.

"At first, none of us knew how to act. Dad kept buying us stuff, and we kept thanking him and being real polite. It was pretty painful. Then all of a sudden, he looks at us and says, 'Listen. There's something I need to say.' And he lets out this big, long burp. *Ur-r-r-r-r-r-r-p.* It just kept coming and coming. Sam and I started laughing so hard we almost peed our pants."

Josh grinned. "Sounds like he was a great guy."

"He was." She smiled briefly. "I just wish there'd been more time."

Josh put a comforting hand on hers, but he was thinking about his own parents. He should have had a lot more time with them, too—maybe forty more years of vacations and phone calls and gathering at holidays. They would have made terrific grandparents, too—they'd already talked about taking everyone to Isles of Wonder for family reunions.

Now he didn't even have pictures of them—he'd lost his dad's camera the day the plague struck. And Maddie . . . she'd barely remember their parents by the time she was his age.

He'd have to become the memory keeper for them both. He'd tell his sister stories about their family every day. Even stupid stories, like when Caitlyn tricked him into eating a banana peel by saying she'd pay him ten bucks if he did. He wouldn't let Maddie forget them. He wouldn't let himself forget, either.

He nodded once, promising himself. And then he decided: it was time to move on. He sat up a little straighter and looked at Zoe with what he hoped was a determined expression.

"I don't know about you, but I'm tired of sitting with sand up my butt. Why don't we go see what everyone else is doing?"

Zoe looked over in surprise, then smiled as his intention registered. She jumped to her feet. "Spam! Bratty! Race you to the Palace!"

As they sprinted across the courtyard, laughing like two-year-olds, Josh felt a brittle shell crumbling away, releasing him to a new life. Other kids smiled at them as they ran, and Josh sensed something unexpected—a feeling of peace. Maybe it had to do with the soothing words of King Neptune. Or perhaps the fire had burned away their fears. Or maybe it was just that the worst that could happen to them already had.

Of course, not everyone was ready to let go of the past. Sara, the dreamer, lived only about ten miles from the park, in a small town near the airport. Even if there were no adults, she said, her friends might still be there. And her dog, Jasper.

There were hundreds of kids just like her, many the children of park employees, who lived close enough to reach their towns by foot or on bicycles, and who wanted to return to whatever remained. They began to find each other, these hopeful ones, and talk together about returning home.

Milo quickly called on the original volunteers to discuss this new development. Josh went, of course, and this time Zoe came with him, refusing to be left out of another important meeting. (Hamim had offered to watch Sam and Maddie, and he seemed grateful when the offer was accepted.) They gathered again at Neptune's Theatre, and Milo once more took charge of the assembly.

"So," he said, once everyone had arrived. "What do we all think? Is it really okay? People leaving?"

"Why wouldn't it be?" Josh asked. "We said before that no one has to stay. And a lot of kids really don't want to."

Toad—who'd already decided his real name was boring and had sheepishly asked everyone to use his nickname again—nodded his agreement. "Besides, they can always come back, right?"

Milo was silent for a moment.

"I don't know. Maybe we can't let them."

Everyone looked at him in surprise.

"I mean, what if there's disease out there, or some kind of infection? We had the funeral pyres here, made sure everything got cleaned up. Our food is safe, and our water gets recycled. We know we're okay. At least right now. But we don't know what's happening outside."

"That's crazy," said Chelsea, the Girl Guide. "Kids out there would be getting organized, too, wouldn't they? Doing the same things we are?"

"Only if there's someone like Milo around," said Moira. "Someone who knows how to make things happen."

Chelsea suddenly looked less certain, and Josh, remembering the first terrifying days of the plague, realized that Moira was probably right. He glanced over at her, and saw her looking thoughtfully at Milo.

"Anyone want to hear what I think?"

It was Caleb. Josh felt a rush of dislike—he remembered thinking that Caleb and his Three Stooges hadn't seemed to mind the "cleanup" as much as everyone else. In fact, they'd made fun of the bodies, commenting on their clothes, or their weight, or the expressions on their faces. Finally, Milo had taken them aside, and whatever he'd said had shut the four of them up.

Now Caleb faced the group. "Okay, here it is. We got it pretty sweet here. But if everyone starts knowing what we got, they're gonna head over and steal it. Then we're screwed." He looked at the others belligerently. "I say everyone stays. We make everyone stay."

Zoe jumped up as though sprung from an ejector seat. "What do you mean, we *make* everyone stay? You can't make people stay if they don't want to."

Caleb folded his arms across his chest. "Sure I can."

"How? Tie 'em up? Throw 'em to the sharks if they resist?"

"Maybe."

Zoe looked at him in disgust. Then she pointed to her rear with her right hand and made a circle with the fingers of her left, mouthing matching words. Josh burst out laughing, and Caleb's face turned purple. Milo broke in.

"Okay, everyone chill." He looked at Zoe. "Who're you? I don't remember you from before."

"She's okay," said Josh. "She's with me."

Zoe flashed him an irritated look.

"Or maybe not," he said.

Zoe nodded, then turned to Milo. "I'm not 'with' anyone. I'm here because I have a right to be. I want to know what's going on."

"Fair enough. What's your name?"

"Zoe."

"Hi, Zoe." He smiled at her, but his charm had zero effect. She just folded her arms and stared at him. "Okay, you're right. We can't make anyone stay here. But we've gotta watch out for ourselves, too. It's . . . it's about staying alive."

Zoe didn't respond, but she lowered her arms and her expression changed, grew more thoughtful. For a few moments, conversation stopped. Josh racked his brain for another solution to the problem and listened while a few halfhearted suggestions were made. But it was soon clear that, really, there was only one option.

Moira suggested that King Neptune be the one to tell the Islanders.

"Why?" asked Josh. "They know it's just Milo."

"Maybe," said Moira. "But did you see everyone on the night of the farewell? They weren't thinking about Milo when they heard Neptune's speech. All they hear is the King."

She had a point, Josh had to admit. Even he had fallen under the spell of Neptune's powerful voice.

Milo was nodding. "I think she's right," he said. "Better the King than one of us." He looked at Moira, who seemed to be waiting for his next question. "Will you help me write the speech?"

She nodded, raising her green eyes to him. "Of course."

The next day, around noon, "Neptune's Fanfare" erupted from the speakers. Everyone turned automatically toward the Palace, and Neptune's voice addressed the Islands for the third time.

"My friends," it said. "Some of you have asked to leave the Islands. You're hoping to find friends, or you just want to go back home. But if you leave, there is something you need to understand.

"My Islands must be kept safe for those who remain. We can't risk anyone returning sick, or bringing back others who might want to take what we have. So here is my decree: anyone who leaves, leaves forever. You won't be allowed to return."

Silence followed his statement. But no one challenged it. Moira had been right about the power of the King.

"All of us here will miss you. But we hope that you find what you're looking for. And we wish you good luck on your journey."

For a few minutes, no one spoke or moved. But then the Islanders turned to each other—talking, arguing, weighing options. Josh and Zoe wandered together through the crowds, Maddie and Sam in tow. They moved from group to group, listening.

Was it stupid, some of the survivors were asking, to leave a place they knew was safe? Even a lot of the employee-kids, recent transplants who were new to the area, figured it was better to stay. There were food and supplies, like Milo had said. And they really had no ties to anything outside the park. Plus, the Islands were a sort of memorial to their parents.

Hundreds more, though, were pretty sure they didn't want to be trapped on five islands in the middle of an artificial lagoon. For them, the real world held more promise. After all, if one place wasn't good, they could always try another.

"Maybe they're right," Zoe whispered. "Maybe it's better to leave."

Josh shook his head. "I don't know. What Milo said about infection and diseases . . ." Fear squeezed his chest, making it hard for him to breathe. "I couldn't stand seeing Maddie sick again. And what if she—"

Zoe grabbed his arm, stopping the words. "It's okay," she said. "We'll stay. We'll stay here where we know it's safe."

He shook his head. "You don't have to—"

"Shut up," she said quietly. "We're kind of connected, now, you know? Besides, I don't think I could pry Sam away from Maddie if I tried."

Josh relaxed. And realized, to his surprise, that he and Zoe had become friends.

Around them, though, an exodus began. Kids found backpacks in the souvenir stands and began gathering up enough food and water for a journey of several days. They said good-bye to recently made friends, connected with other travelers who would be heading in the same general direction, and began to move toward the monorail station. Soon a river of refugees was leaving along the tracks. They left an eerie silence behind them, as each person who remained wondered if he or she had made the right decision.

Greg, who told Josh and Milo that he came from three generations of builders, volunteered to put together a work team and begin the backbreaking task of constructing their defensive structures. His crew gathered materials from the Boneyard—hidden warehouses on each Island where old attractions were stored or awaited repairs—then moved them on rolling repair platforms to three different locations along the monorail tracks on both sides of Atlantis.

Soon they'd built a series of barricades. If something went wrong on the Islands, or if they ran low on supplies, they'd be able to dismantle the barriers and leave. But they'd also have plenty of warning if anyone tried to get in.

To reinforce the security provided by the barricades, Milo posted sentries at the top of the Coral Palace and at the highest point on each Island to keep watch. He also told them to be on the lookout for any other kind of trouble that might arise on the Islands, like if someone got hurt and needed help. Each sentry, as well as most of Milo's other volunteers, was given a Skreecher Creature air horn, once considered the most annoying of the Animation Alley souvenirs. They worked out a series of signals that could be used to alert the Islanders to danger, or to call each other to a particular location.

"We'll call you the Protectors," Milo told them, smiling at the new recruits. "Everyone will feel safe because of you." The kids looked at each other, grinning and high-fiving.

Milo put Caleb in charge of the Protectors, and made sure that Farrel and the other warthogs were among them. Josh felt a spike of disgust at the blond kid's smug expression.

"Why would you put that cretin in charge of anything?" Josh asked. "And why that stupid name?"

"It's better than Goon Squad," Milo said, grinning. "As for Caleb—this'll keep him and his idiot buddies busy. And away from everyone else."

The night the last barrier was completed, Zoe and Josh returned once more to their beach, though they weren't quite sure why. It had been a little over a week since the plague hit, but it felt to Josh more like a year. He and Zoe sat silently for a while, gazing across the water to where a few half circles of light still glowed from distant towns. But whatever was there might just as well have been in another country. Or universe. Josh could just make out the shape of the nearest barricade, looking like a misshapen bear brooding on the monorail tracks.

"So," he said. "I guess that's it."

"Yep. That's it."

"I hope we decided right."

Zoe looked at him. "Not the best time for second-guessing, Josh."

"Right. Sorry."

They were quiet for a moment. Then Zoe shook her arms and head, like she was trying to wake herself up. "God. This is all so bizarre. It's like we've been dropped into some kind of weird reality show. Only there aren't any cameras."

"And we don't get a million bucks if we win."

"I just hope no one votes us off the island."

"Yeah," said Josh. "That'd *really* suck."

They looked at each other and burst out laughing.

DARK SIDE

Once the refugees were gone, the remaining Islanders suddenly realized what kind of world their new home was. A place with no school. No rules. No closing time, no bedtime, and no one waking you up in the morning. Five islands to explore, music blaring from the speakers, and a couple thousand kids to party with. There was nothing to do but eat and play, and, in the process, erase memories of the first week's nightmares.

Days became a nonstop holiday. Thanks to geniuses like Evan, the Visioneer's son; the eternally helpful and willing Greg; and a dozen others who had an aptitude for mechanics, many of the rides were soon functioning again. Kids ran from one to the next, circling the park, riding them for hours.

Maddie, to Josh's dismay, revealed herself to be a pint-sized daredevil. She kept dragging him onto the Maelstrom—a truly heinous water ride that spun riders around in an ever-tightening death spiral—and forced him to stay on it until he turned green. She also loved the Hydra, whose ten whirling heads whipped from side to side on long, segmented necks.

"Please, Maddie," Josh begged after the eighth time. "Can we go on something else? Something horizontal?"

"No."

Zoe was in a similar predicament. In fact, she had it worse, since Sam was so young and for the most part wanted to stay on Enchanted Island. Josh bumped into them once, coming out of a ride called Lop-Ear's Warren.

"Singing bunnies," she moaned. "Frickin' singing bunnies."

"Sorry," Josh said, grinning.

Other kids, unencumbered by younger siblings, were able to make more creative use of the park. Some swam with the dolphins in Neptune's Theatre. Others experimented with the inventions and games on Inspiration Island. And the more athletic Islanders climbed the coaster mountains, scaled the temples in the Ancient Cities, or clambered through the massive rain forests of the Lost World, swinging through clouds of mist on sturdy cables masquerading as vines.

The party continued 24/7, with little thought or planning. When the Islanders got hungry, they grabbed food. If they got bored, they switched Islands. And when they got tired, they made a nest of blankets or clothes inside one of the shops and went to sleep.

It was every kid's fantasy. And it lasted three days.

On the fourth day, Josh and Zoe took a break from entertaining the kids to help Paravi gather supplies over on Timescape Island. Despite the wild atmosphere, the original work crews had periodically continued their tasks, bound by the camaraderie of the first, dark days, and the knowledge that food would not magically appear, not even on Enchanted Island.

Josh and Zoe parked their siblings at one of the impromptu babysitting clubs that had sprung up around the Islands on the second day, headed by older kids who were already looking for an excuse to stay in one place for a few hours. Maddie, eyeing a couple of girls who looked about her age, solemnly promised Zoe she would keep an eye on Sam while they were gone.

They hurried through Atlantis and over the arced bridge into Timescape, then headed to the entry of the Coliseum where Paravi, capable as always, had arranged for them to meet. She was already there with a dozen other kids, including Hamim, Aiko, Micki, and Eli. They waved when Zoe and Josh appeared.

"Rug rats taken care of?" Paravi asked Josh.

"Yep. Chained to a tree."

"Whatever works," said Paravi, a grin gleaming in her dark face. "So I guess we're ready to go."

"Sure," said Zoe. "As long as you can guarantee I won't see any musical rodents."

Paravi and the others looked at one another.

"Don't you dare," said Zoe.

But it was too late. They all linked arms, began to sway, and broke into song.

We have soft fluffy tails and big floppy feet,
Fields full of flowers and clover to eat.
The sky's full of birds and the air smells so sweet.
We're funny, sunny bunnies!

Zoe grabbed her stomach and fell moaning to the ground. Everyone laughed, then scrambled into the passenger cars of the trams. Paravi hopped into the driver's seat, thrusting one arm out in front of her.

"Next stop—Egypt!" She punched a button on the control panel and headed down one of the Island tramways.

They traveled for several minutes, passing a dozen empty Snack Spots. No one was really surprised—the most critical of the provisions, like the perishable food and the medical supplies, had already been brought to the largest restaurant on each island.

Now the work crews were searching out the less obvious storage facilities.

As the volunteers hummed along in the tram, costumed kids ran alongside, eyeing the cars to see what was being stockpiled, then dropping away in disappointment. Others decided to use the tram for target practice, chunking stones at the metal roof from hidden positions in the trees or from ledges on the fake mountains.

Eli flinched as a rock bounced off the seat next to him. "Cut it out!" he yelled to a shadowy form perched in a swaying bough just overhead. "You're gonna hit someone!"

Zoe peered toward one of the attractions. "Look at that," she said, pointing to a huge gouge in the arm of the Egyptian Sphinx. A few kids were scrambling onto the shoulder just above it, scaling the surface by ramming some kind of pole into the statue and then using it to pull themselves up.

"Jerks," said Josh. "They gotta remember these things aren't real stone."

The tram continued its journey.

"Eli!" Hamim called suddenly, pointing to a tall, narrow pyramid that was covered with hieroglyphics and surrounded by low palms. "Is that one?"

"I think so," said Eli. "Yeah, it is."

Hamim grinned, and Josh slapped him on the back. "Good eye, Hamim!"

"Yes," the boy replied, nodding. "I am the man."

Josh cracked up.

Paravi stopped the tram, and the volunteers jumped off. Eli pried open an almost invisible door with a crowbar, and they all looked inside.

They'd hit the jackpot. Fifty cases of Pharoah's Gold (health food bars in disguise); a hundred boxes of symbol-shaped crackers, called Glyphs; and Mummy Yummies, chewy candy in a dozen different buglike shapes. The volunteers formed a chain, quickly loading the boxes on board the tram, and then continued through the Island, locating three similar structures. As they finished their circuit, a swarm of hungry kids began following the tram back to the collection center. They clustered around the cars as the volunteers got off.

"Whatcha got?" someone yelled. "Anything good?"

"Yep!" Paravi said cheerfully. "Pharoah's Gold, tons of Glyphs, all kinds of stuff."

A boy wearing a Barbary Coast head scarf and a fake gold earring shoved his way to the front of the crowd. "Toss some over here."

Josh scanned the growing crowd, which already numbered more than two hundred kids. He shook his head. "We're just collecting right now," he called. "Evan's going to give stuff out later, at the big dining hall."

"Says who?"

"Says . . . everyone."

Hamim stepped next to Josh, eyeing the pirate boy nervously but attempting to support his friend. "Josh is right. It is what we all agreed."

The other kid snorted.

"It is what we all agreed," he said, exaggerating Hamim's accent. "Well, too bad, camel jockey. I want it now."

The boy leaped onto the tram. Josh and Hamim tried to block him, but the kid grabbed hold of Hamim's shoulders and hurled him from the steps. Then he ripped open a box of Glyphs and began tossing bags of the crackers into a sea of cheering kids and grasping hands.

Now others swarmed toward the cars, shoving smaller kids out of the way and tearing boxes out of one another's arms. Some ran away with whole crates, while others literally stuffed their faces where they stood. The volunteers tried to stop them, but they were no match for the hungry invaders.

The mob pressed closer, and Josh could hear the screams of younger kids being crushed in the press of bodies, could see people who'd been knocked to the ground trying to crawl out from under the forest of trampling feet.

"Stop," he yelled. "People are getting hurt!"

No one heard him. Then someone grabbed his shirt and yanked. He flew from the tram and slammed into a lamppost, hitting his head hard. Dizzy, he turned and slumped against the pole, looking back at the cars.

Some of the scavengers, unable to push through the crowd, had pulled themselves onto the roofs. They clambered along on top, shoving others out of their way and swinging themselves into the least filled of the cars.

The tram began to rock.

Josh watched in horror, then spotted Hamim lying on the ground nearby, far too close to the mob. He wasn't moving.

Josh's stomach dropped. He staggered over to the boy and saw that his eyes were open but unfocused. Josh looked around frantically.

"Zoe!" he screamed, spotting her nearby trying to wrestle a box away from a kid wearing a Seemore Sea Horse T-shirt.

She glanced over, saw Hamim, and immediately let go of the box. The other kid almost fell, then hooted in triumph and ran off.

Zoe raced over to Josh, and the two of them pulled Hamim away from the crowd, over behind a concrete boulder. But before they could even take a breath of relief, there was a crash as one of the tram cars tipped over. They heard Paravi screaming.

"I'll watch Hamim," Zoe cried. "Go get help!"

Josh tore off, not sure where he was going. Around him, the chaos was spreading. Other kids, unable to get near Paravi's tram, were streaming toward the bridge, hoping to hunt down work crews on the other Islands. Josh sprinted past them, heading to the only place that made sense.

Josh reached the Coral Palace, the cries of the mob growing behind him. He yanked his air horn from his belt and began blasting it. "Milo," he yelled. "Milo, you there?"

Even the hoots of the horn were nearly drowned out by the shouts, the music blaring from the speakers, and the sound-effect machines that created birdsong whether birds were around or not. Miraculously, Milo and Evan appeared a few seconds later, talking excitedly as they emerged from a stairwell near the base of the Coral Palace. But their smiles faded as the sound of bedlam rolled over them.

Josh raced over to them.

"What's going on?" Milo asked.

"Everyone's gone nuts." Gasping for breath, Josh described what had happened. As he spoke, Milo's expression grew cold, and his jaw tightened.

"Morons. What do they think will happen to us if they wreck everything the first week?" A gang of kids tore by, the one in the lead screaming something about the BioPods. Milo stared after them. "Okay. We need an army."

Caleb appeared around the corner, responding to the howls of Josh's air horn.

"What the hell's going on?"

Milo repeated what Josh had just told him. "So here's what we're going to do. You and Evan, call the Protectors together. Divide 'em up and send squads to each Island. Grab the biggest kids you can find along the way. Then do whatever you have to to get things under control."

Caleb's eyes gleamed.

"*But*," added Milo, "you've got to tell them not to hurt anyone, if they can help it. If they do, it'll just get worse. They'll just turn against you, and we'll have a war."

Caleb snorted. "So whadda we do? Just say please?"

"I'll try to give you an opening—you'll know when. After it's over, post guards in each location to watch over the supplies. We'll work out distribution later. Got it?"

Caleb didn't look pleased, but he nodded and lumbered off. Josh began to back away. "I'm going back to Zoe and Hamim. He's hurt bad."

"Right. Absolutely." Just then Toad came puffing into the courtyard.

"Can I help?"

Milo nodded. "Yeah, you can. I saw Moira heading toward the dolphins before. Go get her and tell her to meet me back in the tower."

"What do I tell her?"

"That Neptune's pissed."

Josh sprinted back toward Timescape, shoving his way back through crowds of kids thundering across the connecting bridge. He reached the tram and saw that the mob had knocked the entire train on its side. They were crouched around it, muttering, tearing into boxes like lions ripping apart a zebra.

Josh spotted Zoe not far from where he had left her, cradling Hamim's head in her lap. Her shirt was stained with blood.

"How is he?" he asked.

"Still out," she said, eyes wide and panicked. "Josh—what if he doesn't wake up?"

A crack of thunder shot from the speakers, then a second and a third, followed by a deep rumble and the shrieking of winds.

"THIEVES! COWARDS! PUT DOWN WHAT YOU'VE STOLEN AND LISTEN TO ME!"

The mob froze, then turned slowly toward the distant Palace.

"YOU, WHO WERE HOMELESS. YOU, WHO WERE FRIGHT-ENED. I TOOK YOU IN. I KEPT YOU SAFE. AND HOW DO YOU REPAY ME? BY DESTROYING MY ISLANDS! BY STEALING WHAT I'VE GIVEN YOU!"

Josh saw some of the Islanders look around guiltily, food dropping from their hands.

"MOST OF YOU ARE INNOCENT AND CANNOT BE BLAMED FOR THE ACTIONS OF OTHERS. AS FOR THE REST–"

The voice trailed off ominously, punctuated with another thunderclap.

"FROM NOW ON THERE WILL BE ORDER. FROM NOW ON, THERE WILL BE RULES. AND IT ALL BEGINS TODAY."

There was a movement at the edge of the crowd, and the Protectors moved in. Within minutes, the riots were over.

FIRST COUNCIL

The manic energy that had poisoned the Islanders disappeared, leaving behind exhaustion, shock, and shame. Most were horrified by the fallout from the riots. The beautiful gardens had been trampled into muddy pits, the mosaic walkways torn up. A few of the smaller buildings had been destroyed, and even some of the larger attractions were scarred or damaged.

There'd been a human toll as well. Some kids had concussions, bloody gashes, or broken bones, and there was no doctor to take care of them. Chelsea and her Girl Guides, along with a few kids who had camping experience, set up a makeshift hospital in the Exploratorium and did what they could to sew up wounds and create splints and slings. But there was a real danger that infection would set in, or that some of the injured would be permanently crippled.

Worst of all—two toddlers had died, trampled by the mobs.

Zoe took it upon herself to care for Hamim. He'd remained unconscious for several hours, and she and Josh had stayed with him by the overturned tram, watching until he began to stir and they could be sure that nothing was broken. Then the two of them carried the injured boy to the "hospital," where she and Sam visited him at least twice a day.

At first, Hamim didn't respond, keeping his face turned away from her on the blankets where he lay. So she filled the silence by chatting about her family and where she grew up, or by reading from books she found in the souvenir stores. Or sometimes she said nothing at all, just sat quietly nearby.

"Why are you doing this?" Josh asked one day, accompanying her and Sam on one of their visits.

Zoe shrugged. "Beats me." She thought a moment. "Maybe because he helped us with the kids. Or maybe 'cause I'm bored."

"Or maybe," said Josh, "because you're a good person."

"Doubt it." But she gave a quick smile, which swiftly disappeared. "He just seemed so alone."

The days continued in fits and starts. For a long while, it seemed as though nothing would feel normal again. No one trusted anyone else, and evidence of the riots was everywhere. So nobody complained when Milo asked Moira and Evan to set up a strict schedule for the distribution of food and clothes. And everyone seemed relieved when he added more Protectors, to make sure no one acted out again.

Then Milo came up with what everyone later agreed was his most genius idea: a weekly Island Council. Anyone could attend, he explained, and everyone would have a voice. For a call-to-meeting, he picked the familiar notes of "Neptune's Fanfare." And for a gathering place, he chose the huge IMAX theatre on Inspiration Island, where 3-D movies about space flight or undersea cities had once been shown every thirty minutes during the day.

The setup of the theatre made it ideal for the Council: the audience seats rose steeply from the bottom in long, slightly curved tiers, assuring everyone an excellent view of the stage. And the domed ceiling and curved sides formed a perfect sound chamber.

At the first meeting, seats were filled almost to the top of the auditorium. Josh sat near the front with Zoe, Paravi, and Toad. Farther down the row were Greg, Eli, and Chelsea. Looking around, Josh could see other familiar faces. Micki. Aiko. Even the skeletal Seth was there, sitting in one of the upper rows. He was surrounded by a group of equally oddball kids, most dressed in black, some with more piercings than Zoe.

Ari arrived just before the meeting started. He made his way slowly down the steps, looking like he could barely keep his eyes open. He stumbled a little as he walked.

"How're the Little Wizards?" asked Josh, sliding over to make room for him. Little Wizards was the name of the child care center Ari and Lana had set up on Enchanted Island during the first few days. They'd gathered the supplies they needed to take care of the babies and toddlers, then found about a dozen older kids to help them.

Ari collapsed onto the seat. "The Little Wizards are great," he said. "Just great. All hundred and seventeen of 'em." He shut his eyes, swaying slightly.

"You sure you're okay?" asked Paravi, leaning over to look at him.

"Yeah," he said. "I just hope Lana and the others are still alive when I get back."

"Hey!" Toad said suddenly. "Here he comes! Here comes Milo!"

Josh looked up and saw Milo, Evan, and Moira standing on the right side of the stage. Milo was looking at a piece of paper that Moira had just handed him.

"What do you think he's going to say?" asked Paravi.

"Prob'ly just gonna yell at everyone," said Toad apprehensively. "Looks like he has some kinda speech ready."

"No," said Josh. "I know what it is. And it's good stuff."

The others looked at him questioningly, but he shook his head.

He'd been proud when Milo and Moira had approached him earlier that day, wanting to get his opinion on their plans for that night's Council. Josh had never been part of any kind of important group before, and he'd never been friends with someone like Milo. He'd always been too busy being the good kid for his parents: studying hard, helping out around the house, making sure they didn't have to worry about him when they were already so worried about Maddie.

He watched as Milo walked out to the center of the stage, Moira and Evan just behind him. Everyone leaned forward.

"Okay," said Milo, his voice echoing through the chamber. "Thanks for coming to our first Island Council. I'm glad that everyone wants to work together to make things safe on the Islands. Because I know that none of us wants anything like the Riots to happen again."

An embarrassed murmur swept through the theatre.

"Anyhow, here's what I think Council should be about. It's going to be a place to talk, to get things out in the open. Anyone can come here with an idea or problem or . . ." He looked at Moira.

"Grievance," she said.

"Right. Grievance. And this will also be where we decide how the Islands should be run, and who should do what."

"Who's 'we'?" whispered Zoe, bristling a little. "Who decides?"

"I think he means all of us," said Josh.

Zoe looked skeptical.

"Just to get things started," Milo continued, "a few of us got together and came up with some rules."

Zoe turned again to Josh, eyebrows raised.

"Just wait," he said.

"Moira's going to read them to everyone," said Milo. "And then, I guess, we'll have a vote."

Moira stepped forward, retrieving the paper from Milo and holding it above her head with both hands. She turned from side to side, displaying the page like it was some kind of sacred parchment.

"Here are the proposed rules. If accepted, they will become known as the Three Laws." She lowered the paper, cleared her throat, and read:

- *Respect the Islands and each other.*
- *Protect those who are smaller or weaker.*
- *Take only the supplies that you need.*

Heads were nodding around the theatre, and kids smiled in relief.

"Well?" said Josh, looking at Zoe. "Those okay with you?"

"Maybe." She stood and waved for Milo's attention.

He saw her, then nodded in her direction. "Zoe. You have a question?"

"Yeah, I do. Who gets to say how much we need?"

"What?"

"Your last rule," she said. "Who decides how much everyone needs? And what if we start running out of stuff? It's going to take a while for us to get the gardens going, and who knows if we can even keep the fish alive?"

Milo smiled. "Don't worry. We'll have plenty of time to learn how to do all that. We're not going to run out of food."

"How do you know?"

Moira took a step toward the edge of the stage, irritation flickering across her face. "Don't you think Milo's earned a little trust, Zoe?"

Zoe folded her arms. "Sure," she said. "But I'm not going to let you guys order me around unless I *know* you know what you're doing."

Moira's eyes narrowed, but Milo stopped her before she could say anything else.

"It's okay," he said. "Zoe, I *do* know we're going to be okay. I know because Evan and I found out the Islands have a secret." Josh looked up at him, confused. No one had mentioned any secret to him.

Milo scanned the sea of faces, building suspense. "After the Riots, I started thinking. We've all been living off the stuff we already knew about—food from the concession stands and the restaurants. But where did all of that come from? How did it get there?"

The crowd was silent, suddenly wondering about things they'd never thought of before.

"So Evan and I started exploring the Islands, to find out. And guess what? We've got enough supplies to last for months."

"Where?" asked Zoe.

"Right beneath our feet."

Everyone looked at Milo like he was crazy. But then Josh had a flash. The UnderGround! Milo was talking about the Under-Ground! Josh remembered reading about it in one of his dad's books, *Inside the Wonder*. It was an unauthorized look behind the scenes at the Isles of Wonder, something Josh's dad had been unable to resist buying.

The UnderGround was a large tunnel system, actually considered by the Visioneers to be the first floor of the park as well as its life support system. It resembled a huge, spoked wheel. The hub was centered under Atlantis, and four wide corridors stretched out from it, burrowing under the lagoon and opening up again under each of the other Islands. There, strategically placed stairwells and elevators led up to the surface, enabling supplies to be brought up invisibly to the concession stands, the restaurants, and the souvenir shops. A final huge pathway connected all four tunnels on the outside.

It was the hub, though, that was the real heart of the Under-Ground. It was subdivided into several areas: the computer center, which housed the controls for the main power systems; the wardrobe and laundry, where hundreds of thousands of costumes and uniform pieces were sewn, stored, and maintained; and, most important, the central kitchen, with industrial-size ovens, mixing bowls the size of kiddie pools, walk-in freezers, and storehouses with literally tons of food stacked on steel pallets.

"We found it by accident," Milo said. "Evan saw this unmarked door near the drawbridge controls of the Coral Palace. We got it open, went down a couple flights of stairs, and, well, there it was. And it's huge. Just the kitchen is about the size of a city block!"

"How come none of you knew about it before?" asked Chelsea. "I mean, your parents worked here, right?"

"I know the answer," said Josh, getting up from his seat and turning to face the crowd. "In this book my dad had, it talked about the tunnels. The builders called them the UnderGround. No one under sixteen was allowed down there, and everyone was supposed to keep it a secret, even from family. Part of keeping the place magic."

Chelsea nodded. "So was the guy who wrote the book executed for treason?"

Everyone laughed.

"*Any*how," said Evan, looking a little annoyed that the spotlight had moved off him and Milo, "you should see what's in the storehouses and refrigerators. Bags of flour and sugar, thousands of eggs, boxes of frozen burgers, cans of fruit . . ."

"We figure there was probably enough to keep the whole park going for a week or so," said Milo. "And that's for, like, sixty thousand people a day. We only have a couple thousand left now, so if we ration it out, we could get by for months while we get the gardens going and learn how to take care of the animals."

"There are even cots and blankets down there," said Evan, "because the tunnels were supposed to work as a hurricane shelter, too." Evan looked out at the crowd, his eyes stopping on Zoe. "So now is everyone okay with the third rule? No one's going to have to go without anything. Ever."

Everyone started cheering and clapping. Any fears they'd had, any uncertainty about their decision to stay on the Islands, seemed to have disappeared with Milo's news.

Zoe sat down, looking a little embarrassed, and Josh squeezed her arm. Then something else surfaced in his memory. As the crowd continued celebrating, he moved closer to the stage, motioning to Milo. The other boy walked forward and bent down.

"I was just thinking," said Josh. "Isn't there a special road, too? That they used when they brought supplies from the outside to the hub? We could use it like a secret entrance."

"Yeah," said Milo, looking impressed. "You're right. There's a road, and we found it. Except—" He glanced at Evan.

"Except it's useless," Evan said. "There's this big steel warehouse door just where the road reaches Atlantis. And someone shut it down, somehow. Maybe trashed the controls from the outside. It's like they were trying to keep anyone from leaving the Islands."

"They must have thought the plague started here. And that if they kept everyone trapped, they'd keep the plague in, too." Milo's voice was bitter.

The idea made Josh feel sick. How could people do that to each other? Trap them in a place they knew would kill them?

The cheers were dying down. Milo called for everyone's attention, then said they would end the meeting with a vote on the three rules. He asked for a show of hands, and not an arm stayed down. The three rules officially became the Three Laws.

"Now we just have to make sure everyone knows about them," said Milo.

"I can make posters," Moira offered. "We'll put them up all over the Islands."

"Great," said Milo. "Thanks, Moira. And thanks for everything else you've been doing."

Moira dipped her head modestly. "Happy to help, Milo." She looked up at him through her long veil of hair, then tossed it back over her shoulder, like a model in some shampoo commercial.

"Oh, barf," muttered Zoe. "Not too obvious." But Josh barely heard her; he was staring at Moira, wishing he needed some kind of assistance, too.

Milo flushed, and Moira smiled at him. Then she turned toward the audience, raising one hand. "Listen, everyone. There's someone else we should be thanking. And that's Milo. He's making everything happen here."

The crowd began applauding again. Josh saw Moira gesture to Evan, who nodded and ran offstage. "In fact," said Moira, as soon as she could be heard, "I think that we should make him Island Council president. Right now. Who agrees with me?"

Milo looked stunned. But the crowd began clapping and stomping, their cheers echoing off the high domed ceiling. Josh joined in, shouting louder than anyone. Zoe, though, made only the feeblest pretense of applauding.

Moira turned back to Milo. "Looks like it's unanimous," she said. Just then, Evan ran back onstage, carrying an oversized trident from one of the souvenir shops. He stopped when he reached Milo, then bowed low before him, holding the staff in front of him.

"Your scepter, my King."

Milo laughed, almost doubling over, but then straightened and took the trident from Evan's outstretched hands. Moira whispered in his ear, and he nodded, grinning. He turned back to the audience, raising the scepter over his head.

"I thank you, my subjects, for this great honor. And I promise you this: I will use my power for the good of us all, and never for evil."

The crowd cheered again, and Moira stepped back from Milo, giving him the stage. But Josh noticed that she looked as pleased as if she'd been elected herself.

OFF TO WORK

"All right," said Milo, pointing to one of the lists that he'd taped to the whiteboard. "So how do we tell these guys they're on garbage detail?"

Evan shrugged. "We just tell them, I guess. I mean, everyone'll have to do it eventually."

"Oh yeah, right, that'll work," said Chelsea. "Especially when they find out that these guys"—she pointed to a second list—"get to take care of the dolphins and the animals in the aquarium."

"So we give the garbage people some status," said Moira. "Call them the Health Patrol, and tell everyone they're responsible for the survival and well-being of the Islands."

Josh shook his head. "Really think they'll buy it?"

"If it comes from the King, they will."

The little group, called the Core Council, had been working for nearly a week to get the Islands organized. Some of the participants, like Micki and Greg, kept things running on the surface; the rest met for hours each day in one of the employee briefing rooms of the UnderGround, identifying key tasks and figuring out work assignments.

Members of the Core had been appointed by Milo soon after his unexpected election. It was important, he'd told them, to get some rules and plans in place quickly. And he didn't think that decisions could be made only during the weekly Island Council—especially not with a hundred kids voicing their opinions.

"A smaller group will be better," he said. "With the smartest kids we know, and the ones who worked hardest during the first days."

"Won't people get upset, though?" asked Josh. "Especially after what you said at Council about everyone being involved?"

"We'll still share everything. I mean, we won't do anything without a vote or something."

So Core Council was established. Milo immediately made Moira his Word Wizard, in charge of keeping records and handling Island communications. Evan became his lieutenant, jokingly referred to by the others as mighty Number Two. His job would be to help run the weekly meetings and, later, to keep track of the work assignments.

Josh, Eli, and Paravi were also among the chosen ones, along with Aiko, Toad, and about a half dozen others. Josh had been a little overwhelmed by the responsibility, at first—the welfare of the Islands was going to rest squarely on the Core and its ability to make good decisions. But he wasn't about to say no to Milo.

When Zoe heard what was going on, she asked Josh to get her into the group, too. He tried, but Moira quickly persuaded the others that the Core was already too big.

"Besides," she said to Josh, wrapping each word in regret, "Zoe seems smart, but we all know she can be a little . . . difficult. We need people who are easy to work with."

"You just don't know her," Josh said. "She's really a good person. And she *is* smart."

"Maybe we'll get to know her later," said Milo. "But for now, I think Moira's right. We've got to make things happen fast, and Zoe . . ." He looked at Josh and shrugged. "Sorry, Josh."

Josh continued to argue, but finally he had to give up. When he explained the decision to Zoe later, he told her only that everyone wanted to keep the group small. She flinched as though she'd been slapped.

"What?" asked Josh.

"Nothing." She turned away, silent for a moment. "You don't have to lie. I get it."

Josh blinked. He'd imagined a lot of reactions, but not this one. He wasn't exactly sure what to do. And then . . . he was.

"Listen," he said, putting one hand on her shoulder. "I won't go either. They don't want you, then they don't get me." But he felt a pang as he said the words, feeling his insider's status disappearing. Zoe helped him out.

"No, you keep going. At least then I'll know what's going on." Josh felt a flood of relief. "You sure?"

"Yeah. Just promise to keep an eye on them for me." She turned back to face him, forcing a smile.

Josh returned to the office in the UnderGround, throwing himself into the work and dutifully reporting to Zoe on all developments.

The first thing the Core discussed was the Protectors. Everyone agreed they would remain in place, and that Caleb would continue to be their chief. Josh almost objected. But then he realized what would happen if Caleb ever found out, and he decided it was smarter to keep his mouth shut. He did suggest, though, that a few other kids be made Protectors, too—kids who acted a little more like actual human beings.

The second big topic had to do with Ari and Lana. Just as the Core finished talking about the Protectors, the two caregivers had staggered into the meeting room. Ari was in even worse shape than at the first Council, and Lana looked like she'd been through a battle, her clothes split at the seams and covered in mysterious stains.

"Jeez," said Milo, jumping up. "You guys okay? Is there a problem?"

"Yeah," said Ari. "There's a problem, all right. There's a hundred and seventeen frickin' problems!"

"They just don't shut up," Lana moaned, her shyness obliterated by exhaustion. "Little cretins are always needing something, and the toddlers keep whining, and they don't let go of my clothes, and the stupid babies won't stop crying. We haven't slept for a week!"

"And we're drowning," added Ari.

"Drowning?" asked Josh. "In what?"

"Poop," Ari said, despairing. "Poop, pee, and spit-up."

Josh thought he'd choke. "I thought you said you were good at this kind of thing. That you liked little kids."

"Yeah? Well, you try being parents to more than a hundred of 'em! See how long you last!"

Milo was fighting to keep his expression serious. "What about the others, the ones who were helping you?"

"Most of them deserted," said Lana, bitterness lacing every syllable. "They couldn't handle it."

"Cowards," muttered Ari.

"Okay," said Milo. "We'll get you some help, I promise."

Ari leaned forward, grabbing Milo's shirt. "Make it fast."

Milo was as good as his word. He and the rest of the Core immediately created their first list of work assignments, and soon Ari and Lana got the help they needed. Not only were two dozen of the older kids sent to help, but in-betweeners, like Maddie, were brought in to help entertain the toddlers. A couple of days later, Josh saw Ari and Lana in the dining hall. They waved at him, looking almost human again.

Next, the Core began figuring out the more critical of the job assignments.

First, they had to make sure that the power systems continued working—no one wanted the lights to go out or the freezers to shut down. So they identified the smartest kids and techno geeks and wrote down their names on the job sheet for the central computer center. Another group was slotted for the kitchens, storage facilities, and dining halls; their task would be to figure out how to keep two thousand Islanders fed three times a day. And those with farming backgrounds or a love of animals were assigned to the aquariums or BioPods. They'd be the ones charged with increasing food production before the supplies in the UnderGround ran out.

The more mundane tasks—recycling, laundry, and grounds maintenance, for example—had to be handed out as well. These would be rotating assignments, given to everyone not on a specialty team. (The busier everyone was, the Core figured, the less likely they'd be to get into trouble.) Even kids Sam's age would have their jobs, like helping to clean up the dining halls after meals.

Finally, the Core was ready to share their plans with the rest of the Islanders. Evan presented the work teams and assignments at the next Council meeting, and then Milo spoke, using talking points prepared by Moira, encouraging everyone to think of each job as an honor and stressing the importance of each one. There was some grumbling, but not too much—only a few blockheads had thought they'd be able to live on the Islands without doing some work.

Plus, Josh had remembered weekends.

"We can't expect people to work every day," he'd said to the Core. "They'll need some kind of break. And it doesn't have to be a Saturday-Sunday thing, either. We could have like four or five days of work, and then one day for fun." He grinned. "We could call it FunDay."

"That's a *great* idea," said Milo. "We could have sports on those days, or games, or whatever. And that's when we can run all the rides."

"And not just sports and games," said Aiko. "We can have culture, too. Like, we still have all the band instruments and costumes from the big productions. And there's paint and brushes that the set decorators used."

"We'll just have to ask people to take turns with the food and stuff whenever we have a holiday," added Paravi, always practical. But she beamed at Josh. "It really *is* a great idea."

And it was. After the jobs were announced at Council, Milo asked Josh to present the concept of FunDay. The crowd roared its approval. Then Milo asked if anyone wanted to volunteer to be in charge of activities.

"We will!" yelled a redheaded kid, jumping to his feet. He was stocky and muscular, his face an explosion of freckles. "Me and my brothers'll do it." He indicated two other flame-haired kids who had shot up on either side of him. They looked almost identical, but one had stick-straight hair, and the other looked like his scalp had sprouted springs.

"Great," said Milo. "So who are you guys?"

"I'm Ryan," said the first kid.

"I'm Matt," shouted the straight-haired brother.

"And I'm Kyle," added the curly-headed one. "Just call us the O'Bannion Boys."

"So you think you guys can organize games and sports and stuff?" asked Milo. "Maybe set up some teams across the Islands?"

"Hell, yeah!" Ryan said.

Matt grinned up at Milo. "We were gonna do that anyhow. I mean, it's almost baseball season, and there's no frickin' baseball!"

"Can we use the Coliseum?" asked Kyle. "It's a stadium, right?"

"Use whatever you want," said Milo. "Just be sure to block off all those trapdoors and sliding panels they used in the shows."

"We're gonna need uniforms, too," said Kyle. "And lots of equipment."

"You could look in the wardrobe department for the uniforms," Moira suggested. "And there are different kinds of balls and bats and clubs in the souvenir stores."

"We'll take care of it," said Ryan, throwing his arms around his brothers' shoulders. "When it comes to fun, you can count on the O'Bannions."

Other kids volunteered as well. Alex, the English kid whose mom had been on the theatre crew, offered to set up some theatre troupes. And a girl Josh always heard singing around the parks said she'd try to put a chorus together, and maybe a band.

Josh returned to the audience, sitting down again with Zoe.

"So," he asked. "What do you think?"

She shrugged. "Let's see if it all works. Then I'll let you know."

Josh smiled. Zoe's way of dealing with her rejection by the Core was to be as skeptical of their plans as possible. Josh didn't have a problem with that. It kept her happy.

"Thanks, guys," Milo said to the O'Bannions and the other volunteers. "So, is that it? Anyone else have anything they want to say?"

A dark-brown hand shot up. It belonged to a girl with a mass of braids gathered on top of her head, and a fierce expression on her face.

Evan pointed to her. "Okay, you. You have a question?"

"No. It's a suggestion. But it means you're going to have to redo some of your nice little work charts." She folded her arms and glared at him. "And by the way, my name's Latisha. Not 'You.'"

"Latisha. Sorry." Evan squirmed. "So why did you say we're going to have to redo the charts?"

"Because I'm going to need people, too."

"For what?"

"For my school."

The crowd reacted in horror.

"School?" one kid yelled. "Are you mental?"

"I hate school," said another. "We *all* hate school!"

Evan shook his head. "Sorry, Latisha. Doesn't look like your idea's very popular. Besides, we've already decided—"

"Hold on," said Milo. "Let her talk first."

"Thanks," said Latisha. "It's good to at least pretend this is a democracy."

Zoe sat up a little straighter, looking at the girl with interest. "I think I like her," she said to Josh.

Around them, though, the hoots and jeers continued.

"Hey, loser, we got enough to do around here without school."

"He's right. And who's gonna go, anyhow?"

"This is a really stupid idea. Just plain stupid."

Latisha listened for a moment, eyes narrowing. Then she stalked to the front of the theatre, her braids jerking like angry snakes. She spun around to face the crowd.

"Now you all listen to me. My folks were both teachers. And *no* one's gonna tell me that what they did was stupid." She glared at the crowd, and the noise subsided a little.

"Besides," she continued, "we can't afford for the little kids to grow up ignorant. Us either. We've *all* got to be able to read the engineering manuals, and do the math for the power systems, and handle first aid, and take care of the animals. If we don't learn how, we're probably gonna die." She put her hands on her hips, looking from face to face. "Anyone want to call me stupid now?"

That pretty much shut everyone up.

And Milo declared that school would start within a week.

"Good Council," said Milo to the rest of the Core, when the meeting finally ended. They were standing just outside of the IMAX, basking in their success. Josh saw Zoe standing a little farther down the entry path, talking to Latisha. The two were laughing, occasionally glancing back at Milo and the others with expressions that Josh decided not to try to interpret.

"So," Milo said, "you'll make sure everything's ready at all the job stations, Evan?"

"I got a bunch of people at each place now, setting stuff up."

"And Moira . . ."

"I'll make sure the assignments are posted. Don't worry."

"Thanks," he said, and took a deep, satisfied breath.

We're going to do okay, Josh thought, watching Milo and pleased with how the Core had handled its first week. Maybe taking care of the Islands won't be that hard after all.

And it wasn't. Until one of the rides turned on them.

TSUNAMI

Josh lay contentedly on his cot in the Holodome, where dozens of kids had been camping, relishing his first FunDay and the fact that he didn't have to get up to meet with the Core. He stretched and let his eyes drift closed again. And then Maddie began shaking him by the shoulder.

"Come *on*," she yelled. "You promised we could do all the coasters today. And my favorites three times each, you said. So we gotta get going *now*!"

"Jeez, Maddie, why does everything always have to be *now*? The coasters aren't going anywhere."

"I don't care. Come *on*!" She kept pulling and prodding and nagging until Josh finally got up, yawning, and pulled on his shirt. He looked over to where Zoe and Sam usually slept and was surprised to see they were already gone.

"You know where Zoe went, Mad?"

"She said she had to get something."

"They coming back?"

Maddie shrugged. "I dunno. So, we going?"

"Yeah. But let's get something to eat first." Just not too much, he warned himself. Or it would all reappear after three turns on the Maelstrom.

They headed over to the main dining hall on Atlantis, the morning so beautiful it might have been ordered as a backdrop. Along the way, they passed a dozen groups of happy, laughing kids who were already running toward the rides. Josh saw others heading toward Timescape, tossing balls to each other as they walked, and he remembered that the O'Bannion Boys had already organized the first set of Island games, including relays and soccer and a hoops tournament, using bottomless buckets nailed to wooden posts.

They reached the dining hall, and Josh led Maddie over to the serving tables where rolls and juice boxes had been piled. There was a mound of apples, too, and Josh grabbed at those, knowing that fresh fruit would be the first of the UnderGround supplies to go bad. He dragged Maddie over to a table, despite her insistence that she could eat and walk at the same time.

"Yeah, but I don't want to," said Josh. "Just sit down for five minutes, okay?"

"You're stupid."

"Mad! Sit!"

Maddie plopped herself down on one of the benches, grumbling, and Josh positioned himself across the table from her. Weeks without parents or rules were starting to take their toll. He decided it was time for a brotherly lecture.

"Listen, Mad. You gotta start listening to me a little better, okay? I have a lot of work to do, and I can't be arguing with you all the time."

"You don't work. You just talk all day. *I* work," she said, referring to her job at Little Wizards.

"I work. It's just a different kind of work." Maddie looked like she was going to argue some more, but then her face lighted up as she saw something over his shoulder. Josh twisted around and saw Zoe and Sam heading toward them. With Hamim.

Josh jumped up from the bench and ran over to them.

"Look who I found," said Zoe, proud of herself. Josh grinned, grabbing Hamim's arm.

"Hey, man. How you doing?"

"I am fine," the boy said softly. "Thank you."

He didn't smile. Josh let go of his arm, feeling a little awkward but not really surprised. Although Hamim had recovered from his physical injuries, this was the first time he had left Chelsea's makeshift hospital. And there was a sadness about him that hadn't been there before the riots. Apparently Zoe had decided enough was enough.

"I told him he wasn't allowed to miss the first FunDay," she said. "And that I needed him to save my life."

"What do you mean?" asked Josh.

"I mean, if I have to visit those damn singing bunnies again, I'll kill myself."

Josh laughed, and saw a ghost of a smile drift across Hamim's face. Then it vanished.

A moment later, Evan came up to them. Zoe's smile disappeared, and she stiffened.

"Josh, sorry, but Milo wants to know if you can meet with us for a little while. We've got a problem."

"Can't we talk later?"

"Now'd be better."

Josh didn't even have to look at Maddie to know she had just turned into a little volcano. "More talking," he heard her mutter, and he braced himself for the explosion.

Zoe came to his rescue. "Hamim and I'll take Maddie," she said. "We can go on some of the rides, and we'll meet you back at the Palace."

"But I don't want to see the damn singing bunnies either," said

Maddie, her face darkening. Zoe grimaced an apology to Josh—he'd been warning her about her language. "I want to go on the coasters."

"Sam's too little for the coasters," said Zoe.

"I don't care."

Josh blew out his breath, ready to whack her. But then Hamim crouched down next to her. "Maddie, I would be most honored if you would let me take you on the big rides. Would that be all right?"

The clouds vanished from Maddie's face, and she grinned.

"Yeah. That'd be all right."

Hamim straightened, and Josh mouthed a thank-you. He warned Maddie to be good, ignored the tongue she stuck out at him, and walked off with Evan to find the Core.

"So what's the emergency?" asked Josh when they entered the UnderGround meeting room. Aiko was there, along with Moira and Caleb.

"It's not really an emergency," said Milo. "But Aiko noticed that a couple of the dolphins are looking pretty sick. Some of the kids want to swim with them today, and I was wondering if we should stop them."

"Well, yeah," said Josh. "If the dolphins are sick, then the kids could get sick, too."

"Plus, the water's looking pretty scummy," said Aiko. "I'm not sure anyone ought to go in it anyhow."

Milo nodded. "Caleb, think you can find enough Protectors to close off Neptune's Theatre until we can figure out what's wrong?"

"Yeah. Most of 'em are still upstairs stuffing their faces."

Suddenly, one of the doors to the UnderGround crashed open, and footsteps pounded down the stairwell. Someone was yelling for Milo.

Milo looked at the others, then headed toward the entrance of the briefing room. Before he could reach it, Greg burst through the door.

"You guys better get up top! Something's happening!"

They all jumped to their feet, following Greg back to the surface. The moment they got outside, Josh could hear air horns screeching from the west side of Atlantis. A stream of kids were racing toward the sound.

Chelsea ran up to them, soaked with sweat.

"It's the Tsunami," she panted. "It's stuck."

Josh panicked. The Tsunami was Maddie's favorite coaster, the first one she'd gone on when their family had come to the Islands. What if she and Hamim . . .

Josh shot toward the ride, muttering a prayer over and over under his breath.

"Don't let her be on it, don't let her be on it."

A minute later, he was tearing across the shadowy web cast by the metal backbone of the bright blue coaster, looking up into its crazy loops and corkscrew spirals. A light mist floated over them from the water jets that sprayed screaming passengers as they shot by on the tracks. But the screams Josh heard now were screams of terror.

One of the coaster trains was stalled halfway up the first of the big loops. About a dozen kids were clutching the safety bars, heads dangling backward, legs kicking frantically in the air. Josh squinted, heart pounding, and looked frantically from car to car.

"It's okay, she's not on it." It was Zoe, rushing toward him and holding Sam tightly by the hand. Hamim and Maddie were just behind her. "I figured you'd be freaking." Josh grabbed Maddie to him, almost collapsing in relief.

Nearby, Milo was yelling for volunteers to help figure out what to do. Evan and Greg put their heads together, gazing at the coaster and pointing to the stairs, catwalks, and maintenance platforms that were built into the tracks. Caleb gathered together the Protectors he spotted, and anyone else who looked like he or she had some muscle. Then Josh saw a trio of redheads pushing their way through the crowd, yelling that they could help.

The three O'Bannions stopped when they got to Milo.

"We can climb pretty much anything," said Ryan. "Our folks used to take us rappelling."

"Great," said Milo. "What do you think we need?"

"Ropes and belts, to start," said Kyle. "We need to make harnesses and rig safety lines."

Milo signaled to Eli, Paravi, and some of the other Core members who knew where the supplies were stored. They nodded, jumped on a nearby tram, and set off with the O'Bannions, Paravi honking madly to clear the way in front of them. Greg ran after them and yanked himself up onto the last car, yelling at Paravi to head toward the nearest Boneyard.

Evan headed back over to Milo, and Josh moved closer to hear what they were saying.

"We've been stupid," said Evan. "I remember my mom telling my dad what kind of upkeep these things take. They used to get checked every night: electrical systems, hydraulics and stuff. They had a whole army of people. People who knew what they were doing."

"Which we don't," said Milo, kicking angrily at the ground. "We didn't even think about taking care of the rides. We've been idiots."

Josh silently agreed, feeling sick.

The crowd went quiet, waiting anxiously for Paravi and the others to return. Finally, the tram reappeared, and those on board began tossing out a small mountain of ropes, cords, and other supplies, including work vests with embedded metal loops holding tools and flashlights.

The O'Bannion brothers grabbed up the supplies, yelling directions to anyone who could help. Josh, Zoe, and Hamim joined them, knotting ropes together, making loops for arms and legs and attaching hooks to the back of each finished harness, carefully following Ryan's directions.

Within an hour, a team of rescuers—the O'Bannions, Greg, and a number of the more agile Protectors—were using the access ladders and stairs to scale the metal frame of the Tsunami. Most stopped along the way, positioning themselves so that they'd be able to guide the riders from person to person as they were pulled from the coaster train.

Only the O'Bannions and Greg climbed all the way to where the coaster was stalled. Josh held his breath, watching as the four of them checked and rechecked their gear and took turns swooping from the catwalks to the cars, helping the terrified passengers into harnesses, attaching the harnesses to their own work vests, and then swinging back over to the platforms.

They worked slowly, carefully, moving like patient spiders across the still-wet tangle of metal. Then one of the younger kids panicked as Matt O'Bannion pulled him from under the safety bar. The boy grabbed Matt's vest, pulling him off balance, and for a moment the two of them were swinging between the train and the platform, the kid not yet secure. The crowd shrieked, and Zoe put her hands over Sam's eyes.

But then Greg jumped down from a slightly higher platform. He wrapped one arm around the nearest beam and reached out with the other until he caught hold of the rope. He pulled it toward him, arms shaking from the strain, until Ryan could grab Matt up by the collar and pull him and the younger kid to safety. A cheer rose from below.

The rescue operation continued most of the morning, with almost every Islander now gathered around the coaster, watching as though hypnotized. Finally, just as the sun began retreating from its highest point in the sky, the last rider was brought to the ground, and the final rescuer climbed off the tracks.

"Let's hear it for the O'Bannion Boys!" yelled Evan. "And everyone else on the rescue team!"

The O'Bannions grinned and waved, and Matt pulled Greg over next to them, wrapping the big kid in a guy hug and pounding him on the back. Josh joined in the cheers, but he was still feeling a little sick inside, realizing how differently things could have turned out.

Taking care of the Islands wasn't going to be that easy after all.

FINDING A HOME

One thing was simple, at least: the establishment of colonies. As the weeks drifted by, kids started leaving the communal dormitories, searching out permanent places to stay. No formal assignments were made, no meetings were held. The character of each Island simply attracted different kinds of kids as surely as if the ground contained personality magnets.

The most traditional of the colonies was Enchanted Island, where kids with younger siblings settled because the storybook buildings, comic book settings, and cartoon colors provided a familiarity and comfort that the little ones needed. Many of the kids even formed little family units, re-creating as much as possible the semblance of a home.

The more romantic, daring, or athletic kids were drawn to Timescape Island, with its exotic locales and atmosphere of mystery and adventure. The land was subdivided into even smaller territories, with some kids living in the towns of the Barbary Coast; others settling in the Great Halls, forums, and pyramids of the Ancient Cities; and a few camping out in the caves and jungles of the Lost World. The O'Bannion Boys settled on Timescape, and so did their new best friend, Greg.

Inspiration Island had the oddest assortment of Islanders. Most of the Brainiacs headed there, immersing themselves in the dazzling robotics and prototype technology in a daze of geeky happiness. And since Inspiration was where Latisha had set up her school, she and many of her Teachers decided to make their homes in SkyTown. Living alongside the Geeks and Teachers, though, were nature lovers and rural kids who were attracted to the gardens and livestock in the BioPods. Quite a few of the "families" decided to stay on Inspiration as well: the combination of rides, gadgets, and animals made the place almost irresistible for younger kids who missed their pets and Game Boys.

Not surprisingly, those with a darker streak—kids like Seth, the silent boy from the Night Crew, as well as his swarm of Goth wannabes and embryo Emos—hid themselves on Nightmare Island. Some lived in the crooked buildings of Necropolis, others took up residence in Dracula's Castle, and a few stayed in the shacks of the Dismal Swamp. And although most kids wandered comfortably between Islands, exploring the new settlements and establishing friendships, the Nightmare residents seldom ventured out.

Soon, no one except those who lived there ever went through the fanged entrance gate at all; although everyone had enjoyed the Island as a theme park, its new inhabitants made the place just a little too freaky. This attitude suited the Nightmare dwellers just fine. In fact, they fed into the image, popping up unexpectedly at night in remote corners of the Islands, or appearing like ghosts in the windows of empty buildings. The other Islanders, unnerved by their spook shows, started calling them the Ghoulies.

Atlantis, by unspoken agreement, belonged to the original volunteer group and most of the Core Council. After all, they had been the ones to get the Islands functioning, so they seemed most deserving of the royal setting. And once Milo took up residence in the Coral Palace, the other Islanders came to think of Atlantis as their capital. It was considered a great honor to live there.

Which is why Milo was disappointed when Josh decided not to join them.

"Why not?" Milo asked. "You've sure earned it."

"Thanks," said Josh. "But Maddie wants to live on Enchanted Island. That's where all her friends are."

"There's some kids on Atlantis, too." Milo thought a moment. "Okay, how about this? What if I got you into one of Neptune's Chambers? Then would you come?" Neptune's Chambers were the special suites in the Palace that had once been reserved for VIPs and the families of Wonder World executives. They were lush rooms with downy beds, comfortable sitting areas, and gorgeous marble bathrooms.

Josh was tempted. "I could ask. Maddie acts like a princess anyhow. And Sam will do whatever Maddie says."

Milo hesitated, and Josh suddenly realized that Zoe and Sam hadn't been included in Milo's offer. Josh spared him the awkwardness of saying so.

"You know what?" he said. "The more I think about it, I really think it's better for Maddie on Enchanted Island. We'll just stay there."

"You sure?" said Milo.

"Yeah."

"Okay. Too bad, though."

Josh felt a flicker of concern at Milo's words. But no. This was the right thing to do. He decided not to let Zoe know about the invitation, though, or why he'd turned it down. Unfortunately, Moira had a different agenda, cornering Zoe in the dining room the next day.

"You know you're messing things up for Josh, right?" she said.

"What are you talking about?"

"Milo invited him to live in the Palace with the rest of us. But he figured he had to stay with you."

"I didn't ask him to do that," said Zoe, glaring at her. "I didn't even know."

Moira shook her head. "Right. Whatever you say. But it's not going to be easy for him to stay part of the Core if he's not living in the Palace. And if that happens, it'll be your fault. Why don't you just cut him loose?"

Zoe flipped her off. But that night, she told Josh what Moira had said. And then she told him that he should join the others on Atlantis.

"Sam and me'll be fine," she said. "And it's not like we won't see you."

But Josh shook his head. "Remember when you stayed here on the Islands with me and Maddie, when you really wanted to leave?"

She nodded.

"Well, this is the same thing. Like you said, we're connected now."

Josh could see the relief in her eyes.

Once the decision was made, Josh and Zoe moved into one of the large cottages on Starlight Lane, which was actually a row of souvenir shops built to look like a small village. They boxed up all the merchandise that hadn't already been taken by the other Islanders and put it into the storerooms. Then they arranged the empty shelves to form separate living spaces. There were sleeping areas, with cots brought up from the UnderGround; a little living room, where they could sit and talk together at night; and a "playroom," its shelves filled with books, toys, and games.

Sam and Maddie thought it was heaven, and they both gave

Josh and Zoe huge hugs. Then Maddie's face scrunched up, a look Josh knew meant she was thinking hard.

"Why don't we invite other kids to live here?" she asked.

"What other kids?"

"There's a buncha kids at Little Wizards that're all alone. An' we got lots of room here. Why don't we let some of them stay with us?"

Josh and Zoe looked at each other, and Josh shrugged. "Why not?"

They rearranged the walls, making more sleeping sections.

The first addition to their family was Shana, one of the toddlers Maddie had been assigned to watch over at Little Wizards. The little girl refused to wear anything but fairy costumes, and Maddie's main job had been to constantly reattach her wings.

Next came Giz—short for Gizmo—a sweet, bright four-year-old who loved gadgets and had a killer grin. He'd been badly hurt during the Riots and still had trouble walking. Josh had seen him on one of their visits to the hospital and had never forgotten him.

Finally, there was Devon, who was just a little older than Maddie but had foraged on his own for two weeks until she spotted and befriended him. He resisted their invitation at first, but Maddie kept nagging him until he gave in. He insisted on retaining his tough-guy attitude, though, calling everyone Dude and moving with a swagger rather than a walk.

There was just one person missing. Hamim. So Zoe invited him over one night to see what they'd done with the cottage, a plan already in place.

Everyone smiled when he walked in the door. He'd become their regular companion on FunDays, never refusing any request from the little ones and always finding ways to sneak them candy. Shana toddled over for a hug, while Maddie, Sam, and Giz waved happily. Then Devon sauntered toward him, head bobbing.

"Hey, Dude," he said, starting one of his long, ritual handshakes.

"Hey," said Hamim, patiently completing the elaborate sequence. He and Devon had formed a special bond—maybe, Josh thought, because the two of them had been so much on their own.

Hamim lifted Shana up for her hug, carefully avoiding her wings. Then he balanced her on his hip as he walked around the room.

"So, what do you think?" asked Josh.

"It is very nice," he said, leaning in toward one of the pictures of classic animated characters that they had hung on the walls. "You have made it very much like a home."

"Yeah," said Zoe, fingering her navel ring. "Creeps me out a little. So . . . where are you going to stay?"

He shrugged. "I am still deciding."

Josh and Zoe glanced at each other, smiling.

"Why don't you stay here?" Josh said.

Hamim shot him a quick look, then dropped his eyes. "I could not impose."

"Why not?" said Zoe. "The kids all like you, and Josh and I could probably put up with you, too. I mean, if we have to."

Hamim bit back a smile.

"Come on, man," said Josh. "You can be Uncle Hamim."

The hidden smile blossomed into a full grin. "Thank you. I will."

And with that, the family was complete.

Similar scenes played out all over the Islands. Friendships developed, families formed, homes were chosen, and the colonies grew and took root. The work groups set up by the Core settled into a comfortable rhythm, and the O'Bannions made sure that no one forgot to play. And one evening, while watching his sister and

Sam play tag with their friends in Starlight Lane, Josh realized that Neptune's Promise on the night of the Last Farewell had actually come true: the Islands were now their home.

No one ever talked about what had been lost, and no one said anything about wanting to leave. The Protectors stationed at the top of the Coral Palace continued to keep watch, but there was now very little to see. Each week, the halos of light from the towns around them grew fewer in number. Then, one night, the sentries reported that the world on the other side of the lagoon had gone completely black. After that, no one thought about Outside at all anymore.

CHANGE OF SEASONS

Josh sat with Hamim and Devon at one of the long tables in the main dining hall of Enchanted Island, waiting for Zoe to return from taking Shana and Giz to Little Wizards. All three were crunching on spoonfuls of cereal from molded plastic bowls that were decorated with glued-on "jewels." Nearby sat a cluster of kidlets (the name everyone now used for the youngest Islanders), and above them, a large mounted dragon's head looked down longingly on the diners from a large oak plaque.

"You gonna eat that biscuit?" it asked one of the kids, who happened to be Zoe's brother, Sam. "You wanna toss it up here?"

"You don't got a stomach!" Sam yelled back. "You're just a head!"

The dragon head rolled its eyes. "So? A head's got a mouth. I can still taste it."

"That's dumb."

"You're dumber," said the dragon.

Josh grinned. Alex, the English kid who'd organized the Islands' theatre troupes, always did a great job voicing the dragon. After nearly a year, some of the kids still hadn't figured out the thing wasn't alive.

The argument continued, with Sam getting increasingly

incensed. Finally, he picked up the biscuit and hurled it at the dragon's head. The creature opened its mouth, trapping the missile between its jaws.

"Ha!" it said, and Josh was impressed that Alex managed to sound as though his mouth was full. "Gotcha!"

Zoe's voice cut through the laughter. She was standing at the head of the table, trying not to smile.

"Josh! Hamim! Move your butts! I'm already late for the Pods."

Josh shoved another spoonful of cereal in his mouth. "Hamim and I aren't finished yet. Neither are Spam and Bratty."

"Then get 'em ready. Latisha's waiting. And I told you not to use those stupid names anymore."

"They like 'em."

Zoe sighed and turned to Devon. "Think you can get everyone moving?"

"Sure." Devon pulled a sleeve across his mouth, then leaned over and rapped on the table in front of the other two kids. "C'mon, Dudes. Gotta go."

"Devon's gotta go," Sam said to Maddie solemnly. "He's gonna poop his pants." Maddie screamed with laugher, and Josh grinned, remembering the days when Sam didn't talk.

They all pushed away from the table and headed over to Zoe. She seemed about to continue her lecture, but then leaned toward Josh, squinting at his chin. "Wait a minute. You getting a beard?"

"No. Yeah. Kind of. Just a few hairs." But he couldn't help grinning.

"Ooooh. I'm impressed."

"Yeah." He almost said something about what was happening to Zoe's chest, but decided against it.

At least they didn't have to worry about these physical changes anymore. When the first kids hit puberty, they'd all been terrified, waiting to see if the plague would somehow return and claim them. Nothing had happened, though, and further "developments" were watched with great interest. In fact, some of the older kids had already paired off, including Ari and Lana. This had necessitated some awkward facts-of-life conversations between Josh, Zoe, and their mystified kidlets, especially when a few of the girls started wearing looser clothes to accommodate softly rounded bellies.

Hamim was one of the Islanders who had benefited most from the hormone surge. He'd grown three inches and slimmed down, and a lot of the Island girls were starting to find reasons to ask him for help or get assigned to his work teams. So far, he'd been flattered—and slightly embarrassed—but he'd shown little interest in any of them. Except for Zoe, maybe. Josh noticed that he followed her around a lot, always looked for things he could bring her or do for her. And Josh wasn't sure how he felt about that.

"So," said Zoe, breaking into his thoughts. "Where you guys stationed today?"

"Kitchen," said Hamim. "Sometimes I wish I had never said that my mother taught me to cook."

"I'm over at the Oceans," said Josh. "We gotta put some of the babies into a separate tank so the big ones don't eat 'em, like last time. Or pretty soon, no more fish fry."

"This is interesting," said Hamim. "You save them so I can cook them. Somehow, it does not seem right."

"Then stop making them taste so good."

"Perhaps I should not cook them at all."

"Wouldn't work," said Zoe. "We'd just start ordering sushi."

"Then I seem to have no choice," sighed Hamim. He grinned. "See you at home." He headed off toward Atlantis and the kitchens, and Zoe and Josh ushered the kidlets out the door.

Josh sensed something falling before he saw it.

"Watch out!" he yelled, yanking Maddie backward. A huge plaster leaf crashed to the ground in front of them, shattering into dust. Josh looked up and saw that it had broken off one of the giant vines that wrapped around the dining hall doorway, like Jack's beanstalk.

"Damn," said Zoe, staring at the rubble. "Some of these places are falling apart faster than Greg and his crew can fix them."

It was true. Without the army of maintenance workers that had once cared for the park, the buildings and grounds were definitely beginning to suffer. The paint was peeling, streets and walkways were cracked and pockmarked, and the exotic gardens and topiary hedges had run wild, creating strange, junglelike terrains that gave each Island the look of a lost civilization or an alien city. Even the Coral Palace had lost some of its splendor, its colors fading and some of its fragile spires breaking off in high winds.

The problems weren't restricted to the buildings, either—the Islands had also lost many of the animals. At first, no one had known how to monitor or maintain the chemicals and ph-levels in the aquarium tanks, or how to determine the amount and type of food needed to keep the larger land animals healthy. So some of the creatures in the BioPods sickened and died, as did many of the larger sea creatures. After two of the much-loved dolphins were lost, the Core decided the rest should be released into the lagoon, to survive as best they could. The aquarium workers focused their efforts on maintaining a few of the smaller tanks and the more edible fish.

Still, the park remained remarkably functional, primarily because the Brainiacs had made sure that the extraordinary computers and power systems didn't fail. And though most of the big rides had been shut down after the Tsunami, morale was pretty high thanks to the O'Bannion Boys and a raft of other FunDay volunteers.

You just had to watch out for falling plaster leaves.

"That was really close," said Zoe. "Glad your Spidey-sense was working."

"Yeah," Josh said, fear-sweat prickling under his arms. He decided not to think about what had almost happened. "So what're you doing in the Pods?" he asked Zoe.

"Veggies." She grimaced. "The boringest, stupidest job in the world. Prune and pick. Prune and pick."

"Hey, you could be on Health Patrol. Or in the laundry. Besides," he intoned, quoting one of Neptune's platitudes, "there are no bad jobs, only bad attitudes."

"Shut up. You sound like a Clone." That was Zoe's name for the kids who tried to act like Milo and parroted everything he said. "Besides, have you noticed that certain people, like you, always get the good jobs, and others, like me, get the crummy ones?"

"Not true."

"Oh, yeah? So how come the Atlantis kids are still the only ones working on the computers or at the aquarium?"

"I'm not Atlantan."

"No, but you're connected. Ever since the first weeks, when you were so tight with the Core. And connected people get treated better."

Josh didn't say anything: no good could come of this conversation. Besides, as the months passed, he'd become less and less involved with the Core. They had too many impromptu meetings at the Palace, often late at night or after the weekly Council meetings were officially over. For a while, Milo tried to keep Josh a part of what was happening, but his efforts gradually tailed off. Josh sometimes wondered if he'd been stupid not to move into the Palace when he'd had the chance.

Well, nothing he could do about that now.

He and Zoe continued their sprint across the Islands until they crossed over the bridge to Inspiration. In front of them was the Holodome, with its sleek, twisted steel surfaces. To the left of the Holodome was the Kinetic Playground, and just beyond that was Digital Dimensions, a complex of TV and animation studios where shows like *Dr. Meek, Science Freak* had once been filmed for the Wonder Channel. It was where many of the Teachers now held their classes.

Moving the school to Inspiration Island had been Latisha's idea. At first, all of the kidlets had to be dragged to classes and sat like sullen lumps once they were there. Josh could hardly blame them— the Teachers used books from the souvenir stores to teach reading, or passed out old-fashioned worksheets they had downloaded from education Web sites before the Internet crashed for good.

But one day, while watching her friend Kim take apart a motor in the Exploratorium, Latisha had had her brainstorm. Why not take advantage of everything the Visioneers had created? The Holodome was a natural for history lessons and geography, and the LifePods could be used for biology. Kim, a born inventor whose brain worked so quickly that her words stumbled over each other, could teach things like computer science and basic engineering.

Even the littlest Islanders would benefit from the change, Tish pointed out, since several of the sets at Digital Dimensions had been designed for kid-sized game shows and educational programs. What better way to teach the basics? Soon, the kidlets were begging to go to school and protesting when it was FunDay. Some of the older kids became regulars, too.

Josh and Zoe entered the main studios and led Sam, Devon, and Maddie down a long hallway to one of the smaller soundstages. They went through the entrance doors, which were near the top of the audience seating area, and surveyed the room.

Latisha and another Teacher named Miguel stood in the middle of the set for *What Do YOU Know?* Miguel, a happy little math geek who once tried to explain to Josh why the number seven was "intrinsically interesting," had his hand poised above an oversized timer. In front of him were fifteen kids, all sitting in contestants' chairs behind high counters. Each had a pad of paper, a pencil, and a determined expression.

Zoe and Josh began herding their kidlets down the stairs, and Latisha turned and waved.

"Come on, guys," she called. "We're doing Mad Mad Math. Prizes galore if you're last on the floor!" Sam and Maddie whooped and raced down the stairs to join their friends. Devon followed more slowly, trying not to look eager. Latisha tapped each of them on the head with a set of flash cards as they went by, then moved toward the stairs, where she hugged both Josh and Zoe.

"Hey, handsome. Hey, girlfriend."

"Hey, Tish," said Josh. "Hey, Miguel." The other boy saluted.

Zoe pretended to pout. "Thought you guys weren't going to do Mad Math 'til the next time I could make it."

"We weren't," said Tish. "But the six-year-olds started complaining. Said you were winning all the stuff."

"Whiners."

"Don't worry. I'll save you a prize."

"Oh. Okay, then." They laughed.

"Got any field trips planned this week?" Josh asked.

"Yeah. Maria's going to take the 'tweeners to the Pods, teach them about mammals. A few are going to start apprenticing there soon, so it's good timing."

"Let me know when they're coming. I can show them the hydroponics," said Zoe.

"That'd be great. Thanks."

Tish motioned to Miguel to start the math game while she and Zoe shared a few more minutes of news and gossip. Josh waited patiently for them to finish. But then Zoe motioned Tish closer. Her voice dropped.

"You going to Council tonight?"

"Sure," said Latisha. "You know me. Gotta put my two cents in."

That's for sure, thought Josh. Tish and Zoe made their opinions known at almost every meeting, much to the annoyance of the Core. Josh himself just liked to hear about new ideas, new plans. Milo was always coming up with something worth listening to.

Zoe took another step closer to Latisha. "I was thinking that maybe it's time to mention . . . you know."

"Yeah. I think you're right."

Josh looked from one to the other. "What?"

Zoe glanced at Tish, who nodded. "We were thinking that no one's talked about Outside for a long time. That maybe it'd be good to see what's going on."

Josh was startled. "But it's gone black. Months ago. The sentries said."

"I know. But that doesn't mean there aren't people. Or things we should know about. Anyhow, Tish and I want to talk about it."

Josh shook his head. "But you guys are always causing trouble at Council, Zoe. First you're complaining about the food rations—"

"Because Milo and the Atlantans always seem to get a little more of the good stuff. And don't pretend you haven't noticed."

"Well, but maybe they deserve it. They work pretty hard."

"Harder than you? Harder than Tish? Come on."

"Okay, okay. But then at last Council you were complaining that Caleb—"

"—is a moron. Well, he is. Him and the rest of the Goon Squad.

Too much power, not enough control. And what about that little jail of theirs that no one talks about?"

"It's not a jail—just some place UnderGround for kids who need time to cool off, like when they get into fights or something."

"Or for kids who break the rules. Or don't do their jobs."

"Well, the Core needs some way to keep things under control. And by the way, it doesn't help that you call Caleb's group the Goon Squad."

"Why? They *are* goons."

Josh sighed. "Fine. I'm just saying that if you keep causing trouble, Milo and the rest of the Core are gonna get really pissed."

Zoe looked at him coolly.

"I'll take my chances. I mean, do you really think we can stay on the Islands forever? Think about that leaf that almost cracked Maddie's head open a few minutes ago."

She looked back at Latisha.

"So, Tish. Tonight?"

"Tonight."

Suddenly, Josh wasn't looking forward to Council anymore.

THE GLOW

That evening, just after dinner, Josh, Zoe, and Hamim headed toward Inspiration Island and the IMAX. Latisha waved to them as they entered, and they joined her in the front row. Miguel and Kim sat just to Tish's right, so Zoe parked herself on her friend's left. Hamim quickly slid in next to her, and Josh sat on the aisle.

"You ready?" he heard Tish ask Zoe.

"I'm always ready."

Josh decided to try one more time. "Come on, you guys. Why cause trouble now, when everything's going fine?"

"Because," said Zoe, "it's not all fine. Things are starting to fall apart. And we've got to be smart, Clone boy."

Josh bristled at the name, and he looked to Hamim for support. But the other boy just shrugged.

"Wait," said Josh. "You're okay with this?"

"I think they make good points," Hamim replied. In his eyes, Josh knew, Zoe could do no wrong.

Josh gave up. To take his mind off what was coming, he scanned the audience, thinking that maybe Milo needed to move the meetings to a smaller place. At first, almost every kid over ten had attended Council—it was a break from the daily routine and a chance to make new friends. But after a few weeks, most of them had gotten bored and were happy to leave the running of the Islands to the more ambitious among them.

Now, roughly the same clusters of kids from each Island or work group attended regularly, totaling fewer than one hundred and fifty people. These included some of the Brainiacs from Inspiration Island, reporting on technology developments; the O'Bannion Boys, who were now making Timescape a sort of vacation and sports resort for everyone else; Ari and Lana, along with some of the "parents" from Enchanted and Inspiration Islands; and, of course, representatives of the Core. There was also a handful of Ghoulies, off by themselves in the upper tiers.

Milo, Evan, and Moira sat up on the main stage, behind a long table. Caleb and a few of his Protectors were positioned just a few yards in front of them, at the base of the stage, scanning the gathering crowd.

Milo spotted Josh and smiled, raising one hand in greeting. Josh waved back, pleased to be noticed.

Watching Milo as he checked out others in the crowd, Josh was struck yet again by his friend's quiet power. With his strange blue eyes and thick black hair—now grown down almost to his shoulders—he had half the older girls on the Islands in love with him, most of the boys wanting to trade places with him, and all of the kidlets planning to grow up to be like him. Some of the littlest ones had even decided that he actually was King Neptune, and they stared, awestruck, whenever he appeared.

Milo stood, and the crowd immediately quieted. Moira picked up his trident and held it toward him. As Milo tried to take it from her, she clung to the handle just a second longer than necessary, forcing him to look down. She laughed, and he smiled back.

"I think I'm gonna be sick," Zoe muttered. "She actually batted her frickin' eyelashes."

Milo banged the handle of the trident on the floor three times. "This Council is now in session. All problems and ideas will be heard." He sat down again, and Evan looked out at the crowd.

"Okay," Evan said. "Anyone have anything to share from last time?"

The O'Bannion brothers stood first. "We're about ready for the first All-Island Olympics," Ryan said. "Probably in, like, two weeks. We want to get some teams together, so we were wondering if Neptune could maybe make some announcements."

"What kinds of teams?" Milo asked.

"The usual," said Matt. "Soccer. Baseball. Maybe people for some special events, like Robot Wars or Segway races."

Milo raised an eyebrow. "No gladiator battles?"

The brothers stared, and Milo laughed. "Just kidding. Yeah, Neptune'll make some announcements. Just tell Moira what you want him to say."

"Thanks." The boys sat down, and they and their fellow Timescapers immediately put their heads together. Moira jotted a few notes on a pad of paper.

"What else?" asked Evan.

Aiko, who now directed the work teams in the BioPods, hesitantly got to her feet. "We need some more help in the gardens. A few people stopped showing, and the system is breaking down. A lot of veggies need harvesting, and some of the animals aren't looking so good."

Ari stood up nearby. "The same thing's happening at Little Wizards. People aren't coming."

Milo frowned. "How long's this been going on?"

"A couple weeks, maybe."

"Okay. We'll take care of it." Josh saw Caleb glance up at Milo, who nodded and looked back at Aiko and Ari. "And get me the names of the ones who aren't showing up, okay?" Caleb grinned over at his pal Farrel, and Moira made some more notes. The two speakers sat down slowly, both looking uncomfortable. And Josh found himself wondering just what did go on in the hidden room in the UnderGround.

Now Zoe and Latisha stood. Milo saw them, and shook his head.

"The Dynamic Duo," he said. "Means more requisitions or another problem. Or both."

Josh cringed. "You sure you want to do this?" he whispered to Zoe.

She ignored him. Moving a little closer to the stage, she took a deep breath.

"Latisha and I have been talking," she said. "A few of the others, too. We've been here almost a year now, and things are going pretty good. But we haven't ever talked about what's next. Like, what happens in a few more months, or if something goes really wrong."

"What do you mean?"

"I mean, are we just going to stay here forever? We're starting to have some problems, we all know that. Maybe it's time we sent some scouts Outside to see what's going on."

"There's nothing going on," said Evan condescendingly. "It's gone dark. There's no one out there."

Latisha walked up next to Zoe. "But it can't be just us left in the world. That's like saying Earth is the only planet with people. There have to be others. Anyhow, Zoe and I think we should find out for sure."

Moira shook her head, pointing to a list of rules she brought with her to all of the meetings. "Remember Neptune's first decree. 'Whoever leaves, leaves for good.' We can't risk an invasion, or infection."

Zoe spoke again. "That's just it. Do we really think there's still a risk? If people were going to come, it would have happened already. And if there was any kind of disease Outside, it'd be gone by now."

"You don't know that for sure," said Evan. "Maybe people haven't come because they don't know we're here. Because Milo was smart enough to start turning off the big lights at night and having Dark Hours."

"And that was really smart." She paused, and Josh could tell she was choosing her words carefully, struggling to praise a group she didn't quite trust. Finally, she turned away from the stage and faced the rest of the audience instead. "Look. The Core's done a great job keeping us safe and getting us organized. But we don't know if what we've got here can last forever. What if the power finally shuts down? What if the food supply goes bad?"

"And what if someone gets sick?" added Latisha. "Really sick, I mean. We've got bandages and antiseptic creams and aspirin, but no real medicine. It was bad enough after the Riots, and when we lost some of the babies at the beginning. And remember"—she glanced at some of the girls in the stands—"there are going to be new babies soon, too." Josh saw one girl worriedly place her hand on her stomach.

"We might have to leave anyhow," said Zoe. "Only we wouldn't know where to go, or who could help us. But maybe someone Outside has done the same thing we have. We could join up with them, combine what we know."

Ryan O'Bannion raised a hand. "She kind of has a point. I mean, why shouldn't we at least see who's out there?"

Caleb grunted, breaking out of Protector mode. "Because they might be like a buncha animals, eating garbage and crap. Then what?"

Hamim stood. "Then we help them." He smiled at Zoe, who mouthed a thank-you. And Josh felt an unexpected pang of jealousy.

Then he realized that an excited buzz was traveling through the crowd, growing louder. What Zoe and Tish were saying seemed to be hitting the right notes, and the Council was responding. Zoe turned back to face Milo, who had walked out from behind the table. His expression was unreadable.

"So what do you think?" she asked. "Can we do something?"

"No."

Zoe's eyes widened in surprise.

"What? Why? We don't have to send more than—"

"I said *no!*" Milo struck his trident on the stage floor, and the sound echoed throughout the theatre. "We made the rules, all of us, and no one's going to break them. We stay here, and we stay safe."

"But—"

Moira leaned forward like a disapproving mother.

"You heard him, Zoe. Milo said no. So why don't you and Tish just sit down."

Zoe's face went crimson. "Shut up, Moira. No one's talking to you."

She strode toward the stage, but Caleb put out an arm to stop her. She swung her fist down on it, hard, and Josh scrambled to his feet, frantically trying to figure out how to defuse the situation.

"Zoe, stop. Let's just—"

"Don't!" she said, spinning toward him. "Don't you side with them."

"I'm not," he said, astonished she would think so.

The trident was pounding once more. Everyone looked toward the stage, where Milo now stood completely still.

"It's my job to watch over the Islands, Zoe. And I've made my decision. So that's it."

"That's it? That's *it*?" Zoe went rigid, anger pouring from her. "And what do you mean, *your* decision? Who made you king of the world?"

Milo smiled, but his eyes were cold. "You guys did. About a year ago."

Josh stared at him.

"Yeah?" said Zoe. "Well, then I take it back. Up yours, King Neptune!"

She turned, took the stairs two at a time, and stormed out the door.

"Oh, man," whispered Latisha. "This is bad." She was looking at Caleb, who was rubbing his arm and muttering to one of his Protectors. The kid was staring intently at the doorway through which Zoe had disappeared. Josh lifted a hand and caught Milo's eye. "I'll get her," he mouthed, tapping his chest and pointing to the door. Milo hesitated, then nodded.

Josh raced up the aisle and through the exit, chasing after Zoe and yelling her name. He could barely see her in the dim late evening light, and she ignored his pleas to wait. She didn't stop running until she reached the connecting bridge to Atlantis, where she stood leaning over the guardrail as though she wanted to stride across the lagoon and get off the Islands that way. Josh ran up beside her.

"Zoe . . ."

"Shut up. If you don't stand up to him, then you're part of what he's doing. You think he's so damn great."

"Zoe, calm down. I just . . ."

"I said shut up."

She stalked back and forth on the bridge, outlined in the glow of the guide-lights that had blinked on along the walkway.

"What a jerk! What a complete and total ass! He doesn't just think he's king, he thinks he's God. Thinks he can control all our lives, tell everyone what to do. And that we'll all just *listen!*"

"But someone needs to be in charge. Otherwise everything would go crazy."

"Oh. So I should just kiss his butt, never use my brain, never *question* anything?"

"I didn't say that. But he knows what he's doing, Zoe. He pretty much saved us when—"

"'—*when we were wandering around, lost and scared* . . .' Oh, please. That's just the crap that Moira and the Core have been spreading around since they took over this place."

"Because it's true." But even as he spoke, Josh was feeling hollow inside. Milo's anger in the Council had unnerved him.

Zoe sighed and shook her head. She turned and took a few steps toward him. "It's not good what's happening, Josh. They don't let anyone else make decisions anymore. They don't let anyone else think."

"We . . . have Council," he said weakly.

"Yeah. But have you noticed that the only ideas that get passed lately are the ones they agree with?" She looked up at the Coral Palace. "And there are other things that don't make sense."

"Like?"

"Like all those extra meetings that they never invite you to. And sometimes I see Ghoulies going over to Atlantis, sneaking over there late at night. That's a little weird, don't you think?"

Josh didn't say anything, but his mind was whirling.

Zoe waited a moment, then folded her arms. "So? You gonna back me on this, or not?"

Josh felt paralyzed. If he said no, Zoe'd never forgive him. But if he opposed Milo, he'd lose his last connection to the Core. Plus, even though some things looked bad right now, didn't all the good things Milo had done make up for it? And wasn't he right about needing to keep the Islands safe?

"Well?" asked Zoe.

Josh stalled for time. "Let me talk to him first, okay? Maybe he had some other reasons, things he didn't want to say at Council."

"Josh—"

"Just let me talk to him. Besides, he's pretty pissed right now. We don't want to make things worse."

Zoe just looked at him, her disappointment knifing through him.

"Whatever, Josh. Do whatever you want." She looked away, gazing again at the silent water that stretched out around them. Then she stiffened, and Josh heard her gasp.

"Zoe?"

"Josh. Look."

She was staring wide-eyed into the darkness across the lagoon. Josh turned to look in the same direction. At first, he didn't understand what she was seeing. And then . . . he did.

There was a glow in the distance.

"What is it?" he whispered.

"The lights have come on again. Somewhere not too far away." She looked at him, her face a mix of excitement and fear. "Come on. We gotta go back to Council."

ZOE'S VICTORY

Zoe sprinted back toward the IMAX. Josh stared at the glowing light a moment longer, the enormity of what he was seeing washing over him like a tidal wave. If there were lights, then there were people. People at least as organized as they were. But even as he watched, the glow began to flicker.

"Zoe, wait!"

She slowed, looking back at him, then stopped and followed his gaze. As they watched, the lights dimmed, went out, came on again, and then vanished.

"What's going on?" Josh called.

"I don't know." She took a few steps back toward him. "Maybe whoever's over there is still working on the power. Maybe they don't have it all figured out yet. But we still have to let people know." She waited. "So. You coming?"

Josh hesitated, knowing his answer would define their friendship. But then he realized that the glow gave him a solid reason for saying something, for doing something.

"Yeah," he said. "Absolutely."

Zoe grinned, then turned and took off again. Josh followed just behind, and a minute later they burst through the doors.

Every face turned toward them. Latisha and Hamim smiled in

relief, but those on the stage looked at Zoe coldly. Caleb seemed to take a cue from their reaction; his eyes narrowed, and his hands became fists. He lunged up the stairs, meeting them halfway, and grabbed Zoe roughly by the arm.

"Come on. You're outta here."

"Let go of me, buttwipe!" She twisted sideways, then plunged her elbow into Caleb's rib cage. He yelped in surprise and Zoe pulled free. Josh jumped in front of Caleb to stall him—at the very least, the guy might stumble when he ran him over—and Zoe continued to tear down the stairs, gasping out her news as she went.

"We saw lights!" she cried, over and over. "There are lights across the water!"

Shocked silence greeted her announcement. Then an explosion of voices.

"Lights!"

"From where?"

"Ignore her," bellowed Caleb. "She's just lying to save her a—"

A loud pounding broke through the babble. Milo's trident. The noise quickly died.

"Okay, Zoe," he said quietly. "Tell us what you think you saw."

"I don't *think* I saw anything. I saw it. Josh, too." Josh, hurrying down the stairs with Caleb breathing down his neck, saw Milo glance up at him. He nodded. Zoe quickly began describing what had appeared across the lagoon, and the room grew still.

Evan interrupted.

"You sure it wasn't just heat lightning or something else in the sky? Or, I remember reading once about gas that sometimes comes out of the ground and glows. Are you sure it wasn't something like that?"

"I'm sure. It was too bright, and too large. And it was steady, too."

"Not to mention convenient," said Moira. "Interesting that it shows up just when you're trying to talk us into going Outside."

"She's not making it up," said Josh, relieved that he could finally support Zoe. "It was the same kind of light we used to see coming from the towns. Starting at the horizon and glowing off the clouds. It stayed on a few minutes, then flickered and went off."

The excited chatter rose again. Milo sat as still as stone, not saying a word. Finally, he stood, raising his hands to silence the crowd. He took a deep breath.

"Then I guess we need to check it out. Like Zoe said." She blinked, startled, and Milo shifted his gaze to her. "You were right, Zoe. You and Latisha. You were right, and I was wrong." The next words seemed to struggle from his lips. "I'm sorry."

Moira and Evan stared at Milo, their mouths slightly open.

Now Latisha got cautiously to her feet. "So does this mean you'll let . . . Does this mean we'll really do something? Send people out?"

Milo hesitated, but then gave a reluctant smile. "We'd be idiots if we didn't, right?"

Moira leaned toward him. "But Milo—"

He cut her off. "We can't ignore what they saw." Moira glared daggers at Zoe, but didn't say anything else.

Milo looked out at the silent crowd, and his smile faded. "The thing is, we can't just rush out there, either. Some lights have gone on, but we don't know who or what did it. It could be whoever caused the plague in the first place. Maybe they finally got here."

The mood in the room changed. Now it was more subdued. Anxious. Even Zoe lost her triumphant glow.

"So what do we do?" asked Josh.

"I'm not sure. But something." He lowered his head for a

moment, then looked back up. "Let's take some time to think, okay? Core Council, and any other group who wants to. We'll all meet back here again tomorrow to share ideas. Same time. That okay with everyone?"

Everyone in the auditorium voiced their approval, except for Moira, who was still brooding up on the stage, and Caleb, who was frowning at Zoe and rubbing his side.

Milo turned to Zoe deferentially. "That okay with you, too, Zoe?"

She gaped at him. But then she nodded.

"All right. See everyone tomorrow night."

The crowd exited the theatre in a babble of voices. Zoe and Latisha slapped skin, doing a little victory dance. Hamim joined in, hugging both girls but lingering a little longer with Zoe. Once again, Josh felt the strange twinge.

"I am proud of you," Hamim said to Zoe, finally pulling back from the hug and grinning at her. "You made them listen."

Zoe actually blushed. "*We* did. Tish and me."

"What about me?" asked Josh.

"Well, yeah," she said dismissively. "After the lights came on."

Josh almost protested. But she had a point. At least she wasn't calling him a Clone anymore.

"Hey. Guys."

It was Milo, standing on the edge of the stage just above them. He crouched, then hopped down to the floor. The little group stopped their celebration, their expressions guarded. But Milo appeared more uncomfortable than they.

"Listen," he said. "I . . . just wanted to apologize."

Everyone looked at him in surprise.

"I'm not sure what happened to me before. I kind of lost it, I guess."

"Yeah," said Zoe. "You sure did."

"It's just . . . it's hard, you know? Sometimes you just get tired." His shoulders sagged, and he ran one hand through his hair, pushing the long dark strands back off his forehead. His eyes looked weary.

Josh felt a wave of relief. This explained why Milo had gone ballistic. He was just exhausted. Everyone acts a little nuts when they get too tired. Like Lana and Ari had, after the first week of Little Wizards.

"Well, yeah," said Josh, eager to forgive him. "You've been taking care of everyone from practically the first day. Fixing things. Solving problems." Zoe closed her eyes.

But Milo ducked his head, surprisingly humble. "Well, a lot of us have. You guys, too. Still. It's kind of hard when someone talks like we're doing something wrong." He looked at Zoe. "But you were right to say something, Zoe. You, too, Tish. I just . . ."

"It's okay," said Zoe. "We get it." Looking at her, Josh wasn't sure she did get it, exactly. Or that she even believed him. But at least she was talking to him.

"So everything's okay with us?" Milo asked.

"Yeah," said Zoe. "We're good."

Josh suddenly felt like two torn halves of himself had been joined back together. He and Milo smiled at each other. Zoe looked at the two of them, then shook her head.

"C'mon," she said to Tish and Hamim. "I think these two need to hug it out. And that would make me throw up." She smiled sweetly, then started toward the exit with the others. "See you back at home, Josh."

Milo looked over at Evan, Moira, and Caleb, who'd been standing off to the side. "You guys go on back, too. I want to talk to Josh a minute."

Caleb grunted, but both he and Evan turned to leave. Moira lingered, then walked slowly over to Milo.

"Don't be too long," she said, sounding like one of the late-night cable movies Josh used to sneak a look at when his folks weren't around. She touched Milo's arm, letting her finger trace a curved path down to his hand. His face changed slightly, and his breath came a little faster. Satisfied, Moira turned, said goodbye to Josh, and ran lightly up the stairs. Her hips and rear end swayed strategically from side to side, straining against skintight jeans. Josh looked at Milo from the corner of his eye.

"Yeah," Milo said, answering his unspoken question. "For a while now."

"Well . . . good. That's great." Josh wasn't exactly sure what a person said in this kind of situation. *Congratulations* didn't seem right.

But Milo's thoughts had already gone somewhere else. He looked at the floor. "We really okay, Josh?"

"Yeah. Sure. I mean, as long as you're not too pissed at Zoe."

"Hey, she wouldn't be Zoe if she wasn't crazed about something."

They both laughed, and Milo looked at him curiously. "Speaking of Zoe," he said, "are you and her—"

"No! No."

Milo laughed. "What're you waiting for?"

"It's not like that. We're just friends."

"Why? Except for the attitude, she's looking pretty good."

Picturing Zoe leaning out over the lagoon, her body taut with anger, Josh felt his own body react. His face caught fire, and he glanced at Milo to see if he'd noticed. Milo was grinning, but generously chose to look toward the exit.

"Well, I guess we should head out."

"Before Moira gets mad, you mean," said Josh, attempting to deflect some of his own discomfort.

"Yeah. Something like that."

Josh caught his meaning and flushed again. Milo laughed and soft-punched his shoulder. Then the two of them headed up the stairs and onto the darkened paths of Inspiration Island.

THE PLAN

The next night, the crowd in the IMAX had nearly doubled. Which wasn't surprising, Josh thought. The appearance of the lights was the most exciting thing to have happened in months. And everyone wanted to hear what would happen next.

Josh, Zoe, and Hamim sat once again with Tish, Miguel, and Kim, whose combined brain power had been used to flesh out the group's original plan. Miguel had estimated the length of the trip and listed the supplies that would be needed. Then, under Kim's direction, they'd combed Inspiration Island, collecting heat goggles, navigation systems, and other technology from the Exploratorium that might be useful on the scouting expedition.

Similar groups were huddled elsewhere in the auditorium, going over their own proposals. The rest of the Islanders were listening in or talking among themselves. What was interesting, though, was that the Core wasn't up on the stage. They were down on the floor in front.

"What's up with that?" said Latisha.

Hamim considered. "Maybe they are showing that they are one with us. That all ideas will be considered equally."

"Maybe," said Tish, though she didn't look convinced.

Evan called for everyone's attention. He asked for a representative from each planning group to report to Moira, who would add their names to a speakers list. The whole Council—everyone in the auditorium—would hear the ideas and discuss them one by one.

To Zoe and Tish's disappointment, though, there weren't many suggestions; as usual, most of the Islanders had left the thinking to someone else. And the few ideas that were presented were pretty lame.

A gang from the Ancient Cities, for example, had donned fake armor from the Caesar's Treasures store and attached wooden shields to their forearms. They wanted to march out like Roman soldiers to show any Outsiders that the Islanders were a powerful force, not to be messed with. A second group, pirates from the Barbary Coast, had a similar plan, suggesting that they raid nearby settlements and bring back stolen booty.

To Josh's amazement, Milo listened carefully to each screwy idea, and Moira took detailed notes.

"Looks like Hamim was right," said Josh. "They want everyone to feel listened to."

"Sure," said Zoe. "Before they go ahead and do whatever they want."

Josh almost said something, but decided not to.

Now it was their turn. Everyone had agreed that Latisha would present their ideas, since she was the kidlets' favorite Teacher and everyone respected her. She launched into a description of their plan with all the enthusiasm and energy she usually brought to her classroom. By the time she'd finished, Milo was nodding approvingly. So were the other Core Council members. Even Moira.

"That sounds great," said Milo. "Really great. A bunch of us came up with almost the same idea. But you guys are a lot farther along."

The group looked at each other, taken off guard by the positive reaction. Even Josh was surprised—he had thought there'd be a little more resistance.

"In fact," Milo said, now speaking to the rest of the assembly, "does anyone here see any reason we just shouldn't go with what Tish's group said?"

Heads turned and bodies shifted as people looked around the room. The Timescapers looked a little disappointed that they wouldn't be able to pillage and plunder, but no one, including them, objected to Milo's suggestion.

"Okay," said Milo. "Then that's our plan."

Zoe looked like she was in shock.

"What's going on?" she muttered to Tish and Josh.

Tish raised an eyebrow. "What do you mean?"

"He didn't challenge a single thing. None of them did."

"And that's bad?" asked Josh.

"No. But it seems too easy."

Milo hoisted himself to sit on the edge of the stage. "Okay, here's what I think. We lower the barricades on just one side of the tracks. That'll still keep us protected, in case something goes wrong. Then we'll send Scouts toward where the lights were. Just a few people, though, in case it's dangerous out there."

"Wait," said one of the armor-clad Timescapers. "If it's dangerous, why aren't we sending an army out, like my group said?"

"Because we don't want anyone to get killed. A big group's easy to spot. Easier for any gangs, or mutants, or whatever's out there, to see coming and get ready to attack. Three or four people can stay hidden a lot better. I mean, this is just to—what did they used to call it in the old war movies? When they just wanted information?"

"Gather intelligence?" suggested Moira.

"Yeah. Gather intelligence. We don't want to start a war, right?"

Everyone nodded. Even most of the Timescapers.

"So all that's left now is to choose the Scouts. Any volunteers?" Milo scanned the crowd.

Conversation rippled around the theatre as everyone talked with a friend, a neighbor, a sibling. But no one was jumping up. Josh figured that Milo's comments about gangs, mutants, and dying must have dampened everyone's sense of adventure.

But then he noticed Milo talking to Evan and Eli, both of whom were nodding. Zoe was looking at them, too, and Josh saw her whole body stiffen.

"That's it," she said. "That's why he's been so mellow. He goes along with our scouting idea, but then he rigs it so the only ones who go Outside are Atlantans. Or Clones."

Latisha shrugged. "So? Let *them* risk their necks."

"No," said Zoe. "Don't you see? Whatever 'intelligence' they brought back would be useless. They'd say whatever Milo told them to say." She sniffed. "Or whatever Moira wrote for them to say."

Josh blew out his breath. "You still don't trust them? C'mon, Zoe, Milo's doing everything you wanted!"

"Exactly," said Zoe. "He's doing everything I wanted." She was silent for a moment. "I'm going to volunteer."

"What?"

"I'm going to volunteer. That's the only way I'll know if the information we get back is real."

"You can't volunteer," said Tish. "And neither can Josh."

"Why not?"

"Sam and Maddie. What if something happened to you? Think they'd ever get over it?"

Zoe swore in frustration.

Hamim's quiet voice interrupted. "I could go."

They looked at him.

"You are my friends. You took care of me when I was hurt, and you made me part of your family. This would be a way for me to thank you. And you know you can trust me."

Zoe's entire body relaxed. "More than just about anyone on the Islands." She jumped forward and hugged him. And Josh knew that he himself had just lost serious points in a contest he had only recently realized he was competing in.

Milo motioned for Moira to hand him his trident. He stood, and pounded it on the stage. "Well?" he asked. "Who's going to volunteer?"

Eli stepped forward. "I'll go."

"Me, too," said Evan immediately.

Paravi raised her hand. "You may need a driver, if you find a car or something. I'll volunteer, too."

"See?" Zoe hissed. "What'd I tell you? Three Atlantans."

"But it's Paravi. And Eli," said Josh.

"I don't care."

"Thanks," said Milo. "But I think just one from the Core is enough. Maybe Paravi, because of the whole driving thing. Anyone else?"

"Me," said Ryan, from among the Timescapers. "I'll represent the O'Bannion Boys."

Josh whispered to Zoe. "Your conspiracy theory is falling apart."

"Maybe," she said. "But do we really know who Milo's friends are? Let's see what happens when Hamim volunteers."

"Jeez, Zoe!"

Now Hamim raised his hand. "Milo. I will be one of your Scouts as well."

Milo didn't even blink. "Great," he said. "Perfect." He looked at Moira, who was scribbling down the names. "So we have . . ."

"Paravi, Ryan, and Hamim."

"And me," said Kim, raising her hand. "You need someone who knows how to use all the gadgets we found."

"Right," said Milo. "Thanks, Kim." He looked again at Moira's list. "I think that's plenty. So now—"

"Wait."

A lean figure detached itself from the silent group clustered like bats in the upper tiers of the auditorium. Everyone watched as he descended. He had straight black hair, even longer than Milo's, and a thin, angular face with high cheekbones. He stopped at the bottom of the steps, scanning the crowd. When his gaze crawled over Josh, Josh had the weirdest feeling of being pinned down, like a bug on a display board.

The boy turned back toward the stage, facing Milo. He put his hands together, steepling long, ice-white fingers and touching them to his lips. He bowed slightly. "Namaste."

Milo looked unsettled. "What?"

"Namaste. It means, 'the spirit in me meets the spirit in you.' It's a greeting."

"Oh." Milo dipped his head. "Namaste." He paused. "Do . . . I know you?"

"You should," the boy said softly. "I've been to every Council. And I was part of the Night Crew. My name was Seth, but now they call me Shadow."

"I remember him!" whispered Zoe. "God, he's really changed."

"That's for sure," said Josh.

"I mean, he is really *hot.*"

"Huh?" Josh saw Zoe's eyes skim over the other boy appreciatively. "You've gotta get your hormones checked."

Milo had regained his composure. "Sorry I didn't recognize you."

Shadow gave a thin smile. "I understand."

"So . . . what do you want?"

"I want to volunteer."

Milo paused. "I think we have enough."

"You have representatives from all the Islands except Nightmare. I think you need one more Scout."

Zoe suddenly grabbed Josh's arm. "Wait. Something's not right. He's one of the Ghoulies I've seen heading over to Atlantis at night."

"You sure?"

"Almost positive. Which means Milo's only pretending not to know him."

They watched as Milo consulted with Moira and Evan, and then shrugged. "All right," he said to Shadow. "You're number five. So we have one from each Island."

The boy nodded coolly. "Excellent." He bowed again, then returned to the upper seats where the other Ghoulies waited.

Zoe was watching him. "Maybe Hamim shouldn't go."

"What?" Josh was surprised. "Why?"

"I'm not sure. Just a bad feeling."

"Yeah. It's called being paranoid." But even as he spoke, Josh shivered at the memory of Shadow's eyes on him. He tried to shake off the chill. "Look, you wanted someone you could trust. You know you don't have to worry about Kim, and I really think Ryan and Paravi are okay, too."

"I know. But still . . ." She was staring at Shadow, rocking nervously, her fists shoved up against her chin.

Milo called for everyone's attention.

"Okay. Looks like we have our Scouts. Why don't we try to have everything ready in about three, four days. Barricades down. Supplies ready. And from now on, Dark Hours start right from dusk."

"Why?" asked Kyle O'Bannion. "If we do that, we can't have night games at the Coliseum."

"Sorry, Kyle. But we saw their lights. We don't want them seeing ours, if they haven't already. So no lights at all, except inside where there aren't any windows. And we put more Protectors on sentry duty." He looked down at Caleb, who nodded.

They worked out some additional details, then Milo got to his feet and raised his arms. "So—are we ready to find out what's Outside? Ready to see what's waiting for us there?" The crowd cheered and applauded, and Milo flashed his mesmerizing smile. Josh swore he could hear female sighs underneath the applause.

The noise died down, and everyone began heading toward the exits. Josh and the others turned to leave as well.

"Hey. Josh."

He turned back toward the stage. Milo was still standing there, like he wanted to say something. "Go ahead," Josh said to the others. "I'll be there in a minute." He walked over to where Milo waited.

"What's up?" he asked.

Milo just looked at him for a moment, his expression unreadable. "I just wanted to tell you thanks," he said finally. "You've been a good friend, through everything. I just wish—"

He stopped, and there was an awkward pause.

"It's okay," said Josh. "It was my choice." Milo nodded. Then he headed to the side of the stage, where Moira stood waiting.

THE DEPARTURE

Every evening after Zoe and Josh first saw the Glow, clusters of Islanders made their way to the tops of the Palace and coaster mountains, waiting to see if the lights came on again. The first night they waited for hours, but the darkness remained undisturbed.

On the second night, though, the skies lit up once more. The soft glow warmed the misty air, silhouetted the trees and buildings on the mainland, and edged low-hanging clouds in gold. The Islanders went crazy, cheering and whistling and applauding like they were at a fireworks display. The Protectors had to silence them, reminding them not to advertise their presence on the Islands.

Then the lights pulsed from strong to weak, over and over, and finally shuddered out again. Everyone groaned. They waited a little longer, hoping the show would start again, but nothing happened. Not that night, or the next two. Still, the lights had been on long enough for Miguel and some of the other math wizards to get a sense of the direction and distance the Scouts should aim for. And to prove that Zoe and Josh had been telling the truth.

"We still can't be sure what it is," said Josh, trying to keep everyone's expectations from getting too high. "It could just be some last gasp from an old generator. Or something finally short-circuiting. Even animals, gnawing on power cords."

"Or it could be people," said Zoe. "Anyhow, we've still got to check."

Preparations for the expedition went smoothly. Greg's construction crew began dismantling the barricades almost immediately, and the Scouts added to the supplies that Miguel and Kim had collected for their journey.

They figured they had to bring enough for a week, maybe more. The farthest recognizable landmark was a tower at the airport, which they already knew was roughly ten miles away. The glow was coming from some distance beyond that. Looking at one of the hundreds of tourist maps still stacked in Guest Relations, Miguel decided that the lights might be from a small town called Heron's Landing, about eighteen miles away. If the Scouts could find bicycles or any other form of transport, they could get there, check things out, and return in a couple of days. If they had to go on foot, it would take much longer.

Zoe grew more and more anxious as the time for departure drew closer. She followed Hamim with her eyes whenever he was around, kept making him promise to be careful. He, in turn, seemed to thrive on her concern, enjoying the unfamiliar role of hero. Finally, after another of Zoe's warnings, Hamim put an arm around her shoulders and gave her an affectionate squeeze.

"Stop worrying," he said. "I will be careful. I promise."

She turned, throwing both arms around his neck and hugging him tightly. Watching them, Josh had an unexpected reaction: he wanted to strangle Hamim.

Later that day, back at their cottage, Josh waited until the kidlets were off playing and Hamim had left to meet with the rest of the Scouts. He wandered over to where Zoe was pointlessly reorganizing some of the shelves, intending nothing more than a casual conversation. To his dismay, that wasn't what came out of his mouth.

"So. You in love with him or something?"

Zoe gave him a look normally reserved for Sam at his brattiest. "*What* are you talking about?"

"Hamim. You in love with him?"

"Don't be stupid."

But now that he'd started, Josh couldn't seem to shut himself up.

"Well, he's always had a thing for you. And you seem pretty obsessed the last couple of days. Always following him around, talking to him, touching his arm . . ." Then one more word escaped, despite his attempts to swallow it. "Hugging."

Zoe jumped to her feet, eyes flashing. "And you want to know why? Because he's doing this for me, Josh. For *me*. Because I'm paranoid, like you said. Because I opened my big fat mouth and he wanted to make me feel better. So now he's going Outside. With that Shadow creep. And we don't know what's out there." Her eyes began to fill, and she turned away. "You are *such* a jerk."

Josh could feel his face burning. He tried to put a hand on Zoe's shoulder, but she shook him off. Then he found more words. The right ones this time.

"You're right, Zoe. I'm a jerk. A big, stupid jerk." He reached out again, and this time she didn't stop him. Tentatively, he slid his arm around her, then touched his lips to the top of her head. "Hamim will be okay," he murmured. "Don't worry."

She relaxed slightly and leaned against him. They stood that way for a long time.

That night, though, Josh had trouble sleeping.

At first, he just kept jerking awake, always certain that Zoe had disappeared—kidnapped, or taken away somehow. Eventually, though, he did fall asleep. But now his mind drifted to the expedition that was about to take place, and he wandered down different dreamscapes, imagining what Hamim and the other Scouts might find on their journey.

In the best-case scenario, the Scouts quickly encountered other little settlements: some kids living in the resort hotels, some in malls, and some, farther away, on farms or ranches. Like the Islanders, they'd gotten organized, located supplies, and started figuring out how to get the power on again and the water running. They'd begun finding each other, too, connecting their little communities and sharing their resources. Josh even imagined Hamim running into Sara, the girl who had begun the exodus from the Islands. In his dream, she was throwing a stick for her dog, Jasper, and playing with a group of her old friends.

But then the dream stuttered and restarted, dragging Josh down different paths to barren cityscapes inhabited by hungry packs of diseased, vaguely human creatures preying on each other, stealing from each other, hunched over the remains of rotten food and animal carcasses. Gnawing on other things as well. Unspeakable things.

Finally, the Scouts were ready. Each had a backpack strapped over a pocketed jacket or hiking vest, pulled from a warehouse where outgrown or discarded clothes were stored and where everyone "shopped" when they tired of items with Island logos. They divided the food and water among them, and each took responsibility for some of the specialty items, like the GPS and medical supplies. In addition, every Scout had infrared goggles for night vision, and two knives: one larger, to serve as a tool in case they had to cut their way through or into anything, and a hidden one that was smaller, sharper, and easy to access.

"I wish they had guns," Zoe complained. "Why don't they have guns?"

"I don't know," said Latisha. "I'm sure I saw lots of Uzis and semiautomatics in the gift shops."

Zoe didn't even smile. "Yeah, well Outside isn't a theme park. Anyone out there is going to have them."

Neither Josh nor Latisha had a clever answer for that.

The Scouts gathered at the monorail station in the dead of night, when most of the Islanders were asleep. This time, there were no speeches from Neptune, no carefully choreographed farewells. Everyone agreed it would be better not to broadcast when the Scouts were leaving. Then fewer people would become worried if their absence stretched into days. Or weeks.

Other than Milo, Moira, and a few other members of the Core, only close friends and family were on hand to say good-bye. There were Matt and Kyle, talking quietly to their brother, Ryan. Miguel, with his arm around Kim. And of course, Josh, Zoe, and Latisha, clustered around Hamim and Paravi.

A short distance away, Shadow silently watched all of them.

Looking at him, Josh felt icy fingers slide down his back. Without thinking, he turned and grabbed Hamim's arm.

"You don't have to do this, you know. You could just stay here."

Hamim looked at him in surprise.

"Why would I do that?" he asked. "This is something that could help all of us. And it will be an adventure." He grinned. "I have never had an adventure."

"What do you call the last twelve months? A frickin' *party*?"

Both girls stared at him.

"You okay?" asked Latisha.

Josh almost blurted out his fear, but instead gave a weak smile.

"Worried about Uncle Hamim, is all." But he could see that Zoe wasn't fooled, was feeling the same sick apprehension he was.

Finally, Milo walked over to the tracks. He turned toward the Scouts, looking more subdued than Josh had ever seen him. "You guys ready?" he asked.

All five nodded.

"Then good luck," he said. "We'll keep watch 'til you come back."

The Scouts hitched up their backpacks and said quick, final good-byes. They went up the ramps of the monorail station, disappearing inside only to emerge seconds later in the groove on the concrete track. For a while, everyone but Shadow glanced back periodically to receive a wave or a smile from those left behind. But finally they stopped turning, and the watchers slowly trailed off. Soon only Zoe and Josh remained, looking after Hamim until he disappeared around the curve of the monorail tracks.

WAITING

The next few days crawled by. At first, Zoe could barely function. She wandered back to the beach on the afternoon the Scouts left, staring across the lagoon until she fell into an exhausted sleep. She repeated this the next day, and the next, as though by standing watch she could keep Hamim safe.

Josh remembered his own long-ago vigils in the hospital, and he left Zoe alone. With Maddie and Devon's help, he got the kidlets fed and off to school each morning, then lost himself in his assignments at the Living Oceans.

He hoped they'd been right to send the Scouts. But he, too, had finally accepted the fact that they couldn't all stay on the Islands forever. Like Zoe and Tish said, more systems would eventually break down, or supplies would run low. On the other hand, if Outside was the horror show he'd seen in his dreams, maybe it was better not to know that for a while.

On the fourth day after the Scouts left, Josh and the kidlets were sitting at the midday meal, grinning at a pompous speech being delivered by the dragon head, when Zoe walked in. She was hollow-eyed and exhausted, but to Josh's relief, she seemed more herself. Sam let out a whoop and ran over to her. He hugged her around the waist, then backed off, frowned, and punched her arm.

"Where you been?" he demanded. "Josh said you were on a special 'signment for the King, but I think he's a big, fat, stupid liar."

"Real nice," said Josh. "See what happens next time you want to go visit Lop-Ear."

"Sorry, Samster," said Zoe, crouching down and pulling her brother in for another hug. "I just needed to do some things."

"Well, don't do 'em again!" he said.

"Deal." She looked up at Josh. "Sorry I freaked out," she said.

"It's okay."

"No. It wasn't fair to you. And you're just as worried as I am."

"I said it's okay." He leaned over and kissed the top of her head. Then he started, realizing what he'd done. He felt his face burn.

But Zoe just smiled, then looked back at Sam. "Okay, bud. No work today. No school, either. I'm all yours until dinner. What do you want to do?"

Sam pursed his lips, thinking. Then his face brightened. "Let's go to the collie place!"

"The what?"

"The collie place! Neptune said they'd be playin' soccer there today!"

"He means the collie-see-um," said Maddie patiently, with the air of someone much older and wiser. Josh had noted with amusement that the more obnoxious Sam got, the more mature Maddie tried to act. "They been practicing there. Getting ready for the 'lympics next week."

"It's our team today, too," said Sam, fiercely loyal. "So we gotta go."

"Perfect," said Zoe. "Okay. The collie place it is."

"And Josh's gotta come, too. And Maddie and Devon and . . ."

"We'll all go," said Josh. "Giz and Shana, too. We'll have a real family day."

Sam's suggestion turned out to be the perfect antidote for the tension of the previous week. They entered the Coliseum and found seats on the north side of the stadium, right in the center and just a few rows beneath the Emperor's Box. They had lots of company—the stands were full of spectators who'd come to visit with friends, watch the two teams practice, and enjoy a few hours stolen from work.

Just across the arena, below the Dignitaries' Box, Josh could see Tish and some of the Teachers taking a well-deserved break from school. He stood, waving until she saw them. She waved back, then cupped her hands around her mouth.

"Inspiration's going to kick Enchanted's butt," she yelled, referring to the two teams warming up below them.

"In your dreams," Josh yelled back. Tish stood, turned, and wiggled her backside at him. The kidlets screamed with laughter.

"Nice role model," said Zoe, grinning. But then a whistle blew, and they turned their attention back to the field.

The players threw themselves into the game. They were still a little awkward, not quite having adjusted to playing soccer with one of the half-size basketballs that once had been sold as souvenirs. Their uniforms were irregular, too. The Enchanted team wore long orange T-shirts with tufts of fur down their spines, courtesy of the Heart of Africa stores. The Inspiration team wore shiny gray knights' tunics, tied around the waist.

No one cared—especially not Josh's family. They yelled like crazy people when their team scored, and booed just as enthusiastically at every wild kick or failed block.

One of the Inspiration forwards leaped at the ball, bulleting it past the goalie. The kid sank to his knees in despair.

"YOU SUCK!" Sam yelled happily.

"Sam!" said Maddie. "That's not nice. What if it was you playing, and you messed up?"

"Then *I'd* suck."

Josh and Zoe burst out laughing. The game continued, and by halftime the score was 2-1, with the Enchanted team miraculously in the lead. Zoe yelled for Tish's attention, then treated the Teachers to a view of *her* backside.

"Hey, guys!" someone called. "Having fun?" It was Matt O'Bannion, yelling up to them from the stadium floor where he and Kyle were acting as referees.

"Yeah!" called Josh. "This is great, Matt!"

"Whadja expect? The O'Bannion Boys never fail!"

He froze, his grin faltering. He's thinking about Ryan, Josh realized. But then Matt recharged his smile, waved, and ran back onto the field, where the second half was about to begin.

"This really *is* great, isn't it?"

Zoe tensed, and Josh twisted to look behind him. Milo was heading down to them from the Emperor's Box, looking as pleased as if he'd organized the games himself. Evan, Toad, and some other members of the Core were sitting in the box as well, yelling down at the players on the field. Toad's eyes were popping more than usual.

Josh smiled. "Yeah," he said. "It's terrific."

Milo sat just behind them, and leaned forward. "Wait 'til you see the opening ceremonies for the Olympics. Alex has this whole spectacular planned. All the musicians are going to be playing, and they're even going to have someone run in with a torch. It's going to be the best thing we've ever done."

Zoe finally spoke, not looking at him.

"You aren't even worried about them, are you?"

"Who?" said Milo.

"Who. The Scouts. You weren't even thinking about Ryan

being Outside just now. Or any of them. All you care about is your next big event."

Josh cringed, but Milo didn't say anything. He just slid over slightly, then moved down a row to sit next to Zoe. She continued to stare straight ahead.

"Yeah, Zoe, I was thinking about Ryan. I haven't stopped thinking about him and the others."

"Could have fooled me."

Milo sighed, looking down at the field.

"I haven't slept the past three nights. But the way I see it, it's up to us older kids, the ones everyone depends on, to make people feel safe. To keep them from worrying. Like you guys do with Sam and Maddie and the kidlets."

Zoe didn't say anything. Milo continued.

"So right now, I can walk around like a zombie, or I can act like I think everything's going to work out great. The second way is harder, but it's probably better for everyone else. Besides ... wasn't the whole Scout thing your idea?"

A flush crept up Zoe's neck.

"Anyhow," said Milo. "I'm doing what I think I have to. Sorry if it bothers you."

He got up and began the climb back to the box.

"Milo." Zoe's voice was subdued. But Milo stopped where he was, listening.

"You're right," she said. "This time you're right and I'm wrong." She paused. "I'm sorry."

"It's okay." He and Josh exchanged quick looks, and Milo returned to where Evan and Toad were shouting colorful advice to the goalie.

Josh was almost afraid to say anything. But Zoe helped him out.

"Maybe I've been wrong about him."

Josh stared, then clutched at his chest. "Two apologies and a confession in one day. You're killing me, Zoe."

"Shut up. Or it'll never happen again."

The rest of the afternoon felt as bright as the sun. The teams practiced until dusk, and then, after dinner, Josh and Zoe entertained their kidlets by playing hide-and-go-seek in the dark. Of course, they had to pretend they didn't see Shana's fairy wings, which stuck out of every hiding place, and they tended to run a little slower when they spotted Devon, who always carried little Giz on his back. They ended the night with Memory Time, laughing with Zoe over another of her stories about her dad.

They tucked Shana, Giz, and Sam into bed, letting Maddie and Devon stay up a little longer, as usual. But finally, even the older two gave up trying to stay awake—the outing and the games had exhausted them. Zoe and Josh sank into the pillows of their little living room, watching the flickering candles they left burning at bedtime, like night-lights.

"This was a good day," said Zoe.

"Yeah. It was."

Outside they could hear a faraway voice, and someone laughing. It gave Josh a pleasant, secure feeling—like the one he used to get when he heard his parents talking in the kitchen after he'd gone to bed.

"Josh?"

"Yeah?"

"Thanks for being such a good guy." To Josh's surprise, she leaned into him, resting her head on his shoulder and putting one hand on his thigh. He felt his body stir, knew that this was the moment he could change their relationship from friends to something else. But then he thought of Hamim, the way his face looked whenever he was near Zoe, and he sighed. Awkwardly, he lifted his arm and put it around Zoe, patting her shoulder as a brother would. They sat quietly together, not speaking, and Josh felt himself drifting toward sleep.

The nightmare lay waiting for him.

In his dream, he heard Maddie cry out, and Shana shriek. There was the sound of things crashing to the floor, garbled words that he didn't understand. He tried to get up, but his arms and legs felt pinned. Peering deeper into his delirium, he saw dark figures lurching around the room, clambering over furniture, grabbing at the kidlets.

And then the true horror hit.

It wasn't a dream.

OUTSIDE IN

Josh shot to full consciousness. Two figures staggered across the floor, dimly outlined in the light of the guttering candles. They were thin, covered in rags, and their skin looked greenish white. The creatures pawed the books and toys from the shelves, knocked over chairs, and bent low over the cots, silent except for harsh, ragged breathing. Josh tried to jump toward them, but found to his horror that he couldn't move his legs and arms. He could feel Zoe struggling next to him, crying out for Sam.

The kidlets were all awake, huddled shrieking in their beds. The monsters lurched over to them and bent down, picking curiously at their hair and clothes with long, talonlike nails. Devon jumped from his cot and swung a fist at one of them, but the thing caught the boy's hand in its claw, shoving him hard into the wall. Devon collapsed and lay still.

"Josh!" shrieked Maddie.

"Get away from them," Josh yelled furiously, still struggling against whatever was binding him. "Get the *hell* away from them!"

One of the creatures paused, then limped over and bent close to him. Its face was covered with open sores, and half of its nose looked eaten away. It laughed dully.

Josh gaped. The thing was human. And, more horribly . . . it was young.

An air horn sounded in the distance. Then another, and another. The Protectors had spotted the invaders.

The creature in front of Josh froze, cocking its head. It lurched away, joining its companion. They poked their claws into the screaming cluster of children, and then a gust of wind came in and blew out the candle. Swearing, weeping in frustration, Josh could only watch the silhouettes of their hunched, misshapen forms limping toward the door.

A moment later they were gone.

"Maddie!" Josh yelled hoarsely. "Maddie, you still there?"

There was no answer, and his stomach dropped and heaved. Then he heard a shaky voice.

"I'm here," she said between sobs. "But, Josh . . ." She gasped, and started crying again. Next to him, Josh felt Zoe stiffen.

"Maddie," she called, "where's Sam? Sam, where are you?"

Josh strained to hear, and saw something crawling toward him on all fours. He jerked backward, then realized it was Maddie, too terrified to walk.

"The monsters took him," she moaned. "They took Sammie and Giz!"

Josh shot a look at Zoe, who raised her head and screamed Sam's name. At the sound, Shana and Maddie cried even louder, choking on snot and tears.

"Everybody shut up," Josh said. "Just shut up!" Zoe froze, and the sobs of the younger ones lessened. Josh realized that what happened next was all up to him. "Maddie, light some more of the candles and bring them over here. We've gotta figure out why Zoe and I can't move."

A minute later, candlelight flickered across his body. All that was binding him were a few strips of something that looked like duct tape, wrapped around his ankles and wrists. But when he struggled, they felt like iron bands.

"Mad, go get something sharp. We've got to cut this stuff off."

The girl was still trembling.

"Maddie! NOW!"

She jumped to her feet and darted across the room, returning seconds later with the bucket of scissors they used for crafts. She grabbed the largest pair and began sawing at the tape. Minutes later, Josh scraped the last remnants from his own legs. Zoe tried to do the same, but her hands were shaking too badly.

"Help Zoe," Josh said to his sister. He stumbled across the room on deadened legs, vaguely aware of an orange glow bleeding through the windows from outside. Devon lay in the corner, stretched out on the floor but beginning to move. Josh pulled him to a sitting position and leaned him against the wall.

"You all right?"

"My head hurts."

Josh felt along his scalp, walking his fingers through Devon's hair. He found a lump on the back of his skull, but no blood.

"I think you're okay. Just sit still for a while."

Devon nodded, and Josh returned to where Maddie was pulling the last shreds of tape from Zoe's ankles.

"Come on, Zoe," he said. "We've got to go after them."

She nodded vaguely, but her eyes were dead. Josh wasn't even sure she'd heard him. So he did what he'd always seen people do in movies: he slapped her.

"What the hell!" she said, gasping. But her eyes snapped back into focus.

"We've got to go after them. Now!"

Zoe clambered to her feet, and together they raced outside,

yelling at Maddie and Devon to close the door behind them and shove the heaviest furniture up against it. A handful of other kids were in the street as well, shouting out names and looking frantically up and down Starlight Lane. Small fires struggled to life in waste bins, and glowing ashes floated toward the cottages.

"Come on," Josh yelled. "They have to be heading toward the monorail tracks. It's the only way in or out!"

"What about the fires?"

"Let someone else put 'em out! We've got to go!"

They ran, followed by other frenzied parents. Doors and windows opened as they raced by, the startled occupants pulled from sleep by the blasts of the air horns and the screams of their neighbors.

"We've been attacked!" Josh yelled as he and Zoe tore past. "Check the other families. See who needs help!"

They sped through the village, terror taking root behind them, then pounded across the connecting bridge into Atlantis. The bridge from Inspiration Island was also spewing out a stream of kids, all with the same crazed look.

The two groups swirled together in the Palace courtyard. Josh turned toward the monorail station, but Zoe grabbed his arm, dragging him toward the other bridge. He started to pull back, then saw Latisha pushing her way toward them. The three threw their arms around one another.

"They got Jesse," said Latisha, naming one of her favorite sixes, a little boy she had adopted along with two of her other students. "I heard screaming and I woke up and saw him being dragged out the door by these sick goblin things with claws." She shuddered. Then she pulled back slightly, looking at Zoe.

"Sam," whispered Zoe. "And little Giz."

"Oh, God." Latisha's face went ashen.

Around them, the crowd was growing, ready to explode with panic and fear. Josh looked at the two girls grimly.

"So are we just going to moan about it?" He raised his voice, calling to the others. "Why are we standing here? Everyone! Let's go!"

The crowd roared, and they all surged through the darkness toward the monorail station.

The speakers rumbled, and hot flames exploded from the reflecting pool, forcing everyone back.

"STOP!"

Josh looked up. Milo stood on the balcony of the Palace, and it was his voice, not Neptune's, roaring through the speakers.

"I SAID STOP! THE PROTECTORS ARE ALREADY AFTER THEM!"

"I'm not staying here while they've got my brother!" someone yelled. The entire crowd pushed forward again.

"WHAT ARE YOU GOING TO DO WHEN YOU FIND THEM? *IF* YOU FIND THEM? DID YOU BRING LIGHTS? WEAPONS? ANY-THING?"

The crowd slowed, and Josh was suddenly aware of his empty hands. Everyone stopped running, confused, and looked up again at Milo. Josh noticed a flicker of movement just behind him, in the shadows. Moira.

Milo's voice dropped.

"I know we're all scared. But we're going to get the kidlets back, I promise. We just don't want any more people lost or hurt. Look out there."

Everyone turned and stared toward the monorail. The station itself was barely visible, and the concrete track had vanished, swallowed by the night.

"They could be out there waiting for us. Ready to attack.

Maybe that's why they took the kids—to lure us." The listening crowd went still. "But the Protectors went armed, and they have lights." He pointed back toward the track.

Less than a kilometer in the distance, Josh could see a string of bright dots clustered together, just beyond the first barricade.

"They're going to find those things," said Milo, leaning forward on the balcony. "And they're going to rescue our kids."

His face and voice were strong and certain. Josh felt the hysteria around him begin to subside.

"So what do we do?" someone asked.

"We wait," said Milo quietly. "Go back to your homes. We'll sound the horns as soon as we know anything."

Josh and Zoe returned to their cottage. Looking in the window, they saw Devon sitting up and Maddie reading a story to Shana inside a ring of candlelight. The fairy wings lay crumpled in a corner.

They called to the kids, then listened to their excited voices and the shriek of furniture being moved away from the door. When they entered, Devon and Maddie looked at them and past them, expressions hopeful. Then their faces fell.

"You don't have them," Devon said, making it more an accusation than a statement.

"Not yet," said Josh. He looked at Shana, who was staring at him wide-eyed, and chose his next words carefully. "But Neptune sent his soldiers after them. With swords and . . . and magic lights. They'll get Sam and Gizzie back."

Devon looked at him with eyes more skeptical than any nine-year-old's should be. "You sure, Dude?"

"I'm sure. King Neptune promised."

Devon nodded, but Josh could see that he didn't believe him.

Every minute that passed felt like an hour. Shana, at least, wasn't aware of the endless night. With her parents back and King Neptune looking for her brothers, she was able to fall into an exhausted sleep. Maddie and Devon stayed awake, huddling together for comfort, sharing guesses about what the King and his soldiers would do when they found the invaders. Josh nodded at Devon, grateful that the boy was helping maintain the illusion.

"So who were they?" Zoe whispered. "Where'd they come from?"

"From Outside, I guess." Josh thought a moment. "They must've seen the Scouts and figured out the barricades were down."

"So why didn't they come right away?"

"I don't know. Maybe it took a day or two for the Scouts to get to wherever they were living. Or maybe whatever made them look so sick has rotted their brains, and they can't think straight."

"Like the zombies in those old *Living Dead* movies."

"Yeah."

Zoe nodded, then stared straight ahead. "Did you get a good look at them?" she asked, her voice quiet. "They were kids."

Josh didn't respond. But he had noticed. And realized that he and Maddie—all of the Islanders—might be looking like that, if they'd gone Outside. Milo had been right.

Nothing more was said, and night crept toward morning. Maddie and Devon finally fell asleep, but Zoe's and Josh's eyes remained wide open. Occasionally, Josh would realize that nothing was going through his mind. Absolutely nothing. It was as though his brain had decided it couldn't take any more and just switched itself off.

An air horn split the silence, and everyone jumped. Hearts pounding, Josh and Zoe jumped to their feet, hope tearing at them.

"AWAKE, EVERYONE," thundered the voice of King Neptune.

"AWAKE AND COME TO NEPTUNE'S THEATRE. THERE IS NEWS TO BE SHARED."

"What does that mean?" asked Zoe nervously.

"I don't know. But we're sure as hell gonna find out." Josh looked at his sister. "Maddie—"

"Forget it," she said. "We're coming, too." Next to her, Devon folded his arms and glared at them.

Josh almost smiled. He gathered little Shana in his arms, and all of them rushed out the door. Minutes later, they were hurrying across the winding entrance paths to Neptune's Theatre, meeting up with hundreds of other kids whose faces all showed warring emotions of hope and terror. They entered the theatre, joining Latisha in the stands, nerves tightening when they saw nothing but an empty stage in the weak, pre-dawn light.

A spotlight suddenly glowed on the trainer's platform. Josh looked back over his shoulder, up to the engineer's booth, and saw Evan working the equipment. Milo stepped into the pale circle of light and looked out at the anxious crowd.

"We have something to show you," he said quietly.

The spotlight swung over to the reflecting wall. A door opened, and Caleb walked out with several of the Protectors. Between them, bound in ropes, were two of the invaders from Outside.

The crowd gasped.

"The Protectors caught these two, and we're going to find out everything we can from them," said Milo quietly. He paused, as though not sure how to continue. Finally, he looked down, and took a deep breath.

"There's something else, too."

The silence in the stands was absolute.

The spotlight swung away from the captives, lighting up the tunnel leading from the side entrance of the theatre. There was a shouted order, the sound of pounding feet, the echo of dozens of voices.

Josh and Zoe jumped to their feet. The missing children streamed out of the entrance, yelling happily, eyes searching the crowd for their families.

"There they are!" cried Tish, pointing toward the middle of the crowd, where little Jesse was jumping like a rabbit. Zoe sobbed as she spotted Sam, and Devon and Maddie let out loud whoops when Giz limped in just behind him. Josh scooped up Shana and they all raced down the stairs. They came together in an explosion of shrieks and laughter, Maddie and Zoe almost knocking Sam over, Devon struggling to lift Gizmo off the ground in a bear hug.

"You okay, little Dude?" Devon asked.

"Yeah," grinned Gizmo, hugging him back. "You okay, big Dude?"

"Am now."

Sam suddenly pulled away from his sister and began bouncing up and down like he was on springs. "You should have seen it," he said, eyes bright. "The Protectors came and got us away and just *creamed* those guys! It was *so cool!*"

"I bet," said Zoe, giving up on the hug but devouring him with her eyes. "And we want to hear everything."

Josh grinned. "So let's go home. Treats are on me."

"Treats with Giz and Sam!" said Shana happily, and Josh gave her a squeeze. Then he and Zoe started making their way back through the crowd. They passed a small mob, then realized it was Milo, surrounded by grateful, cheering families.

"Kids okay?" he called.

"They're terrific," grinned Zoe.

"Good. That's great."

Oddly, though, Milo didn't look as triumphant as Josh would

have expected. His smile was forced, and he barely seemed to be listening to the voices around him.

"Josh, hold up a second, okay?"

"Sure. Everything all right?"

Milo didn't respond. Didn't even look Josh in the eye.

Josh turned back to Zoe. "You take Shana and go ahead. I'll meet you back at the cottage." Zoe nodded, too happy to ask any questions. She pulled Shana onto one hip, and the little group headed off. Josh waited until Milo extricated himself from the happy families, and the two walked off by themselves, to the edge of the pool.

"What is it?" asked Josh.

Milo's white face had never looked so pale. "I've got bad news. It's about Hamim."

Josh's elation drained from him. "What about him?"

"Caleb found him, just past the last barricade."

"And?" Josh whispered.

"He's dead."

CAPTIVES AND HEROES

Telling his family was the worst thing Josh had ever had to do. When he entered the cottage, Sam had just started telling about his adventure, with Giz nodding emphatically and interrupting every chance he got.

"We couldn't see anything 'cause the Outsiders put sacks or something over our heads when they took us. But we could hear them. They were growling, kind of, and talking like their mouths didn't work so good. And at first we were really scared, weren't we, Giz?"

"Really scared," agreed Giz.

"'Cause they were acting real mean, pinching us and squeezing our arms—"

"And they smelled bad—"

"Yeah, like garbage. And some kids were crying . . ."

"Not me," said Giz proudly. "*I* didn't cry."

"No," said Sam, pointing to Giz's crotch. "You just peed your pants. *Any*how," he continued, "all of a sudden we could hear Caleb yelling, and then the Protectors were there, and I felt someone pull me away from the stinky Outsider."

"Then the fighting started," said Giz.

"It was crazy bad. The Outsiders were making these really

creepy noises, but we could hear the Protectors whacking them and punching them, and they started grunting and screaming. Then we heard big splashes, things going into the water. Then I guess the Protectors carried us back, 'cause when they took the bags off our heads, we were back on Atlantis, in Neptune's Theatre."

"Wait," said Zoe, moving closer to Sam. "You had the bags on your heads all that time? Why?"

"Caleb told us to keep them on," explained Giz. "So we wouldn't see the fighting."

Zoe nodded, but still looked confused. Giz returned to the story.

"Then the King came—"

"You mean Milo?" asked Josh.

"Yeah, the King, and he bent down and hugged everyone, and we all hugged him and hugged each other. Then he had us all cheer for the Protectors." He and Sam demonstrated, yelling at the top of their lungs and jumping up and down. Finally, they stopped, gasping for air.

"It was *so cool*," Sam concluded.

"Shoot!" said Devon, kicking at the floor. "Wish they'd taken me."

"That's not what you were saying last night," said Zoe. She turned to Josh. "Guess we owe Milo and the Goons a big thank-you. Maybe I'll even stop calling them Goons."

Josh forced a smile. "Yeah. Bet they'd appreciate that."

"Okay," said Zoe, grabbing a bowl and heading to the cabinet where they stored their special rations. "Let's celebrate. I'll break out the treats."

"Treats with Giz and Sam!" shrieked Shana.

Zoe laughed, glancing over at Josh. "She's been saying that

ever since we left the theatre. It's pretty much the only thing that stuck with her tonight." She rummaged in their supplies, pulling out a stack of Glyphs and Mummy Yummies.

"Candy for breakfast!" gasped Maddie. "Hamim's the only one who ever lets us do that!"

Josh's vision blurred. He turned away, pretending to pick up something from the floor.

"Josh?" said Zoe. "You okay?"

He remained crouched where he was, unable to answer. Around him, the cottage grew quiet.

Zoe walked over to him. Her voice was low. Fearful.

"What did Milo want you for?"

Josh told her.

News of Hamim's death ripped through the Islands. Just as they had after the plague, people gathered in small groups to talk, sifting through details that Moira released after Caleb made his report to the Core.

The Protectors had caught up with the Outsiders just before the last barricade. There had been about twenty of them, but all were slow-moving and dull, just as they'd been in the cottage. It was easy for the Protectors to catch and overpower them, pull the kidlets to safety, and send most of the creatures into the lagoon.

The last six or so let go of their captives and clambered frantically up the side of the barricade. Caleb, who'd been at the lead, was able to stop two of them and yank them back to where his Protectors could restrain them. But when he'd climbed over the last barricade, yelling after the few who'd escaped, he'd found Hamim.

From his position, stretched out toward Atlantis, it appeared that Hamim had been running from something, trying to get back to the Islands. But he'd been overtaken before he could get to safety.

He was the only one the Protectors had found. For a while, the Islanders tried to convince themselves that the rest of the Scouts were just in hiding somewhere, slowly making their way back home. But after another week or so, it had to be assumed that they'd met a fate similar to Hamim's.

Their friends and families went into mourning, struggling with disbelief and unable to say good-bye. To help them heal, King Neptune proclaimed a Week of Remembrance and called the Islanders to gather in front of the Coral Palace for a special ceremony. Josh and Zoe collected their little family and went early, expecting everyone on the Islands to be there. But when they arrived, Josh noted that only a couple hundred had come. I guess death doesn't matter, he thought bitterly, unless it's someone you know.

The sky was mercifully gray, and a light rain fell. Those closest to the Scouts were led to a platform at the entrance. Josh and his family stood up for Hamim. Next to them Kyle and Matt O'Bannion stood shoulder to shoulder, pale and silent. Miguel and Tish were there for Kim, and Eli stood up for Paravi. Only the Ghoulies refused to participate, so Greg offered to represent Shadow. Each person was given a flower to hold, the most beautiful ones Aiko could find in the BioPods.

The gentle sound of spring rain came over the speakers, heightening the illusion that the skies were weeping. And then, softly and sorrowfully, Neptune spoke.

"We are here to grieve with the friends and families of the lost Scouts. To thank them. To give them our support. Please say each name after I do.

"Ryan."

Ryan, murmured the crowd.

"Kim."

Kim.

The other three names were called. Paravi. Shadow. Hamim.

As Hamim's name echoed from the speakers, Josh heard Giz sob and Maddie begin to weep. He bent down and kissed the tops of their heads. Zoe, who already had one arm around Sam, reached out with the other to touch Devon's shoulder. The boy was holding Shana tightly, his face buried in her neck.

"These are our heroes," Neptune said. "They gave their lives so that the rest of us would be safe. So that we wouldn't be harmed by whatever lives Outside. And thanks to them, we are safe. And we know how to stay that way."

Neptune's voice was changing. Looking up, Josh saw that Milo had stepped out onto the balcony, and he realized that the voice of the King had gradually become Milo's own. Slowly, all the faces in the crowd lifted. "Most of us could never have been as brave as they were," Milo continued. "Most of us would never have volunteered to go on that journey. And so, in gratitude, we make them this promise: that we will all live our lives as they, at their best, lived theirs."

After the ceremony, the Week of Remembrance continued uneventfully. The fate of the Scouts had been shocking, but there had been just five of them: five out of almost two thousand. So as long as the kidnapped children had been rescued, and as long as the barricades could be rebuilt, most of the Islanders easily fell back into their routines.

The only thing that continued to be of interest was the questioning of the two Outsiders. Unfortunately, according to Moira's regular postings, the captives yielded little information. Most of what came out of their mouths was useless—they didn't seem to be able to retain a thought from minute to minute. But from the little Milo and the others could glean, everyone outside the Islands had sickened—something about bad food, bad water. There apparently was fighting, too. One of the Outsiders mumbled about knives and guns and "broken" people.

In between interrogations, the Outsiders were kept in an empty aquarium tank in the Living Oceans, guarded by three Protectors. They huddled along the back wall like starving dogs, devouring the food that was thrown to them and sleeping curled up on blankets that had been tossed in the tank. Islanders filed by, horrified by the sight of what-might-have-been, relieved that they'd been wise enough to stay on the Islands.

There was some talk about what should be done to the prisoners after the questioning was over. Most thought they should be kept in the tank permanently, like zoo animals. A few Islanders, angrier and less forgiving, talked about throwing them into the Coliseum, like in old gladiator movies, to face some horrible kind of punishment.

And then, without warning, the Outsiders vanished. They simply escaped one night, clambering out of the tank and overpowering their sleepy guards. There was a brief panic, but then Neptune reassured everyone that they'd been spotted far down on the monorail track, heading away from the Islands.

And perhaps, he said, it was all for the best. After all, the Outsiders couldn't help what had happened to them. Some might even be old friends who had left during the exodus. So hadn't they already been punished, two or three times over?

Ashamed, no one said anything more about revenge. In return, Neptune made good on his promise to protect them. The barricades were rebuilt, taller and thicker than before. The supplies in the UnderGround were all gathered to the central hub under Atlantis, the better to guard and ration them. More Protectors were put on sentry duty.

And there was no more talk of going Outside.

DISCONNECT

Josh steeled himself for Zoe to spiral into another depression. But what happened was almost worse. After a few subdued days, she buried herself in work, no longer complaining about the tasks she was given and volunteering for extra shifts. She worked in the laundry, mopped floors in the dining hall, and wandered the grounds on Health Patrol, picking up everyone's garbage.

The one thing she didn't do was talk. She left the cottage before dawn and usually returned long after everyone was asleep. And if Josh did see her and tried to say something, she cut him short and hurried away.

"It's like she's mad at me," he said to Tish one morning after dropping Sam and Maddie at school. "But I'm not sure why."

"She's not mad," said Latisha. "I think she's just trying to stay away from anyone who might make her think about what happened." Tish shook her head. "I haven't seen her in days."

Josh heard the sadness in her voice. "Sorry," he said. "I guess we've both lost our best friend."

"We haven't lost her. We'll just have to be patient."

Josh tried. But after two more days of waiting, he decided that patience wasn't going to work. That night, he put the kidlets to bed and planted himself in a chair, listening as the Islands grew silent around him. Finally, a long time later, the door opened and Zoe slipped into the cottage. She moved quietly over to where Sam was sleeping, then bent down to kiss him, her face caught in the glow of his candle.

Josh gasped, and Zoe spun toward him, her eyes huge in sunken sockets. In the dim light, her arms seemed little more than skin on sticks, and her cheekbones jutted from her face.

"Jeez, Zoe," he said, horrified by her appearance. "You've gotta stop this. You're making yourself sick."

She looked away from him.

"I'm fine. Don't worry."

"No," he said. "Tonight you're gonna talk to me. You're gonna tell me what's going on, and why we barely see you anymore."

"You see me enough."

"No, we don't. Just at breakfast, sometimes, or dinner. And the kids really miss you—you're not even around for Memory Time."

"Maybe because too many memories are bad now."

Josh stopped. This was the closest she'd come to telling him how she was feeling. He didn't say anything more; he just waited for her to continue.

"Look," she said, turning to face him again. "I have trouble coming home, because as soon as I walk in the door, all I can think of is that Hamim isn't here. I know that's crummy, that I should still want to see you and the kidlets. But I can't help it—that's what happens."

"I know," said Josh. "I feel that way, too."

"Yeah, but you push past it. I can't." She took a breath. "I still can't help feeling like this is all my fault."

"Zoe—"

"I know, I know. But that's how I feel. The only thing that keeps me going is what Milo said."

Josh shook his head, not understanding.

"About not being a zombie. About helping others. And I want to do what he said at the memorial, too." She looked at Josh, her eyes filling with tears. "I want to live my life like Hamim tried to. It's the only thing I can do for him now."

Josh didn't know how to respond. So he did the only thing he could think of: he pulled her close, and he held her while she cried. And when she sank to the floor, exhausted, he held her then, too. Until finally, with a long, shuddering sigh, she escaped into sleep.

The next morning, when he woke, she was gone again.

Josh sat for a moment, staring at the place where she had lain and wondering what to do next. But then he heard Shana whispering to her Seemore Seahorse doll. He sighed. Figuring out how to help Zoe would have to wait.

He got to his feet. "Okay, everyone. Time to get moving."

The other kids stumbled out of their cots. Maddie took Shana and Sam over to the washbasin and tried to wipe the sleep out of their eyes. Devon pulled on some pants, then helped Giz get dressed, which meant he pulled the cleanest items from a pile on the floor, sniffed them, and then wrangled the little boy into them.

Josh suddenly realized that without Zoe to help, the cottage had pretty much fallen apart. Clothes and toys lay everywhere, chunks of mud and stale food covered the floor, and mysterious smells drifted out from the snack area. Looking at the mess, Josh finally figured out one thing he could do to get their lives back on track: he could clean the place up. If he did persuade Zoe to start coming home more, at least it wouldn't be to a pigsty.

Josh asked Devon and Maddie to take the younger kids to breakfast and then to Little Wizards and school. He hugged each of them as they left—except for Devon, of course, with whom he knocked fists. Then he turned back from the doorway and scanned the cottage.

It really *was* a sty. They'd done almost no housekeeping since the night of the Invasion, and now Josh almost couldn't figure out where to begin. Big stuff first, he decided, and he started picking up whatever the kids had left lying around the sitting room and play area. He threw clothes in the laundry box and put it outside for the tram pick-up. Then he shoved toys back onto the shelves and tossed empty snack boxes into the garbage. Finally he headed for the closet where they stored cleaning supplies.

He opened the door and pulled out a bucket, some old rags, and liquid cleaner. He wiped down the shelves and furniture, then decided he might as well go all the way and scrub some old stains off the walls. Finally, he grabbed a broom and attacked the filth on the floor.

The last places he cleaned were the sleeping areas.

These were in the worst shape. He was always yelling at the kidlets to keep their cots neat and their shelves clean, but for the past couple of weeks he hadn't had the energy to fight them. Now, though, something had to be done. Some of the blankets were badly stained, and the dirt and garbage under the cots looked like the beginnings of an archaeological dig.

Josh assessed what had to be done, his eyes moving again from the floor to the cots to the walls and shelves. He froze as he looked at the gouges in the walls by Sam and Giz's cots, reminders of the night the Outsiders attacked. Once again he felt the helplessness, the hideous fear he'd known when he thought Maddie had been taken. But that was stupid. She was safe, and so were the others. He shook off the feeling and went back to work.

He picked up the blankets, shaking them one by one and hearing who-knows-what clatter to the floor from the folds. He piled them up for the laundry, then added a layer of sheets. He noticed that some of the stains had soaked through to the cots themselves, so he sponged them down as best he could and took them outside to air.

Finally, he grabbed the broom and began sweeping again, pulling the dirt out of each corner and from under the metal frames of the cots. He peered at the pile of dust and trash to make sure that there was nothing worth saving.

There were a couple of items he didn't recognize. Frowning, he leaned closer. And saw three long plastic claws, and a small plastic tube of greenish-white makeup.

PUZZLE PIECES

Josh tore out of the cottage. In his right hand, he clutched the three claws, and in his left, the plastic tube. One word pounded in his head with every step: *Fake. Fake. Fake.*

He raced over the connecting bridge and into Atlantis, heading toward the Coral Palace. He saw Toad almost immediately and sprinted toward him.

"Where's Milo?" Josh said.

"Still asleep," said Toad. "You know he doesn't surface much before lunch."

The comment surprised Josh. "No. I didn't know."

Toad grinned. "It's *good* to be the King." His smile faded as he registered Josh's expression. "You okay? You look a little weird."

"Yeah, I'm okay. I just have to talk to him."

Toad shrugged. His eyes strayed toward Josh's right hand, which was nervously opening and closing around the claws.

"Whatcha got?"

Josh tightened his grasp.

"Nothing. Some stuff I found for the kids."

"Yeah?" Toad said, his eyes popping with curiousity. "Like what?"

"Just junk," said Josh. "Listen, I gotta go find Milo."

"Your funeral," said Toad, dragging his gaze up from Josh's hand. "And good luck waking him."

Josh ran toward the Palace, then climbed the stairs to the third level, a hexagon-shaped landing that contained Neptune's Chambers. As the Atlantis settlement grew larger, the VIP rooms had been subdivided into smaller units, housing about five or six Islanders each. Similar, smaller rooms on the second level were home to about twenty more Atlantans.

Milo knocked on the door of the King's Suite, the largest of the chambers. There was no answer. He knocked harder and heard a mumbled obscenity. Josh flinched. Maybe Toad had been right.

"Hey, Milo. It's me. Josh."

"Josh."

There was more muttering, and a moment later the door swung open. Milo stood in the doorway, eyes puffy from sleep, long hair matted against his skull.

"Hey, man. What's up?"

"I gotta talk to you. You alone?"

Milo pointed a thumb behind him. Josh looked over his shoulder and saw a girl padding across the floor, struggling into a shirt. Her head finally popped through the collar.

"Hey, Josh," she said. It was Aiko.

"Hey," said Josh weakly. He looked at Milo, who raised a lazy eyebrow and shrugged.

"So what do you need?" he asked.

Josh dragged his thoughts away from the girl and shook his head. "It's private."

Milo's pale blue eyes fixed on him, and Josh saw a flicker of irritation. But then it vanished. "Yeah. Okay." He turned toward

Aiko. "Why don't you go get something to eat, Kiki? I'll meet you there in a minute."

"Sure," said Aiko. She smiled again at Josh—proudly, he thought—and headed out the door. Josh stared after her, then looked at Milo.

"What can I say?" said Milo, his expression smug. Josh tried to laugh past his discomfort, wondering if Moira knew what was going on.

"So," Milo said. "What's so important?"

Josh squeezed his right hand and felt the plastic claws dig into his palm. For some reason, he couldn't say anything. His brain was trying to shout something at him, something he didn't want to hear. As he tried to organize his scrambled thoughts, Milo's face clouded.

"Jeez. What is it now? Someone break into the supplies? Or wreck another building on Timescape?"

"No. No, nothing like that."

"So that means your girlfriend found something else to complain about, right?"

"What?"

"Zoe hasn't caused trouble for a couple weeks. She's due."

"No. I mean, she's not complaining about anything."

"Then what's wrong?" Milo snapped, his hands bunched into fists. "Sometimes I feel like we're just babysitting a bunch of spoiled brats."

Josh gaped at him. After a moment, Milo blinked.

"Sorry," he said. "Guess I haven't gotten over the last couple of weeks. I mean, I thought I had, but . . ." Milo made a visible effort to calm himself. "So what's up?"

"Nothing big," said Josh, searching for a lie that Milo would believe. "Just another run-in with Caleb. But I'll take care of it."

"You sure?"

"Yeah. Sorry I bothered you."

"It's okay. Sorry I acted like an ass."

"No prob. Catch you later, okay?"

"Okay. And Josh, if you still have trouble with Caleb, let me know. I'll talk to him."

"Thanks."

Josh left the Palace, bumping into Toad again on his way out. The boy grabbed hold of his arm and spun him around, staring at his rear.

"Hey," said the boy. "There's still only one."

"What?"

"I mean, Milo didn't rip you a new one."

Josh tried to laugh. But he was barely seeing or hearing anything.

"Look, I gotta go," he mumbled. "Late for work."

Toad looked at him curiously, but nodded. And Josh headed over to the Living Oceans, hoping it would give him time to sort out his thinking.

He spent the rest of the morning chopping up vegetables and small fish to feed to the turtles. But as he cut and diced, his mind kept spinning, and by midday break, he was going crazy. He needed someone smart to talk to, someone he could trust. Someone who could help him figure things out, or else tell him he was nuts.

He needed Zoe.

After checking the assignment board, Josh tracked her down in the recycling area underneath Inspiration Island. She was with a half dozen other kids, each wearing a stained olive-green jumpsuit and sorting through the previous day's output of garbage. Certain materials, like plastic utensils and aluminum foil, were being pulled out for re-use. The rest was sorted a second time and sent either to the landfill or to the central incinerator, which fed into the Island's energy system.

Zoe glanced up as he approached. She froze, then pasted a smile on her face.

"You okay?" he asked.

"Fine," she said, giving no indication that the previous night had even happened. Josh wasn't sure what to make of that.

"Nice outfit," he said finally, pointing to the jumpsuit.

"Thanks. I like it." She smiled again—a too-bright smile that completely unnerved him. It was like the girl he knew had been sucked out of her skin and replaced with someone else. Like in some old body-snatcher movie.

"So why are you here?" she asked. "Slumming?"

"Not exactly. Listen, Zoe. I gotta talk to you."

The smile disappeared. "Anything wrong? The kidlets okay?"

"Yeah, they're fine. Listen. I found something I need to tell you about. But not here." Josh glanced at the other workers, some of whom were only a few feet away. He lowered his voice. "It's about the Outsiders."

Zoe shook her head, and Josh felt an invisible wall slam down between them. "No. I don't want to hear any more about the Outsiders. I don't want to hear anything about anything for a while." She turned, and Josh found himself talking to her back.

"Zoe, this is important." His voice dropped to a whisper. "The Outsiders aren't what they looked like. They were wearing makeup or something. It was all fake."

She didn't respond, didn't even acknowledge that she'd heard him.

"Come on, Zoe. I need your help figuring this out."

"Leave me alone." She moved a few steps farther away, to

where one of the pneumatic tubes was spitting refuse into a large metal bin.

"Thanks," he said. "Thanks a lot." He felt like punching her, suddenly sick of her dramas. But then he realized he had an option. Turning abruptly, he headed for the exit. But he couldn't resist one last shot.

"Enjoy your garbage, Zoe. Maybe Tish still cares what happens to us."

That night, Josh waited until after Memory Time, then asked Maddie and Devon to watch the younger kids. He told them he was meeting Tish about some science lessons she'd be doing in the marine labs at Atlantis. They agreed a little too quickly, and Josh knew that the snack stash would be down by half when he returned. He said good night to all of the kidlets, gave Maddie an extra hug, then went out the door and headed toward Digital Dimensions, where he'd arranged to meet Tish in her classroom.

For some reason, he felt nervous, certain he was being followed. He kept glancing backward, peering into every shadow and crevice along the way.

"Stop it," he told himself. "If there were any Outsiders around, they wouldn't be after you."

Finally, he reached the TV studios. He looked around to make sure no one was watching, then slipped through the main door and headed to Tish's classroom. She was already there, waiting just outside the studio door, a small flashlight in one hand.

"Hey," she said.

"Hey. Thanks for meeting me."

"You kidding? After what you showed me? I've been going nuts all day. And look." She reached into her own pocket. "I went back to my place and looked around. Lucky I hate cleaning." She pulled out her hand again, revealing another one of the plastic claws and a thin piece of latex with a fake scar running across it. "Guess whoever it was used the wrong glue."

They headed into the studio and down the stairs, leaving the room in darkness except for the dim glow of lights that edged the stage. They sat cross-legged together on the game floor, just in front of the contestant podiums.

"Okay," said Latisha, keeping her voice low. "Here's what I'm thinking. We've been trying to keep the Outsiders from coming here and taking our stuff, right? Maybe some tribe out there had the same idea. They knew we'd taken down the barricades. And we know . . ." She hesitated. "We know they saw the Scouts. So what if they wanted to stop us before we saw what *they* had? Decided to make us afraid to leave the Islands?"

A familiar voice came from above them.

"Nice thinking. But there's another possibility." Zoe was sitting in one of the studio seats, about a dozen rows from the top.

"Hey," said Josh. "You came."

"Nothing gets past you, Captain Obvious."

Josh felt relief wash over him. That was the Zoe he knew. "So what changed your mind?"

She shrugged and started down the stairs. "I started feeling crummy that I didn't listen to you. I mean, you listened to me, about the Glow. Kind of." She reached the edge of the stage, where the other two now stood waiting.

Tish was beaming.

"Good to see you again, girlfriend."

"Thanks," said Zoe, not meeting her eyes. "Sorry I've been—"

"Forget it."

The two stood awkwardly for a moment. Then Tish jumped forward, yanking Zoe into a hug. Zoe squeezed back tightly.

Josh felt a weight lift off him.

"So. Zoe. You said you had another idea?"

She nodded. "Yeah. But you're not going to like it. In fact, maybe you better sit down again."

Josh glanced at Tish. They sank to the floor, and Zoe started pacing like a wolf in a cage. "Okay. As soon as Josh came this afternoon and said that the Outsiders were fake, I couldn't turn off my brain. I came up with a lot of ideas, including the one you just said, Tish. But none of them made any sense."

Tish leaned forward, prompting her. "And then . . . ?"

"Then I realized that there's another group that doesn't want us to leave the Islands." She looked hard at Josh, and he knew she'd reached the same conclusion he had, the one he'd been trying not to let surface in his mind.

"It's the only way everything makes sense," she said softly. He nodded, feeling sick.

"What?" asked Tish. "What makes sense?"

Josh was still looking at Zoe. "She's talking about the Core," he said. "She thinks that they're the ones behind all this."

"*What?*"

"And so do I." As the words came out, he felt like something had been ripped from his chest.

Tish gaped at them.

"That's pretty wild, guys."

"Maybe," said Zoe. "But if they aren't behind it . . . Well, if they aren't, then explain a couple of things to me. We have all these sentries, right? How did the Outsiders get in without anyone spotting them?"

"We've been here a long time," said Tish. "Maybe they just weren't being as careful as at the beginning."

"Or maybe the Outsiders used the stairways in the Under-

Ground. Popped up exactly where they needed to. And here's something else: why did they go only to Enchanted Island and Inspiration Island?"

"Because they wanted the kids, and that's where most of the kids are."

"Right. But how did *they* know that?"

Tish had no answer.

"Plus," Zoe continued, "they acted like their brains were rotten, but they were smart enough to wrap us up with duct tape, and to light fires as a distraction, and to bring the hoods."

Josh's brow furrowed. "What hoods?"

"Remember? Sam and Giz said they had hoods on their heads from the time the mutants took them until they were back at Neptune's Theatre. It just didn't make sense."

"And now it does?" asked Tish.

"Yeah. With the hoods on, the kids didn't know where they really went, or what really happened. They could even have been in Neptune's Theatre the whole time."

"You're right," said Tish, nodding slowly. "It would've been like the old shows my folks used to listen to on satellite radio, all sound effects and illusion. Like, maybe the splashes the kids heard weren't really Outsiders being thrown into the lagoon. The Protectors could have just been throwing stuff into the pool."

"That guy Alex would have been good at figuring all that stuff out," said Zoe. "And did you notice he moved to Atlantis a few weeks ago?"

"Wait a minute," said Josh, knowing she was right, but needing to be one thousand percent sure. "What about the lights we saw on the tracks. Remember? When Milo stopped us from going after the kids, we could see the Protectors moving toward the barricades."

"Just part of the show," said Zoe. "Set up to throw us off."

Josh nodded. It made sense. And everything else seemed to fit, too. No one except the Core had questioned the Outsiders, who had conveniently escaped before they could be punished. And Moira, so good at making things up, so terrific with words, was the one who'd posted the information about what they'd said.

Zoe's eyes suddenly went wide. "Oh, God," she said.

"What?" asked Tish.

Zoe looked sick. "Hamim. Hamim and the other Scouts. If the Outsiders weren't Outsiders, if the Core planned everything else . . ."

Tish gasped as though she'd been punched, and Josh felt the blood drain from his face. Then something inside him finally rebelled.

"No," he said. "No matter what else, the Core wouldn't hurt someone. Couldn't *kill* someone."

"Maybe they couldn't," said Zoe. "But what about the Ghoulies? Remember how I said I saw some of them around the Palace at night? And remember who the last person was to join the Scouts?"

"Shadow," murmured Tish.

Zoe clenched her hands. "He was part of this, I know it. Sick, twisted creepazoid."

They fell silent.

"So what do we do now?" asked Josh. "We can't just go to the Core and tell them what we know."

"No," said Tish. "And whatever we do, it can't be just three of us. We've got to let a few others in on this, people we can trust. Then, at the next Council, we'll all go."

"Right," said Zoe. "And accuse them in front of everyone."

"No. That'll just make us sound like *our* brains have rotted."

"So what, then?"

"We just act innocent, tell everyone what we found. Take the Core by surprise. And then we keep asking questions, the same ones we asked ourselves. If we do it right, everyone will start thinking the way we did, start getting suspicious. The Core'll be squirming up on stage like worms on a hook. And then things will take care of themselves."

Zoe smiled grimly. "I like it. So who else do we tell?"

"We can tell Miguel. A few of the other Teachers, too. They're smart. They'll believe us."

Josh thought. "And the O'Bannion Boys." Since their brother's disappearance, Kyle and Matt had become ghosts of themselves, haggard and silent. They deserved a piece of revenge.

Tish nodded. "Matt and Kyle, yeah. And we can ask them who else from Timescape would be good. Like Greg, maybe."

"What about Lana and Ari?" asked Zoe. "I trust them."

"No," said Josh. "Leave them out of this. They've got all the kids to take care of." He hesitated. "Or maybe we tell them just a little. Then, if something goes wrong, they'll be there to take care of our kidlets."

Tish and Zoe went silent. And Josh knew that, like him, they were suddenly realizing the enormity of what they were about to do. No matter what happened at Council, everything about their lives was going to change.

They continued to talk, identifying a few other Islanders whom they thought could be counted on to keep the secret and support them at Council.

"We'll have to work fast," said Zoe. "We've got just two days until the next meeting."

"We'll contact everyone tomorrow," said Josh. "Then we'll meet tomorrow night, plan what we're going to say."

There was a rustling above them. They stared at each other, terrified, and Tish clicked on her flashlight, shooting the beam up into the darkness.

Nothing. Josh grabbed the light from Tish and ran up the steps, pointing it down every aisle, into every corner. Finally, he gave up, but as he moved back down the stairs, he felt a prickling on the back of his neck.

"What do you think?" asked Tish nervously.

"I don't know," said Josh. "But if someone was up there, we're in big trouble."

TRAITORS

The next morning, Josh and Zoe went through their usual routine, getting the kids ready for their day, taking them to breakfast, reporting for their jobs. But Josh's nerves were raw. He jumped at every unexpected sound, looking over his shoulder to see if Caleb and his Goons had suddenly appeared to drag him off to the secret room.

Nothing happened, though. In fact, when Josh passed Evan on his way to the dining hall, the other boy smiled and waved.

"Guess we were just spooked last night," said Zoe, when she and Tish met up with Josh for the midday meal. "We just thought we heard something."

"I sure hope so," said Tish. "Hope they're not just waiting to grab us all at once."

Josh hadn't thought about that possibility.

"Do you want to forget about doing this?" he asked. "Pretend we didn't find that stuff?"

"We can't," said Zoe. "Remember Hamim."

That ended the discussion. Now they just had to recruit the others.

• • •

"Are you freakin' *kidding* me?" yelled Matt O'Bannion when Josh filled him and his brother in that evening. "Those . . . those . . ." He couldn't seem to come up with a word obscene enough.

"I'm gonna kill 'em," said Kyle, his face like stone. "I'm gonna rip 'em apart."

"No," said Tish. "Then you'll look crazy, and they'll look like martyrs. Let's just go according to plan. Then everyone on the Islands can decide what to do. Maybe put that prison room of theirs to a new use."

Greg was shaking his head.

"I can't believe this," he said quietly. "I trusted them. I *believed* them." He looked hurt at first, and then angry. But Josh wasn't sure if it was at the Core, or at himself.

"Don't beat yourself up," said Josh. "They fooled me, too."

Miguel remained silent, muttering formulas and equations to himself as though trying to lose himself in the numbers.

"They fooled everyone," said Zoe. "But they're not going to do it anymore. After next Council, no one's going to trust them again."

Tish nodded. "And then they'll be out of the Palace, and we'll run the Council the right way. We'll figure out together what we should do next. And that means with everyone. Power to the people!"

"Yes!" Miguel yelled suddenly, jumping to his feet and punching the air with his fist. "*¡Viva la revolución!*"

"Whoa," said Tish. "Where did that come from?"

Miguel looked at her coolly. "There's a side to me you don't know."

"I guess."

"Okay," said Zoe. "Now we have to figure out what we're going to do, and what we're going to say at Council."

"And I have to figure out how to keep you from tearing down the Palace before then," said Josh.

Everyone laughed, but it turned out not to be a joke. Over the next day, every time they saw someone from the Core, Josh could see Zoe's fists clench and her eyes shoot daggers. He had to keep grabbing her arm, hissing at her to stay calm.

But finally, the day of the Council arrived. Josh felt like he spent half his time on the toilet. Part of him was hoping he'd get violently ill, or break a limb, or fall off a bridge—anything that would prevent him from going to the meeting that night. And if that weren't possible, then he wished time would just stop.

Zoe was having a different reaction. She kept glancing up at the sun as though willing it to go down. When she was standing, she paced. When she sat, her leg jiggled and she gnawed her fingernails.

"Calm down," said Josh. "You're making me nuts."

"I want to get to Council, Josh. I want to see their faces when we tell everyone what we know. When the crowd finally sees them for what they are. It's going to be so sweet."

"Sweet?"

"Okay, maybe that's the wrong word. But they're finally going to have to pay for what they've done. And for Hamim." Her voice became quieter. "Then maybe I'll start feeling like me again."

Daylight faded, and they went through their usual mealtime and cleanup routines at the dining hall. Then Zoe told the kidlets they were going to spend the night at Little Wizards.

"A sleepover?" asked Maddie excitedly.

"Yep. Ari and Lana have this big party planned. You get to stay up all night, stuff your faces, play games . . ."

"Why aren't you coming?"

"It's just for nines and below. Besides, Josh and I could use some time away from you brats."

The kids laughed, but Josh saw Maddie and Devon exchange knowing glances. Jeez, he realized, they think we want to be *alone*.

Tish was waiting for them outside her tower in SkyTown. "You guys ready for this?" she asked.

"No," said Josh. "It's going to be nuts."

"Maybe not. I mean, once everyone realizes what's going on, what can the Core do? Maybe they'll just back off."

"Right. And maybe I'll grow wings and fly." Josh took a nervous breath. "It's just that, no matter what, everything's going to be different."

Latisha looked at him closely. "You want to back out?"

Yes, thought Josh. "We can't."

"Neptune's Fanfare" rang from the speakers, calling everyone to Council.

The three of them entered the IMAX and took their place in the front row. Shortly afterward, Milo appeared on the side of the stage. He looked down into the audience, nodding slightly when he saw Josh. Josh automatically nodded back, still hoping that, despite everything he knew, a mistake had been made. That someone else had been behind the attacks, and that Milo was still the boy who'd given them all hope after the plague.

Zoe caught the look and jabbed her elbow into Josh's side. "Don't go soft on me now."

People were still arriving, and the rows slowly filled. Josh saw the O'Bannions come in, along with some of the other Timescapers. They signaled to Josh, then began spreading themselves out through the crowd. Miguel appeared a few minutes later, a gaggle of Teachers behind him. They, too, dispersed around the theatre.

The stream of Islanders began to trickle off. Still, the meeting seemed to be a bit better attended than it had been in months—maybe thirty or forty more people than usual, although Josh didn't know most of them.

Milo, Evan, and Moira took their places on the stage, and the Protectors filed out across the floor. Caleb was the last to appear, but he walked halfway across the floor, planting himself directly in front of Milo.

Milo's trident pounded three times.

"This Council is now in session," he said. "All problems and ideas will be heard."

Evan stepped forward.

"First—does anyone have anything to report from last time?"

Aiko raised her hand, and Evan nodded in her direction. "I just wanted to say that things are back to normal in the Pods again. Everyone's showing up, and the gardens and animals are all healthy."

"Good," said Milo. "Glad we could get things back in shape."

"Yeah. Everything's good." She smiled. "Thanks to the Core."

Josh looked at her curiously. The thank-you was a little odd.

"Anyone else?" asked Evan.

Eli raised his hand. "The new rationing system you came up with is saving us a lot of food. Things are lasting a lot longer than we thought. We're even starting to be able to store some of our own stuff that we're growing."

"That's terrific. Good job, Eli."

"Well, it was your idea."

Now several more kids stood and gave reports, many of them

thanking Milo or the Core for their help. Josh shifted uncomfortably. Why was everyone so grateful all of a sudden?

Then Evan called for new concerns and ideas, and several more Islanders got up to speak. A group from Inspiration Island reported that they'd found a way to recharge some of the old batteries. A Timescaper asked if they could consider leaving lights on a little longer, now that the barricades had been rebuilt. Milo listened and nodded, and Moira took detailed notes.

"Okay," said Evan. "I guess that's about it. If anyone forgot something, just talk to Moira later and she'll list it for next time."

Josh's heart began pounding.

"Wait," he said, and Zoe squeezed his arm. Josh took a deep breath and got slowly to his feet.

"Sorry, Josh," said Evan. "I didn't see you raise your hand. Is there something you need?"

"Yeah. Well, something I need help understanding."

Those up on stage stared at him, Milo most intently.

"Go ahead," said Evan.

"The other day, I was cleaning our cottage." He saw Caleb snicker when he said that. "We hadn't really done that since the Invasion—too much else to deal with. Anyhow, I found some things I hadn't noticed before. Things that didn't belong to us."

"Such as?" asked Moira, feigning interest.

"Plastic claws, the kind you glue on at Halloween. A tube of green makeup."

"So?" said Moira. "Your kidlets were playing dress-up. What's the big mystery?"

Now Tish stood as well. "I found one of the claws at my place, too. All the way over in SkyTown. Plus a fake scar. Right where the Outsiders grabbed my Jesse."

"I still don't get it," said Evan. "What're you trying to say?"

Josh steeled himself. "I'm saying, I don't think we were invaded by Outsiders."

Startled voices rose like locusts. A kid in the front row leaned over, the Timescape boy who'd asked about the lights.

"What d'you mean?"

"I mean, I think the Invaders might have been some of us. Kids from the Islands, wearing makeup."

The Timescaper laughed. "You find some funny stuff in the hydroponic gardens, Dude? You been smoking?"

Laughter rippled across the audience. Then another kid got to his feet, but he wasn't smiling.

"Why're we even listening to this? Who'd do something stupid like that?"

Zoe jumped up, her patience at an end. "I'll tell you who, you idiot." She turned toward the stage, her arm sweeping from left to right. "Your precious Core. Your wonderful Protectors. They planned the whole thing."

"That's nuts!"

Josh shook his head. "No, it isn't. They don't want anyone leaving the Islands. They want to scare everyone into staying. So they dream up an invasion."

All eyes switched from Josh to those on and around the stage. Josh closed his eyes to build up his courage, then turned to face Milo, bracing himself for the rage he knew he'd find.

Milo's face showed nothing but pain.

"I can't believe you're doing this," Milo said.

"I have to."

"Have to what?" Milo's voice got louder. "Lie to everyone? Try to make us look bad?"

Josh blinked. "What?"

"You've been angry ever since we kicked you out of the Core."

"Kicked me—?"

"You didn't want to do the work, but you missed the power. And the three of you"—he gestured at Zoe and Tish—"the three of you have been trying to cause trouble ever since."

Josh's shock turned to fury. "*I* missed the power!" He felt himself shaking. "You're the one who's lying, Milo. And if you're not, then explain these claws. And the makeup."

"Sure. I can explain them. You guys got them from the costume shop in the UnderGround."

Chelsea's voice called out from the audience. "I don't know about anyone else, but something here really stinks." Josh turned to her gratefully, but then his insides turned to water. She was glaring at him, furious.

"Milo's taken care of us from the first day," she said. "He found us food. Got us organized."

"And he stopped the Riots," said another kid. "We would have wrecked the place if it hadn't been for him."

There was a murmer of agreement.

"And we're safe, too." The speaker was a girl who lived just a few cottages down from Josh and Zoe on Starlight Lane. "We're safe, and our kidlets are safe, now that the Core's built up the barricades and added more Protectors."

The Timescaper spoke again. "Right. And it's these guys"—he pointed to Josh, Zoe, and Tish—"who started all the talk about leaving. Who got us to lower the barricades so the Outsiders could get in."

"And now they're attacking the Core," said the Timescaper. "If there's anyone who shouldn't be trusted, it's them."

Josh looked at Zoe and saw that she'd gone chalk white. Milo had loaded the assembly. Somehow, he'd figured out what they were going to do, and he'd put his Clones in place. But how? How had he known?

Then Josh spotted Toad. The boy's bug eyes were fixed on Milo, as worshipful as a pet dog's. Josh suddenly remembered him spotting the claws in Josh's hand on the day he'd made his discovery, and the rustling they'd heard in Tish's classroom.

"Hold on," said Matt O'Bannion, jumping to his feet with his brother Kyle. "This is crazy. You know Josh and Zoe wouldn't do something like that. Neither would Latisha."

The Timescaper glared at them. "And Milo would?" He turned back to the crowd. "Who are we going to believe?" he shouted, his voice barely audible over angry shouts. "The one who saved us, or the ones who let the Outside in?"

"But that doesn't even make sense!" cried Zoe. "Even if the Invaders were real, why would we risk everyone's lives? Our kidlets were captured, too!"

"And what about Hamim?" Josh said. "Why would we hurt our best friend?"

But no one was listening anymore. Frenzied Islanders were screaming at them, drowning them out, every face twisted with anger, shock, or disgust.

He felt someone walk up behind him.

"Did you really figure you could outthink me?" Milo asked quietly. His voice rose to a shout. "Caleb. Now!"

Caleb raised his arm and the Protectors moved in. Panicked, Josh grabbed Zoe's arm and screamed back at Tish.

"Come on!"

He yanked Zoe toward the side of the theatre, where the crowd was less dense, and began tearing up the steps.

"Stop them!" Evan shouted.

A mass of furious Islanders surged toward them, with more moving up and over the rows of seats to cut off their exit. Greg and Miguel were trying to get to them, to help them, but they couldn't push through the crowd. Josh slowed, looking desperately for another way out.

There was none. Then a dark cloud poured down from the upper reaches of the theatre. It swept between them and the mob in a hideous frenzy of snarling white faces and hideous grasping hands.

Zoe had been right. The Ghoulies were in on it, too.

BACK FROM THE DEAD

Josh felt someone grab his arm and turned to see a skeletal boy with spiked hair and an iron-studded collar. Josh tried to pull himself away, despairing, furious.

"Hit me," the kid hissed. "And make it look good."

Josh stared, and the Ghoulie gave an almost invisible nod. Josh swung wide at the boy, who took the punch and fell. Just below him, Josh saw Zoe hesitate as well. Then she aimed a fake kick at a kid's groin. He collapsed, moaning.

The other Ghoulies pretended to trip and stumble over their fallen companions, creating a blockade that stopped the rest of the mob from getting closer. Josh looked up and saw a girl with long white hair scrambling toward the aisle, then suddenly falling to her knees, blocking the Islanders behind her as she discreetly motioned Josh to the top of the auditorium. He and Zoe tore up the stairwell and through the door to the waiting area. An angry roar exploded from the crowd at their escape.

The big doors to the outside were wide open. "Come on!" Josh gasped.

Zoe started to run, then stopped. "Wait! What about Tish?"

Josh looked back, shocked that there were only two of them in the lobby. "Wasn't she behind us?"

"I don't know. I didn't see."

One of the Ghoulies burst out of the theatre, spotted them, and waved them away from the entrance. He pointed off to the side, where one of the employee doors had been propped open.

"Over there," the kid said. "Hurry!"

They had no time to think. Josh pulled Zoe toward the opening, and the Ghoulie slammed it shut behind them, trapping them in a dim hallway. The two of them jumped, and Josh pushed back against the door. It was locked. Then he heard someone creeping up behind him and he swung around, fist raised.

The figure held up one hand, then bowed slightly.

"Namaste," said Shadow.

Outside, they could hear the crowd thundering into the lobby, Caleb shouting directions. But Josh barely noticed, still staring into Shadow's unblinking eyes.

"What the *hell*?" said Zoe. "You're supposed to be dead."

"I am," the dark boy said. "I drowned the night the Scouts were attacked."

"What?"

"Just follow me."

"No way," said Zoe. "Tish is still back there somewhere."

"My friends will do their best to help," said Shadow. "But there's nothing you two can do now."

Zoe looked at Josh, who shook his head. Shadow was right. They couldn't do anything.

"This way," said Shadow.

He led them through the backstage warren of the IMAX, where cast members had once moved between lobby and stage, and where engineers had accessed the equipment behind the screen to maintain the massive speakers and projection equipment.

Finally, they reached what looked like a solid gray wall. Shadow leaned over and pushed a tiny red button in a small recessed square to his right. There was a soft click, and the wall swung open silently.

"Cool," Josh heard himself murmur.

"Magnetics," said Shadow.

"No. I meant the secret door."

"All of the buildings and attractions have them," said Shadow. "Back doors and hidden entrances. Built so the workers could get in and out without being seen by the guests. The Islands have a lot more secrets than just the UnderGround."

"How did you know about them?"

"There used to be a Web site where ex-employees spilled park secrets. And since most of us Ghoulies used to spend a lot of time online . . ."

Josh was surprised. "You call yourselves Ghoulies, too?"

"We actually like it."

They emerged at the rear of the theatre, moving down a gentle slope to a hidden utility path that snaked through the darkness behind the building. Around them, they could hear hoarse shouts and aimless threats as their pursuers spread out through Inspiration Island.

Shadow cracked open a large glow stick, a leftover souvenir from Freddy and Jason's Chop Shop on Nightmare Island. It glowed green, illuminating their path.

Motioning for Zoe and Josh to stay close, he led them around the edge of the Island, through the backlots of the BioPods and the Exploratorium. Finally, they emerged just below the entrance of the connecting bridge to Atlantis. A narrow path split off from the utility road and led to the underside of the bridge.

"I never noticed that before," said Josh.

"You weren't supposed to."

The path joined with another walkway attached to the inner wall of the bridge's elaborate siding. It allowed access to the cables and wiring that crisscrossed the underside of the bridge itself and provided power for the lights and speakers. Shadow led Josh and Zoe quickly onto the walkway and "across" the bridge. Listening to the water lapping against the beams beneath them, Josh felt like a rat scuttling through city sewers.

Once on the far side, they picked up another utility path and began following it around the edge of Atlantis.

"So where exactly are you taking us?" Josh asked Shadow.

"Someplace safe."

"Oh yeah?" asked Zoe. "Where's that?"

"My colony. On Nightmare Island." Josh suddenly had an image of Ghoulies hanging upside down from trees, clutching the branches with their toes.

Zoe stopped on the spot, snorting. "Right. You get us over there so you and your friends can nail us into a coffin somewhere. You think we're that stupid?"

Shadow looked at her coolly. Zoe returned the look, icicle for icicle.

Shadow shifted his attention back to Josh. "Maybe you'll listen," he said.

"Maybe." But Josh's skin was once again crawling with the pinned-bug feeling. "First tell me what's going on, why you're doing this. And how did you know this was going to happen tonight?"

"Toad wasn't the only one in Tish's studio the night you three were talking. We've been watching you for some time, waiting for the right moment to contact you." He hesitated. "Hamim told me you were his friends."

"Shut up," said Zoe. "Don't you even say his name, you murderer."

"Stop it, Zoe," said Josh. "You don't know anything for sure."

"I know plenty. I know this guy came back from the expedition, and the others didn't."

"At least let him talk," said Josh. "You can kill him later, if you want."

"*Fine!*" Zoe said. "But this is such total crap."

Maybe not, thought Josh. He was looking again at Shadow. There'd been a flash of pain in the other boy's eyes when he'd said Hamim's name. Pain too real to be part of an act.

"So," said Shadow, returning Josh's look with his unblinking gaze. "Will you come with me?"

"No," said Zoe. "He won't."

Josh raised one hand to quiet her. "Yeah," he said. "I'll go."

Zoe blinked. "You kidding?"

"No. I think he's telling the truth."

"Oh, sure, and you're this great judge of character. I mean, you were one hundred percent right about Milo."

Josh shot her an angry look, and Zoe quieted.

"Sorry. That was stupid." She took a breath. "Okay. If you're sure, then I trust you." She poked a thumb at Shadow. "Even if I don't trust the Crypt Keeper."

They continued along the hidden paths, moving more quickly as they heard the mob from Inspiration Island begin to cross over the arced bridge to Atlantis. Finally, they reached the next connecting bridge and were able to head back to the upper level, where the fanged entrance of the tunnel to Nightmare Island waited to swallow them.

Josh and Zoe exchanged nervous looks, then followed Shadow into the dark, increasingly narrow passage. Josh stretched out one hand and touched the side, shivering like a little kid at the moist, spongy feel. He remembered how the walls had once emitted a gurgling sound and pulsed with red light, giving visitors the feeling they were being slowly swallowed and digested.

A dim light shone ahead: the entrance to the Island. Shadow stopped, turning slowly to look back at them. The light from the glow stick shone on his face, making dark hollows of his cheeks and eye sockets.

He's enjoying this, thought Josh.

"Ready?" Shadow asked.

They nodded, and he grinned.

"Then welcome to my Nightmare."

They exited the tunnel.

NIGHTMARE ISLAND

Nightmare Island had always been the most twisted of the Islands, a disquieting mix of horrific images and black humor. Now, though, it showed an even darker side, like the weird neighbor who turns out to be a serial killer. Without its carefully orchestrated mood lighting and horror-movie music, it felt more like a bombed-out city after a war: dark, silent, and empty.

Josh looked around, remembering the creepy adventures he'd had here with his family. To the right of the tunnel entrance was the Troll Road, which wandered through Dismal Swamp and some of the slimier Island adventures. Josh's favorite had been the Nightcrawler, an enclosed subway train shaped like a huge, segmented serpent. It plunged under the surface of the Island, then crawled through a subterranean city that was home to pale, shovel-headed creatures with no eyes.

On the Swamp Tour, airboats piloted by hollow-cheeked guides glided through a bank of deceptively beautiful azaleas that hissed at the riders, then pulled back to reveal a gnarled forest of ancient pines and bearded cypress trees. There, trolls and gators waited to drag screaming tourists—actually, disguised cast members—off the boats and into the green waters.

To the left of the entrance tunnel was the midway of the

Midnight Circus, complete with a SideShow that boasted actual geeks and two of the park's more extreme coasters: Bonecrusher and the Screamer. Josh had gone on Bonecrusher for the first time on this last trip—it was not recommended for children younger than twelve.

But Shadow was leading them straight ahead, through Blandford Cemetery toward the central city of Necropolis. Crooked headstones and gaping mausoleums leaned drunkenly all around them, and Josh squinted through the pale moonlight at some of the inscriptions:

Justin Balmed

Barry M. Alive

Frau Malda Hyde

"Real good idea to come here," Zoe whispered in Josh's ear. "Maybe we'll at least get side-by-side crypts."

"Shut up."

Next, they entered the dark city of Necropolis itself. Buildings rose at impossible angles, their roofs slicing the night sky in jagged silhouettes. Each had a handpainted sign advertising a local business: the Shovem Inn, advertised as a traveler's "Tomb Away from Tomb"; the operatories of Dr. Payne, Dentist; and, of course, the comforting showroom of Digger O'Dell, the Friendly Undertaker.

At the far end of the town, they left the main street and turned onto Dead Man's Road, a twisted pathway that led up to Dracula's Castle on the Haunted Hill. Along the way, they traveled through the Howling Forest, glancing uneasily at dozens of giant spiderwebs that floated above them, and hurried past the Taunting Trees, a grove of skeletal trunks with glowing knothole eyes that had once insulted passersby and grasped at them with clawlike branches.

"Why are we coming all the way up here?" asked Zoe, eyeing the looming castle nervously. "Couldn't we have talked back in Necropolis?"

"This is safest," Shadow replied. "Even if someone came to Nightmare, we'd be able to scare them off a long time before they got up here." He glanced back. "We've got sentries, too. They've been watching you the whole time we've been here. And we've created a few 'amusements' of our own."

Josh shuddered, suddenly certain he could feel a dozen pairs of eyes on him. "Like what?"

"Like clinging vines that we've turned into hunting snares. Covered graves in the cemetery, just waiting for someone to stumble in. Or be pushed. I led you around them, but they're there."

Josh's nerves started singing. If something went wrong, if he and Zoe had to run . . .

"Calm down," Shadow said. "If we wanted to get rid of you, you'd already be sitting in a hole."

Finally, they reached Dracula's Castle, an imposing structure guarded by two huge stone griffons that flanked a working portcullis. It was five stories tall, covered nearly two acres, and contained both a ride-through attraction ("Please watch your step as you enter the hearse") and a walking tour led by Renfield, the Count's pleasant but deranged assistant. The tour always ended in the Catacombs, where, Renfield had explained, the Count "stored" his least-favorite guests.

It was to the Catacombs that Shadow was leading them.

They descended a spiral staircase to the lower level of the Castle, past skulls and spiderwebs and curious rats, until they reached a large wooden panel, carved with elaborate scenes from the Count's homeland of Transylvania. Behind it, Josh knew, was the main chamber where the Count had once waited to greet his guests. Shadow hit another of the hidden buttons, and Josh readied himself for the horror he was now sure waited for them.

The panel whooshed up. Josh's jaw dropped.

The chamber had been transformed. It was made of the same faux stone used throughout the castle, but here the rock was almost invisible, hidden by a comfortable assortment of upholstered chairs, thick floor pillows, and plush couches. Candles glowed softly in hurricane lamps, and books and musical instruments sat on gleaming wooden tables and leaned up against the furniture. The room looked . . . homey.

Except, of course, for the Ghoulies. They were everywhere. And they were staring at Josh and Zoe.

A tall girl with long, almost pure-white hair got up from the pillow on which she'd been lounging. Josh recognized her as one of the Ghoulies who had helped them escape from the IMAX. Somehow, she had reached the castle before them.

She walked over to Shadow.

"You got them."

"I did."

"I'm still not sure this was a good idea. Especially Core boy." She nodded at Josh.

"Hey," said Zoe. "You got something to say, say it to us."

The girl looked at her appraisingly. Zoe folded her arms and stared back. Finally, the girl nodded.

"You're right. I apologize. My name's Cassandra."

"Zoe."

"I know."

Other kids were now edging toward them. Most were dressed in black, like Shadow, and Josh saw a lot more piercings, streaked hair, and amateur tattoos than in the general population. He got the creeps, as though he were Bambi and the wolves were closing in. Shadow's eyes glinted.

"Don't worry. They're not going to attack."

Josh felt his face burn, and Cassandra finally smiled. "Okay. I guess you aren't a threat." She patted his cheek. "Poor little bunny."

Josh flushed deeper, and Cassandra gestured at two other girls who had come up next to her. One was frail and mouselike, the other had a strong biker-chick vibe. "This is Meeps," she said, pointing to the smaller girl. "And this is Nasra."

The two girls nodded.

"And I'm Styx," said a thin boy, his face a moonscape of acne craters. "We've already met." Josh saw the spiked collar and recognized the boy who had told Josh to punch him. Then Styx got bumped from behind, and two more kids stepped forward—brothers, it looked like, maybe a year or two older than Devon.

"Hey," they said in unison.

"Hey," said Josh.

"I'm Spike," said one, attempting a snarl.

"RiffRaff," the other added.

Zoe looked over at Cassandra. "You guys really went creative with the names."

"We have a reputation to maintain," said Cassandra, flicking her long white hair.

But Zoe looked around the room. "A lot of you were at the IMAX. Anyone know what happened to Latisha? Is she okay?"

Shadow looked at Styx, who shook his head. "I don't know. Things got insane. The rest of the mob finally pushed through our group, and there wasn't much we could do without giving ourselves away."

"But your other friends were trying to help," said Cassandra.

"The O'Bannions, and that big guy—Greg? And there was this strange geeky kid, yelling something about a revolution."

"Miguel," said Zoe, almost smiling. But when she looked over at Josh, her eyes were sick with worry.

Shadow noticed.

"We'll find out what happened to them," he said, looking over at his Ghoulies. "Nasra. Spike. Go over to Atlantis. Watch and listen. Then come back and tell us what you've learned."

The two nodded, and started to run toward the back wall of the Catacombs.

"No," said Cassandra. "The other way." They stopped, confused, but then Nasra whispered something to Spike. He glanced at Zoe and Josh, and then the two of them backtracked, disappearing through the door that led to the spiral staircase.

"All right," said Shadow, turning back to them. "It's time to talk."

A minute later, they had settled themselves in the main sitting area. Shadow sat in one of two large claw-footed chairs, his long arms draped over the wooden armrests on either side. Cassandra sat next to him, and Josh and Zoe perched on smaller chairs, facing them. The rest of the Ghoulies arranged themselves nearby.

"Okay," said Zoe. "Tell us what happened."

Shadow nodded. "All right. But it's not going to be easy to hear."

THE SECRET

"The first thing you have to know," said Shadow, "is that we Ghoulies have never really trusted the Core." He looked at Josh. "And that included you."

Josh felt all eyes on him, and Cassandra's "bunny" image hopped into his head.

"Why?" he managed. "At least at the beginning, we were all trying to do good things. You know that. You were on the Night Crew with us."

"Agreed. But there wasn't a Core then. We were all just working together. Once Council started, all that changed. Milo and his friends kept taking more control. And Ghoulies don't like anyone who tries to tell them what to do for too long."

He raised an eyebrow at Zoe, as though suggesting they had that in common, at least. She didn't respond.

"That's why we always came to Council," said Cassandra. "We wanted to know what their plans were, keep an eye out for anything that seemed off."

"For example," said Shadow, "the night Milo apologized to Zoe and Tish at the Council, after the two of you saw the lights. That wasn't like him. Milo almost never admits he's wrong, and he never apologizes. Especially not to Zoe."

Zoe nodded.

"So I left before the meeting was over and headed to the Palace, up to Milo's room. That's where they always go after Council."

"Wait a minute," said Zoe. "How did you know that's where they go? Plus, the Palace is always swarming with Protectors. There's no way you could get all the way up to Neptune's Chambers without anyone seeing you." She sat back in her chair. "Sorry, Fear Factor. I don't buy it."

Cassandra shot her an irritated look. "Maybe because you haven't spent the last year scoping out the UnderGround and all the employee passages."

"What? Why were you doing that?"

Styx shrugged. "It started kind of like a game," he said. "A Ghoulie game to creep people out. We'd pop up out of nowhere, show up in locked rooms, make ourselves disappear."

Josh remembered. They'd given Sam and Maddie nightmares.

Styx patted the plush cushion he was sitting on. "It was also a good way to steal stuff."

"That's how we started overhearing things," said Cassandra. "Things we weren't supposed to know about. And it's why we started to keep a closer eye on the Core." She pointed to a nearby storage shelf, where Josh spotted spyscopes and listening devices, obviously "borrowed" from Inspiration Island.

"We found passages in the Palace that even the Core doesn't know about," added Styx. "They were all made for the staff. Like, the tower walls are doubled, with hidden ramps winding inside, and supply cabinets at every level. The cleaning crews used them, so they wouldn't be seen going into guest rooms with mops or carts. I think the guests were supposed to figure there were magic cleaning fairies or something."

Cassandra elaborated. "During the day, when no one was

around, we drilled little holes in the walls, so we could see into the rooms and hear what was going on." She sat back in her chair and stared at Zoe. "So don't talk about things you don't understand. All right?"

Zoe squirmed a little, but Josh's mind was clicking. Zoe had been right. Ghoulies *had* been sneaking into the Palace at night. Just not for the reasons she'd thought.

Shadow tilted his head.

"May I continue?" he asked.

"Yeah," Zoe muttered.

Then Shadow told them what he'd seen.

The night of the Glow, after Council ended, members of the Core poured into Milo's chamber. Milo himself was in the lead, with Moira and Aiko just behind. Evan, Toad, Eli, and several others followed.

"Why can't some people leave well enough alone?" asked Moira, pacing back and forth. "Why do they always have to cause trouble?" She glared at Milo, who stood gazing up at a portrait of King Neptune. "And why did YOU have to apologize to Zoe and Latisha?"

"What was I supposed to do?" Milo said. "Ignore what they saw?"

"Why not? Nobody likes Zoe anyhow. If you'd just blown her off, they would have forgotten what she was babbling about."

"Not with Josh backing her up, they wouldn't."

Moira shook her head. "What a pain he turned out to be."

"So what do we do now?" asked Evan. "A lot of people are going to want to go out now, at least to see what's happening."

"So why not let them?" asked Toad. "I mean, what's the big deal?"

Milo slowly turned to face them. "I'll tell you. If they go Outside, they may find out that it's not as bad out there as we thought. Then people are going to want to leave. And everything here will fall apart. We'll have to leave, too, and start all over out there."

Toad tried again. "But if there are other kids . . ."

"If there are other kids, then they'll already be organized. They'll have the best places to live, and the best stuff, and we'll be living in boxes and begging them for help." Milo's face darkened. "After all this, I'm not going to start taking orders from someone else." He looked at the others. "That sound good to any of you, either?"

No one answered.

"Besides," he said, his voice now more controlled, "everyone here owes us. If we hadn't taken charge, then half of them would probably be dead by now. They owe us to keep things going."

"So, what do we do?" asked Eli. "How do we stop them if they want to go out?"

Milo didn't answer. But Moira looked over at Eli, like he'd said something brilliant. "That's it."

"What's it?"

"You said, 'If they want to go out.' We just have to make them not want to."

"Okay," said Evan. "But how?"

"Here's how. Tomorrow night, at Council, we listen to everyone's ideas. But we work it so that Zoe and Tish's plan is the one we choose."

"You mean, the one about sending Scouts?" asked Evan.

"Exactly."

"But who? Who do we choose?"

"It doesn't matter. Because they're never going to go anywhere. The moment they get to the other end of the monorail tracks, they're going to be attacked by Outsiders. Sick, vicious Outsiders. The Scouts will be so terrified that they'll run right back to the Islands. And no one will ever want to leave again."

"I don't get it," said Evan. "What Outsiders?"

"And how do you know they're sick?" asked Toad, brow furrowed. "And if they are sick, then how could they help us?"

Milo was beginning to smile. "Because they *are* us. Islanders in disguise." He shook his head. "You're a genius, Moira."

"I know," she said, smiling at him. "And it would be easy to pull off. We've got everything we need in the costume shops of the UnderGround. And we could ask Alex to help us plan it."

"But he's not Core. How do we convince him?"

"I could try," said Aiko, sitting up a little straighter and leaning toward Milo. She'd become a real beauty over the last year, her once bubbly voice now soft as a cat's. "I bet I could convince him."

"I bet you could, too," said Milo, his gaze lingering on her.

Moira's eyes narrowed. "We shouldn't get too many people involved, though," she said, a little more loudly than necessary. "Just Caleb and some of the Protectors."

"Right," said Milo, dragging his eyes away from Aiko. "Those guys'll do whatever I tell them to. Especially if I say it's for the good of the Islands."

Evan shook his head. "You guys are brilliant."

"We know," grinned Milo, echoing Moira. "So now let's plan tomorrow's Council. It's got to look good."

Shadow stopped speaking. For a long time, there was silence.

"I told the rest of the Ghoulies what I'd heard," he said finally, "but we knew no one else on the Islands would listen to us. Not after some of us"—he glanced at Styx—"had made ourselves bogeymen for all those months. That's why I volunteered to be one of the Scouts. I thought maybe I could find a way to ruin their plans. Unmask them."

Zoe shook her head, her voice bitter.

"So all this is just because Milo and the Clones don't want to give up living in the Palace."

"Not just that," said Shadow. "It's the power. They like being in charge."

Josh nodded. But he felt hollow inside. Milo had been playing them, and for longer than Josh wanted to believe.

"So what happened?" he asked finally. "Why didn't the Scouts come back?"

Shadow's face went dark. "That's the second part of what I wanted to tell you. But first, I need you to know that Hamim and I really were friends."

"You didn't even know him," said Zoe.

"Yes, I did. We'd been together on the Night Crew, remember. And we'd joined it for the same reasons—to make sure the families were treated with respect."

Josh did remember. Both Shadow and Hamim had stood up to Caleb when he'd talked about throwing the victims into the lagoon.

"We didn't see each other much after that, not until we both volunteered. No one else in that group talked to me any more than they had to—I made everyone too nervous. I don't think I expected Hamim to talk to me, either. But he did." The pained expression returned to Shadow's face. "I guess he understood outsiders."

"He was just a good guy," Josh said quietly.

Shadow nodded. "That's why I trusted him. And why I told him about Milo's plan just before we left. I figured we could watch out for each other." Shadow gave a short, bitter laugh.

"So finally, we headed out. When we got to the end of the

tracks, it was still dark. We were blocked by the monorail train, and we had to climb into the rear car and walk through. It was horrible. There hadn't been any Night Crew at that end to clean up afterward."

Josh felt sick. He'd never let his mind travel that far beyond the Islands.

"Finally, we reached the station platform. And that's when we were attacked.

"They jumped out from everywhere, maybe a dozen of them, howling like something out of a slasher movie. I could see Caleb leading the charge, dressed in rags and carrying a big knobbed stick. He was wearing green makeup and had glued-on scars and face parts. He looked so fake it would have been funny, except that no one else knew what was going on.

"Everyone started screaming and yelling, and I think that's when the Core had figured we'd all go running home. But all of a sudden, Ryan reaches down and pulls out his knife. Paravi and Kim see him and pull theirs out, too. The Outsiders all freeze, and that's when I know none of the other Scouts are in on the plan.

"I start yelling at everyone to put down the knives, that it's just Protectors in makeup. And then I see Hamim running at Caleb, maybe to pull off the disguise. But Caleb's panicking, like some big cornered bear. He swings his stick at Hamim, and I hear a crack. And Hamim just crumples to the ground."

There was a strangled noise from Zoe. Shadow's eyes dropped.

"Everyone stopped moving. I ran over to Hamim, but . . ." Shadow shook his head. "The girls started crying, and everyone else was looking at Caleb. Even some of the Protectors. I could see him sweating. But I didn't expect what he said next."

"What?" asked Josh.

"He said, 'Milo's gonna kill me.'" Shadow shook his head.

"That's all. He didn't care about Hamim. He was just worried that he'd screwed up Milo's plan, and that everyone back on the Islands would find out what was going on."

"And then it would have all been over for the Core," said Josh.

"Exactly. But then Caleb got an idea, probably the first in his life. He told the Scouts that we were going on our expedition after all. But that we were never going to come back.

"Ryan went crazy and asked Caleb how he thought he was going to manage that. 'Because there are a lot more of us than there are of you,' Caleb said. 'So either you leave, or we take care of things right here. And if you ever show up on the Islands again . . .'" Shadow stopped.

"So what did you do?" asked Josh.

"I started running—but back toward the Islands. That was the only way all of you were ever going to know what happened. I tore back through the monorail cars and onto the tracks, but Caleb was right behind me, screaming. I knew I'd never make it even to the first barricade.

"I moved up onto the side of the track and spun around for a second, like I wanted to see where he was. Then I pretended to lose my balance, and I fell backward off the track and into the lagoon. It was like hitting concrete. But I made myself stay underwater, and I swam under the tracks where I could hold on to one of the support beams and where Caleb couldn't see me. Right above me, I could hear him laughing and yelling like some kind of lunatic.

"I didn't move for a couple of hours, just in case he'd left someone to watch for me. Finally, I started swimming from beam to beam, until I got back to the Islands. It took me the whole day. I've been hiding here ever since."

Cassandra's voice was quiet. "Shadow only left the Castle to come look for you."

"So what happened to the other Scouts?" asked Zoe, sounding as though she were afraid to hear the answer.

"There were only three of them left," said Shadow. "Three against all those Protectors. I'm hoping they just did what Caleb said. Left forever."

Josh nodded, piecing the rest of the puzzle together. "And that explains why we had the Invasion a couple of nights later. Plan A hadn't worked. There was no one to bring back a report."

Cassandra nodded. "Plan B turned out better for them, anyhow, because more people saw the mutants. And by saving the kids, Milo and the Core got to look like heroes."

"Even Caleb," said Zoe furiously. "Sam said all the kids were hugging him and the Protectors after the rescue." She looked from face to face. "So what do we do now? We can't just let them get away with this."

"No," said Shadow. "We can't."

"So what, then?" asked Zoe.

Shadow leaned forward, fingertips pressed together in that odd way of his.

"We get even."

NEPTUNE'S REVENGE

Before Shadow could explain what he meant, a tapestry on one of the walls started quivering. It swung toward them, as though on a hinge, and Nasra and Spike squeezed out from behind it.

Josh stared. "What—?"

Cassandra was glaring at the two Ghoulies. "I told you to use the staircase. Until we're sure about these two." She jerked her head toward Josh and Zoe.

"Sorry," said Spike. "My bad."

"What is that?" asked Zoe. "A secret door?"

"Yes," Cassandra said grudgingly. "It leads directly into the UnderGround. It's how we're able to get around the Islands so quickly." She shook her head, looking at Spike with narrowed eyes. "No one except Ghoulies is supposed to know about it."

"Cassandra," said Shadow, "after what Zoe and Josh have heard tonight, the door doesn't matter anymore." She folded her arms, still displeased.

"Now," said Shadow. "Tell us what's happening."

Nasra looked from one Ghoulie to the next. "Okay, here it is. The Protectors organized everyone who was at Council into search parties. Some of our Ghoulies volunteered, too, so no one would get suspicious about us. That meant Spike and I were able to join one of the groups." She looked at Spike. "The others didn't seem to like that much, though, did they?"

"No, they didn't." Spike grinned, eyes gleaming from the dark smudges around them. "For some reason, we creeped 'em out."

"Anyhow," said Nasra, "it's like some old Frankenstein movie out there, villagers looking for a monster. They've all got flashlights, and they're in every corner of Inspiration. A few groups are heading to Enchanted Island, to do a house-by-house search. Then they're going to go to Timescape. But right now, no one has a clue where Zoe and Josh are. And no one's even thinking about coming to Nightmare." She looked smug.

They will, though, thought Josh.

"Listen, Shadow," he said. "Zoe and I should leave. Now."

"What are you talking about?"

"If the Core figures out you've helped us, you'll all be in trouble."

"You're not going anywhere," said Shadow firmly. "After what Milo and the Core have done, we'd be planning a rebellion whether you were here or not. They're dangerous, Josh. And it's just going to keep getting worse."

"Yeah. But—"

"You're staying."

Zoe stepped forward. "What about Latisha? You see her anywhere?"

Spike shook his head. "No. Sorry. Haven't seen her since the IMAX."

Zoe swore. Then she looked up at Josh. "And what about the kidlets? They're going to hear what happened, and they're going to be scared to death."

"I know," said Josh, who'd been thinking the same thing.

"We've got to go get them. We've got to get them now," Zoe said.

"You can't," said Shadow. "The Core will know that you'd head for the kids first. You put one foot on Enchanted Island, and you're dead."

"I don't care," said Zoe. "I'm not leaving our kids up there alone."

Shadow's face went dark, but Cassandra intervened.

"You won't have to leave them," she said. She looked at Shadow sternly, then back at Zoe. "Just give us some time to get organized. We'll bring them back through the UnderGround as soon as we can."

"You swear?"

"I swear." She looked away. "I lost my sister in the Riots."

Zoe gasped. Then she took Cassandra's hand. Josh saw the two girls become friends at that moment.

"We'll talk more in the morning," said Shadow. "The best thing everyone can do now, though, is get some sleep. I don't think we'll have much of a chance over the next few days."

A few of the Ghoulies nodded and drifted away. Zoe wandered over to a nest of cushions in a dark corner of the room. She sank into them, brooding, and Josh knew that every moment until she saw Sam again would be agony.

He stayed with the remaining Ghoulies a while longer, listening as Spike and Nasra shared more of what they'd seen on the surface. But soon their voices trailed off, and one by one the others headed toward their cots.

Shadow looked at Josh. "Why don't you get some sleep, too. You're going to need it."

Josh nodded, and got up to leave. "Shadow?"

"Yes?"

"Thanks."

"You're welcome."

Josh walked to the cushions where Zoe lay sleeping and stood looking at her for a moment. He could see patches of clean skin streaking through the dirt on her face, and he realized that she'd let herself cry again.

Slowly, carefully, he lay down on the cushions beside her, hoping that even as she slept she'd know he was back with her and not feel so alone. Around him, candles and lamps were extinguished one by one, and the room disappeared into darkness. Zoe murmured something, and he stroked her hair. She stirred, waking.

"Josh?"

"Yeah, it's me."

She shifted where she lay, moving closer to him.

"You know," she whispered, "it was never Hamim I was in love with."

"No?"

"No."

Her hand touched his face, her fingers tracing his cheek and drifting over his mouth. His heartbeat quickened, and he frantically tried to decide what to do next. Finally, he rose up on one elbow and leaned over to kiss her forehead. But she took his face in both hands, kissed him full on the mouth, and pulled him back down next to her.

They woke to the sound of feet clattering down the spiral staircase. Josh shot fully awake, clutching Zoe to him, eyes glued to the entryway. He slumped in relief when Spike and RiffRaff appeared. But they didn't come any farther into the room, and Josh stiffened when he saw their faces.

"You better come to the surface," said Spike. "Neptune's calling to the Islands. And I don't think it's gonna be good."

Josh and Zoe raced up to the main level of the Castle, part of a dark mass of Ghoulies. They streamed through the Castle portcullis, to an overlook on the Haunted Hill. The sky was just beginning to lighten.

Neptune's voice, anguished and urgent, was calling from every post, every hidden speaker. "AWAKE, EVERYONE! OUR HOMES ARE IN DANGER. COME OUTSIDE AND HEAR MY WARNING."

Josh shook his head in disgust. Milo was about to put on another show.

The announcement was repeated every thirty seconds or so, the words varying only slightly. No one on the hill spoke or moved. Finally, the voice stopped. A minute passed, then another and another. Finally, Neptune spoke again, his voice deeper this time, and sadder.

"My friends," said Neptune, "I bring you solemn and terrible news. The Island home we have worked so long to build is being threatened once more."

"Freakin' Moira," muttered Zoe.

"When the Outsiders attacked," the voice continued, "we were able to fight back. Our Protectors overcame them and rescued our little ones from a terrible fate. This time, though, the danger is much worse. Because this time—" He paused, his silence more ominous than any words. "This time, the enemy comes from within."

"No," whispered Josh. "He wouldn't."

"There are traitors among us," said the King. "Traitors who pretended to be our friends. They were the ones behind the Invasion. And last night, they attacked the Core Council."

Josh stared at the speakers. "He's making it sound like we went after them with knives."

"We already have some of them in custody, and their names will surprise you. Latisha, the Teacher, and her partner, Miguel.

Greg, whom we trusted, but who has secretly been weakening our barricades as we slept. Matt O'Bannion and his brother Kyle, helping plan the attack even as they distracted us with their games on Timescape."

"Oh, God," said Zoe. "No, no, no."

"It's because of what Toad heard in Tish's classroom," Josh said, sick with the realization that their plans had condemned their friends. "He told Milo who to go after."

Neptune's voice grew stronger, his words swirling through the air like a gathering storm.

"Their leaders have gone into hiding—Josh and Zoe, who first tempted us to leave the Island, and who let the Outsiders in. We have to find them, along with whoever helped them escape from Council last night. Who will help me?"

Frenzied cries rose in the distance.

"I knew I could count on you," said the King, "all of you who are still loyal to Neptune. Together, we will find the traitors. We will find them and we will destroy them, before they can destroy us."

The cries were louder this time and wilder, and they went on and on. Only the group on the hill was silent.

"I thought we'd have a little more time," whispered Cassandra.

"But we don't." Shadow stared across the Islands to where the damaged spires of the Coral Palace pierced thick clouds of gray fog. The Ghoulies turned toward him, waiting.

"I'll need some of you to head out into the Islands," he said. "We need to find out what's going on, what they're going to do. Cassandra. Styx. Pick a dozen or so people and get going as soon as you can." They nodded.

"What about our kids?" asked Zoe. "You said you'd find them and bring them here."

Shadow's jaw tightened. "Right now it's more important to—"

"I'll try to get to them," said Cassandra. "Don't worry."

Zoe looked at her gratefully.

"Fine," said Shadow. "Meanwhile, Nasra, you go down to Necropolis. Spike, head out to the Dismal Swamp. Meeps, go to the Midnight Circus. Tell the Freaks to prepare for a Gathering. The moment the sun sets."

Cloaked in late-afternoon darkness, the residents of Nightmare Island streamed toward a huge black tent slouched at the center of the Midnight Circus. Called the Shapeshifter, it was actually a complex web of rods and wires covered with flexible steel mesh. The tent had been designed to reshape itself in response to a computer program, allowing it to endlessly change form and personality. A few days after the plague, though, the program had crashed, freezing the front of the tent into the visage of a howling demon.

Josh and Zoe followed Shadow into the gaping mouth, and watched his skin turn pale green under the interior mood lights that rimmed the roof. The bleachers on the entry side were already dark with Ghoulies—close to three hundred, and none much younger than Spike and RiffRaff.

Except for their age, though, there was more variety among the spectators than Josh would have thought. He had expected all of them, like the Castle dwellers, to have gone for the Goth look. But Ghoulies from other parts of Nightmare had more varied outfits. Josh saw everything from tattered troll vests, to formal jackets once worn by the mayor of Necropolis, to the shimmering, sequined capes of the Circus Freaks.

Shadow left Zoe and Josh in the bleachers. Then he walked to the center ring, where he perched on a large pedestal that gleamed an oily midnight blue. Unlike Milo, he chose not to use a spotlight or microphone. The moment he looked at the audience, though, the room grew still.

Shadow wasted no time.

"You all heard Neptune this morning," he said. "So you know it's time for the Core to be removed. Otherwise, the Islands are going to fall apart, and none of us will ever get a chance to know what's Outside. Worse, the Core will never have to pay for their crimes."

The Ghoulies leaned forward.

"We've had spies throughout the Islands all afternoon to see what the situation is. I'll let them tell you what they heard." Shadow motioned to the Catacomb dwellers, several of whom stepped forward.

Josh blinked. They looked entirely ordinary. Styx was in jeans and a T-shirt, his studs out, his choker off, and his hair tousled. Nasra, wearing worn sweats, now looked like a jock instead of a biker. And Meeps, free of her makeup, could have been someone's sweet little sister. Josh shook his head. Only Ghoulies could disguise themselves by looking normal.

Styx spoke first. "It's not too bad yet," he said, "because no one was expecting last night to get so out of hand. But Neptune got everyone worked up this morning, and there are tons of kids gathering on Atlantis, waiting for Milo to give them orders. It's just taking them a while to figure out what to do."

"There's a lot of kids over on Inspiration, too," said RiffRaff, looking like some wholesome kid from an old cereal commercial. "They're seeing if anything in the Exploratorium can be turned into weapons."

Cassandra stepped up next to him, wearing faded jeans and a torn hoodie. She'd found some way to color her hair a mousey brown and had gathered it into a scraggly ponytail.

"I went to Enchanted Island," she said. "It's still pretty quiet there, at least. A lot of the parents left for Atlantis to join Milo's army, but the ones who stayed aren't doing much besides keeping their kids indoors."

She searched the audience for Zoe. "I got to Little Wizards, too. There were Protectors all over the place, so I couldn't get the kids out. But I managed to sneak Maddie a note. It just said that you guys were safe, and that they should stay put." She grinned. "Maddie read the note, crumpled it into a ball, and swallowed it."

Josh and Zoe looked at each other, smiling, and some of the tension left Zoe's body.

Now Meeps and Nasra came forward.

"We went to Timescape," Meeps said. "It's worse there. A bunch of Protectors are doing some recruiting. They already had a group of pirate kids from the Barbary Coast ready to form some kind of squad."

"They were talking about sharpening swords," said Nasra.

Josh felt Zoe stiffen again. Back in the center ring, Shadow eased off the pedestal and walked forward.

"It's clear then. The time to fight back is now. Before they get any more organized. And before Milo figures out what so many Ghoulies were doing at Council."

"But how?" asked a boy in zombie rags. "There aren't that many of us. Not compared with the rest of the Islands. And Milo's got everyone on his side."

"Not everyone," said Cassandra. "Most people are just watching. Keeping their distance."

"But after what happened to that Teacher and the other kids, even the ones who aren't with Milo won't want to risk their necks. And we won't know who we can trust."

"We know we can trust anyone on Nightmare," said Shadow. "So we stick with our own. And we do what Ghoulies do best."

"What?" asked the boy. "Pop up and yell 'boo'?"

"No." Shadow looked around, a dark smile spreading across his face. "We're going to rule the UnderGround."

The Ghoulies looked at each other and grinned.

BELOW THE SURFACE

Shadow's plan was simple.

"Milo controls what's on the surface," he said. "But the Islands run on what's underneath: the main computers and power generators, the kitchen and the food supplies. We take charge of those, and we're the ones in control. There's no fighting, and no one gets hurt."

"Okay," said Styx. "But how?"

"We'll move at night, when the Islands are asleep. First, we block off the entrances to the UnderGround. We put guards at each key location and shut off the power. Then we send a message to the Core: Surrender Atlantis. Step down. Or the Islands will die."

Zoe jumped to her feet, and Josh had a flashback to Island Council.

"So now we're terrorists?" she said. "What about the kidlets? You can't starve them. And there are a lot of good kids up there, too. Why should they—"

"It won't ever get that far," said Shadow. "Once the rest of the Islanders understand why we're doing this, they'll join the resistance against Milo and the Core."

"And who's going to make them understand? They didn't listen so great at Council."

"They will now." His next words played out like a winning hand at cards. "Because we'll have taken over the sound system, and Neptune won't have a voice."

Zoe wasn't impressed.

"So what? Everyone thinks that Josh and me are the enemy, and that anyone who was even friends with us is, too. So who're they going to believe?"

Shadow placed one spidery hand on his chest. "How about someone who's returned from the dead?"

Zoe stared at him, and he smiled briefly. Then his eyes once again lasered the crowd. "No one has to do this," he said. "We can stop right now. But if there was ever a time for Ghoulies to take a stand, it's now. Who's ready to fight back?"

Hundreds of hands went up. Hundreds of eyes gleamed.

They waited until moonset, until the Islands were silent again. Then a horde of Ghoulies, costumed to look as gruesome as possible, streamed out from Nightmare Island, some above ground and some below. Each group had its own assignment.

The first ones on the surface were to find and subdue as many of the Protectors as possible. This meant capturing the sentries on the individual Islands, as well as those who patrolled the streets at night. Only those guarding the Palace would be left alone, to avoid alerting Atlantis.

The Ghoulies moved quickly and efficiently. After months spent learning how to avoid Caleb's goons, the Ghoulies now knew exactly where to find them.

Emerging soundlessly from hidden stairs and doorways, they approached their targets unseen, empty canvas sacks from the storerooms stretched open in front of them. Before the Protectors were even aware that anyone was around, they were inhaling dust and food crumbs, their arms bound tightly to their sides. Then they were dragged UnderGround, into the tunnels, and herded back to Nightmare Island.

Beneath the surface, a second group of Ghoulies targeted the Protectors who'd been assigned to guard the storehouses in the dimly lighted Hub each night. It didn't take long to deal with them: they tended to be the least powerful of the guards. Each caved almost immediately, unnerved by moaning swarms of the undead staggering out of the shadows with dangling ropes and bloodied fangs.

Once the guards were out of the way, other Ghoulies began barricading the lower tunnels and blocking off the stairways to the surface. Doors were locked from inside, then made more secure with metal bars wedged between them and the walls of the stair-wells. Tables and chairs from the old employee lounge areas and cafeterias beneath each Island were dragged into the spokes of the UnderGround and piled into an impassable tangle of metal and wood. Only the passage leading to Nightmare was left open, along with the outer corridor.

Josh was on a special mission—to find Tish and the other captives, and fill them in on what was happening. He and Zoe had been assigned to this task because they were the only ones the captives would trust. Cassandra and Styx offered to accompany them, though, so that none of the Ghoulies would mistake them for enemies. It made perfect sense.

To everyone except Zoe.

"This whole plan is stupid," she'd said after Shadow's meeting, when they'd been given their tasks and were standing outside the Shapeshifter. "Too many things could go wrong."

"You got a better idea?" asked Styx, nervous himself but fiercely loyal to Shadow.

"Not yet."

"Then how about making this one work?"

"And leave the kidlets up there while this whole place explodes? I don't think so."

"Zoe," Cassandra warned. "You know you can't go after them. It's too dangerous."

"So's this." She raised her hands to head off any more discussion. "Sorry. I'm out." She turned and strode off.

Josh rushed after her. "Zoe, wait a minute! Where are you going?"

She indicated Styx. "To do what he said. To come up with a better idea." She paused, then put her hands on Josh's shoulders and gave him a quick kiss. "Good luck," she said. "We just need one of us to be right." She ran off, disappearing between the tents of the SideShow.

Josh started after her, but Cassandra came up behind him, grabbing his arm.

"There's no time," she said. "Just hope she doesn't get caught."

Josh looked once more at the spot where Zoe had vanished, then followed Cassandra and Styx back to the main chamber of the Catacombs. There they waited for word that the UnderGround was secure, so they could proceed with their search.

They huddled together, grasping at fragments of information that got brought back to the Castle, reports of little victories. As the hours passed, Ghoulie squads from the surface and the Hub began appearing, all driving captured Protectors ahead of them toward a large passageway off the main chamber.

The passage had once been a waiting line for a labyrinth called Enigma. A dozen alcoves were carved into the wall on either side, each fronted by a heavy wooden door with iron bars on a viewing window. Once, these cells had held animatronic captives, all pleading for release as nervous visitors wandered by. Now, reinforced with chains and locks, they served as perfect holding cells for the prisoners.

Finally, Nasra and RiffRaff pushed through the tapestry door with the last of the captured sentries from the storage areas.

"It's all secure," Nasra said to Josh. "You guys can go now."

Josh nodded at Cassandra and Styx. The three of them exited to the outer hall of the UnderGround, then dashed down the open access spoke toward the Hub, where Ghoulies now stood guard at each entrance. Somewhere in the maze of offices and work areas was the Protectors' secret room: Styx had once heard some of them saying that Caleb had picked a place under Atlantis because prisoners would be easier to guard there.

Josh and the others split up, agreeing to keep returning to the center to see if any of them had found anything. Josh began in the computer section, moving from office to office, closet to closet, looking for his friends.

After nearly an hour, though, the location of the prison was still a mystery. Swearing, Josh headed back to the center for the fourth time, to see if Cassandra or Styx had had more luck.

They hadn't.

"Maybe we were wrong," said Cassandra. "Maybe the room isn't down here at all."

"It's got to be," said Josh, frustration gnawing at him.

"Why?" asked Styx. "Maybe we got bad information. I mean, why couldn't it be above ground, in one of the buildings? Like when they put the Outsiders in the tanks of the Living Oceans?"

"They only did that because the Outsiders were fake, and they needed them to be able to escape."

"We're running out of time," said Cassandra, looking nervously back down the tunnel that led to Nightmare. "We might have to wait and find them later."

"No!" said Josh sharply. "We don't know what's going to happen next, or how bad it's going to get. And I'm not going to lose another friend."

Images of Hamim flashed through Josh's mind. Hamim sneaking candy to the kidlets, watching Zoe move around the cottage, joking about the cooking talent that seemed to have condemned him to a permanent assignment in food preparation.

Josh's head jerked up. "That's it."

"What's it?"

"The kitchen."

He bolted toward the main cooking area, the others on his heels. Racing past the giant ovens and tub-sized sinks to the rear wall, he shoved through the swinging doors that led to one of the three main storerooms. This one hadn't been used for months, blocked off as the original supplies dwindled and were consolidated in the remaining two rooms.

Josh stopped, put his hands to his mouth, and yelled.

"TISH! LATISHA, IT'S JOSH!"

For a moment, they heard nothing. Then, suddenly, there was a dull metallic clanging and a muffled voice.

"Where's it coming from?" asked Styx.

"I'm not sure." He listened harder, trying to match the sound with a place. "Damn. The freezers."

They ran down the central aisle to where three huge stainless steel doors reflected the dim glow of worklights. Like the rest of the storeroom, the freezers hadn't been used in months. But each was secured with a heavy metal lock threaded through holes drilled in the latch. The pounding was coming from the one on the right.

"Why aren't they dead?" asked Styx. "Why aren't they frozen?"

Josh didn't answer. He was staring at the lock.

"We need something strong," he said. "Strong and heavy."

Cassandra darted back to the main kitchen. A minute later, she returned with a metal tenderizing mallet and a thick cleaver. Josh positioned the blade of the cleaver on the lock and swung down hard with the mallet. After two strikes, the lock popped off. Styx leaped forward, yanking at the handle.

The door swung open. Latisha stood a few feet back, blinking as the light hit her face. Behind her were Matt, Kyle, Greg, and Miguel.

" 'Bout time you showed up," Tish said.

The cooling agents of the freezer had been turned off long ago, so Tish and the others had been dealing mainly with darkness and fear.

"Jerks didn't even leave us a candle," she said. "Just buckets to take care of business."

Miguel looked like he was sleepwalking. "It's actually interesting what happens when you're in total darkness for a long time. You start seeing color flashes and weird images, and—"

"Miguel," said Tish. "Analyze later."

"What were they going to do with you?" asked Cassandra. "How long were they going to keep you here?"

"I don't think they'd thought that far ahead," said Matt. "They just wanted to get us out of the way."

"Anyone in the other two freezers?"

"Don't know."

"We'd better find out." Josh picked up the mallet and cleaver again, smashing the remaining two locks. The others yanked open the doors. No one was inside either room. But there were buckets in both freezers, and some stale bread and blackened chunks of cheese.

"Wonder who they had in there," Tish said quietly. "And for how long."

Josh shuddered, his imagination going to dark places.

Kyle broke into his thoughts. "So what's going on out there? And how did you get away after Council the other night? And . . . who're they?" He nodded at Cassandra and Styx.

"Friends," Josh said. "Really good friends." And he told them everything, including what Shadow had revealed to him and Zoe about the Core's plans, and what had happened to the Scouts at the monorail station.

"Animals," whispered Tish. Next to her, the O'Bannions, Greg, and Miguel stared at the ground, deep in shock. Then, suddenly, Matt raised his head.

"Wait. Do you really think everything Shadow told you is true?"

"Yeah. I'm sure it is."

"So then Ryan . . ."

"Might still be alive somewhere out there, along with Kim and Paravi."

Matt and Kyle whooped, leaping to their feet and slapping hands. The others grinned, the horror of the previous moments replaced by hope.

"Speaking of missing people," said Tish, "where's Zoe?"

Josh glanced at Cassandra. "Long story."

"She okay?"

"Yeah," said Josh. "I hope. I'll fill you in later."

Tish raised an eyebrow. But she didn't push. "So what's next?" she asked.

Josh quickly explained Shadow's plan.

"Smart," said Kyle. "Just like in war books. Cut off the supplies, force the bad guys to surrender."

"Except if they don't," said Matt. "Then we'll just be fighting a bunch of hungry, pissed-off Islanders."

"Shadow doesn't think it'll get that far," said Josh. "He thinks we'll be able to get the word out about what we're doing. Rally more people to our side."

"Yes!" yelled Miguel, his alter ego resurfacing. *"¡Por libertad! Por la vida!"*

"Right," said Josh. "But first things first. Let's head back to Nightmare, get you some food and stuff. The Ghoulies will take care of you, just like they've watched out for Zoe and me."

"No," said Matt, brow furrowed.

"What do you mean, no? It's safe there."

"No," said Matt again. "I mean, you're right, it's safest for us, but I don't think it's the best thing for Shadow's resistance."

"Why?"

"Because, a skinny bunch of Ghoulies can't stand up to Caleb and the Goon Squad." Kyle shoved an elbow in his brother's ribs, nodding at Cassandra and Styx. "Sorry. No offense."

"None taken," said Cassandra coolly. She took a step toward him, leaning in slightly. "Though I'm pretty sure I could take *you* down."

Matt seemed to shrivel where he stood. Cassandra stepped back, satisfied.

"So what do you want to do?" asked Josh, and Matt turned to him in relief.

"I want to go back to Timescape," he said. "Me and Kyle. I know a bunch of kids who would never side with Milo. Maybe we can get them to help us."

"It's too risky," said Tish. "If you're wrong, if they've switched sides, they'll just drag you over to Atlantis and you'll be back in the deep freeze. Or worse."

"What'll be worse is if we don't beat Milo."

"Matt's right," said Kyle. "The sooner we take care of the Core, the sooner we can look for our brother. We'll risk it."

"So will I," said Greg. "It'd be hard for anyone to grab all three of us."

"Thanks, man," said Kyle. "Besides, you're kind of an unofficial O'Bannion Boy anyhow."

Greg grinned.

"I'll go, too," said Miguel. "Over to Inspiration. It's time Geeks took a stand." Josh looked at the little Brainiac, surprised again by his fervor. But Miguel was on fire, and Josh realized that he was now channeling Emiliano Zapata or maybe Pancho Villa, ready to lead his people to freedom.

Tish sighed, shaking her head at Miguel. "Then I suppose I'll go with you. Make sure you don't hurt yourself."

Josh looked at the two of them, and at Greg and the O'Bannion brothers, and then at Cassandra and Styx, who had become two of his closest friends in a matter of days. They made him think that maybe, just maybe, Shadow's plan could work.

"Okay," he said, suddenly feeling like a hero himself. "Let's do this."

ULTIMATUM

Milo's war stalled, subverted during the night. Islanders woke the next morning to find that there was no food in the dining halls and no way to reach the kitchen or storerooms—all the doors to the UnderGround were locked. The power was off in the BioPods and Living Oceans. The sanitation systems weren't running. And there were only a handful of Protectors around, looking as bewildered as everyone else.

Fear crept through the Islands, quietly taking hold. Islanders began to cluster in small groups, asking each other what was happening. Speculating about the reasons.

"Generators must have gone down. The Core'll be on it."

"But why can't we get to the UnderGround? And why isn't there any food?"

No one had an answer. And, most unsettling of all, Neptune was silent.

Morning gave way to afternoon. Messengers came from the Palace, telling people to stay calm, that the Core knew what was happening and would take care of them. But nothing changed, and the traitors they'd been told to track down seemed to have been forgotten. Confused and frightened, hundreds of Islanders began streaming toward Atlantis, to gather at the Coral Palace. Waiting for Neptune to tell them what to do.

The sun slid toward the horizon, impaling itself on the broken spires of the Coral Palace. The light dimmed and the air grew colder, but the Islanders were still without food, without lights, without answers. They shivered as they waited, afraid to return home.

Josh wandered among them, unrecognizable in a tattered outfit thrown together from odds and ends on Nightmare, an old beach cap pulled low on his forehead. A dozen equally invisible Ghoulies—among them Cassandra, Nasra, and Meeps; Spike, Styx, and RiffRaff—roamed through the crowd, watching and listening. Waiting for what was about to happen.

Evening crept across the sky.

Suddenly, the speakers hummed, power crackling back on. The Islanders groaned with relief as they turned toward the Palace, all eyes fixed on the balcony. Josh listened as they whispered to each other. Finally, they said, the King would tell them what was happening. He would tell them that there was nothing to worry about.

Except that it wasn't Neptune who called to them. This was a different voice—somber, hypnotic, and chilling.

"CITIZENS OF THE ISLES OF WONDER," it said. "LISTEN TO ME."

The crowd buzzed with confusion, still looking up at the balcony of the Coral Palace. But no one appeared.

"THE LAST TWO DAYS HAVE NOT BEEN WHAT THEY'VE SEEMED. NOR HAVE MANY DAYS BEFORE THAT. THEY'VE BEEN AN ILLUSION, A SHOW PUT ON FOR YOUR BENEFIT."

"Who is that?" murmured a boy next to Josh. "What's he mean?"

"IT'S TIME FOR YOU TO LEARN THE TRUTH, IF YOU'RE FINALLY READY TO LISTEN. AND IF YOU ARE WILLING TO BELIEVE WHAT YOU HEAR."

An explosion shattered the air, and the reflecting pool burst into flames. The Islanders cried out, spinning around and pulling back from the blaze like rats from a lit torch. Just then, Milo, Evan, and Moira burst onto the balcony, Caleb and two of his Protectors just behind them. Like those in the courtyard, they stared at the leaping tongues of fire.

"YOUR LEADERS, TOO, ARE NOT WHAT THEY APPEAR TO BE. THEY'VE DECEIVED YOU, FED YOU LIES ABOUT THE ONES YOU SHOULD HAVE TRUSTED. YOU WOULDN'T BELIEVE THOSE PEOPLE WHEN THEY SPOKE AT COUNCIL. BUT PERHAPS YOU'LL BELIEVE ME."

The inferno shot even higher, driving the crowd farther backward. From the center of the pool, a platform rose, climbing higher and higher in a thick column of boiling water. But this time there was no serpent, no sea nymph chorus, no giant writhing Kraken rising to meet the King.

This time, Shadow rose from the flames.

The crowd gasped. Josh looked back at the balcony and saw Milo's eyes widen with shock. He whirled toward Caleb, whose face was chalk white. The big kid held out both hands, babbling wildly, but Milo swung at him, his fist slamming into the side of Caleb's face.

Transfixed by Shadow's appearance no one in the crowd saw Milo's rage. The kid next to Josh was gaping. "He's supposed to be dead!" he said to a companion. "Him and the other Scouts. Milo said so, and there was that memorial."

His friend shook his head, equally confused. "So what the *hell's* going on?"

Good, thought Josh. They're finally going to figure it out.

"MILO!" said Shadow. "YOU KNOW WHAT I'M ABOUT TO SAY. BUT I CAN REMAIN SILENT, AS I HAVE ALL THESE WEEKS. THE CHOICE IS YOURS."

Milo faced forward again, eyes blazing. His unamplified voice cut through the darkness, hollow compared with Shadow's, but somehow still evoking the power and majesty of the King.

"What is it you want, Shadow?"

"I WANT YOU TO STEP DOWN. YOU AND THE REST OF THE CORE. THE MOMENT YOU DO, WE TURN THE POWER BACK ON AND GIVE BACK THE SUPPLIES." He paused, his voice suddenly quieter. "More important, Milo, my friends and I will keep silent about what I know, and what I saw. We'll wipe out the past, and make new plans for our future."

"And if we don't step down?" said Milo, defiant.

Shadow's voice became even quieter. "Then everyone on the Islands finds out what you've done."

Milo's face twisted into a mask of hate and fury. The crowd in the courtyard turned to look at him, mystified by Shadow's cryptic words. Suddenly, Milo's energy seemed to drain from him. He looked beaten—pain and humiliation wiping out the rage.

Moira put her hand on his arm, and Josh could see her talking earnestly to him. Milo listened, but Josh could see no reaction, no change in his expression. Looking across the courtyard, Moira called to Shadow.

"He just needs a minute," she said. "Can you at least give him that?"

Shadow hesitated, but then nodded, firelight flickering on the white planes of his face.

Milo and Moira disappeared into the Palace. A minute later, Caleb slipped inside as well. Long minutes passed, and the crowd began whispering nervously. Josh, too, became uneasy, wondering if they'd return.

"MILO!" called Shadow. "YOUR DECISION."

Milo stepped back onto the balcony, Moira still by his side. He looked calmer now, more like himself, and for just a moment, memories flashed through Josh's mind of the day King Neptune's voice had first called them to the Palace. He remembered the intensity of Milo's vision, the passion of his words. He had given them hope, and a new life.

And then he'd destroyed it.

Milo walked to the edge of the balcony, placed both hands on the railing, and leaned out over the waiting Islanders. All faces lifted to him.

"I know that all of you are confused," he said, "and that everyone is afraid. Our world has turned upside down for a third time, and you want to know why." He paused, took a breath. "Well, maybe . . . maybe it's because, somewhere along the way, a few of us got a little lost."

Josh caught his breath, astonished at what Milo was saying. But part of him was relieved—Moira had given Milo a way to leave the Palace with dignity.

"This isn't anything I planned," Milo continued. "Not me, and not any of the Core. We believed that all of us could live together, build a perfect world. But maybe that couldn't happen. Maybe some of us weren't ready." Sorrow seemed to push down on him, and he lowered his head.

Then, abruptly, he straightened. His voice grew twice as loud. "I promise you this, though. Our dreams will not die!"

Josh flashed a look at Cassandra, who was frowning. Something wasn't right.

"One thing you just heard is true," Milo continued. "Someone *is* putting on a show, trying to trick you. Only it's not me, and it's not any of the Core." His tone became more urgent. "Earlier today, a message was delivered to me. A threat. From the Ghoulies. They're in league with the ones who betrayed us before, the ones behind the Invasion."

A buzzsaw of horror ripped through the crowd.

"NO!" thundered Shadow. "THESE ARE MORE LIES!"

"Are they?" asked Milo. He pointed toward the ring of flames. "Who turned off the power on the Islands? Who was the only Scout to return from the expedition alive?"

Angry shouts erupted from the crowd.

"NO," said Shadow. "IT WAS MILO AND THE CORE WHO PLANNED THE OUTSIDERS' ATTACK. AND IT WAS MILO WHO—"

Shrieks from two dozen air horns buried his next words, coming from all over the courtyard. Cringing, the Islanders slapped their hands over their ears, trying to block out the sound. The noise continued until Josh thought he'd go deaf. But he couldn't see who held the horns.

"We have to stop our enemies now," shouted Milo when the noise finally died down. "The Ghoulies already have control of the UnderGround. What's to stop them from taking over the BioPods, and the Living Oceans? Why wouldn't they go after the kidlets from Little Wizards?"

The mob howled with anger, and Josh, whirling back toward the reflecting pool, saw Shadow crying out from the platform. But his voice could no longer be heard above the churning water and crackling flames: during the long minute that the air horns had blasted, someone had cut all the power lines to the speakers.

Desperate, Josh tried to shout through the pandemonium.

"Don't listen to him!" he cried. "Shadow's telling the truth. It's Milo doing all this! It's been Milo all along!"

Cassandra grabbed his arm.

"Shut up!" she hissed. "They're not going to listen. Look." She pointed to where Islanders were picking up rocks and chips of pavement, rushing toward the pool and hurling them at Shadow. He crouched, trying to shield himself. Then the roiling waters began to recede. The platform sank once more into the flames, deep into the UnderGround.

Other voices around the courtyard were still trying to scream out the truth about the Core.

"You hear?" Milo shouted, his eyes trying to search out his enemies. "Even now they're trying to spread their poison. But we won't let them. We're going to fight for our home, for everything that's good!"

His subjects raised their fists in the air, roaring approval.

Milo pointed into the crowd, his arm sweeping from left to right. "Head back to your Islands, gather your neighbors, arm yourselves with any weapons you can find. Meet at the entrance to Nightmare Island. We destroy the Ghoulies now!"

WAR

In an instant, the crowd became a mob. They screamed out against the traitors and began chanting Milo's name like a battle cry. Josh and the Ghoulies disappeared into the chaos and raced back to Nightmare Island, reaching the fanged gateway in minutes. They shot through the tunneled bridge and sprinted across the main Island, pairs and trios of Ghoulies peeling off along the way.

"Where are they going?" gasped Josh, glancing at Styx.

"Battle stations."

They panted up the Haunted Hill to Dracula's Castle, scurrying down to the Catacombs. Shadow was already there, pacing the main chamber like a rabid dog. Relief spilled over his face when Josh and the others entered the room.

"You're okay," he said.

"Barely," replied Meeps. "Caleb spotted Josh and started charging through the crowd, but Spike tripped him. He crashed so hard I thought the sidewalk would crack."

"I didn't see that," said RiffRaff, turning to his friend. "Nicely done."

"Thanks."

Shadow looked from one to the next. "How close are they?"

"Don't know," said Styx. "They were all heading back to their own Islands. But they'll be here pretty fast. Milo had them all crazed." He paused. "So. What exactly happened back there?"

"We underestimated Milo," said Cassandra.

"And Moira," said Josh. "When she pulled him back into the Palace."

"Still," Meeps said, "why did everyone believe them so fast?"

Shadow's voice was bitter. "Because we're Ghoulies. And because it's easier. This way, they can go on believing in Milo, believing they're safe." He paused. "They don't have to think."

The truth Shadow spoke was hard to hear, harder to accept. But there was no other explanation.

"So what can we do?" Josh asked. "If logic isn't an option?"

"We do what they're forcing us to do. We fight back." Shadow turned to Styx. "Where are the others?"

"Headed toward their stations. Nasra's going to start a crew building a blockade at the tunnel."

"Good."

"So what do you want me to do?"

"You and Cassandra, head back to Necropolis and the Swamp. Spike can run over to the Circus. Make sure everyone's ready."

"Got it." They raced off.

"What about me?" asked Josh.

"The rest of us have to defend the Castle. If we lose control, their army can go through the Catacombs and take back the UnderGround. And then it's all over."

Josh's heart began pounding.

"Okay," said Shadow. "Let's get ready."

He led the remaining Ghoulies out of the main chamber and into the passageway where the Protectors were being held. Plaintive cries came from inside the cells.

"Come on, man," said one as they passed by. Josh recognized Farrel's voice. "This isn't funny."

"No," said Josh. "It sure isn't."

Shadow continued down the passage toward the entry room for the Enigma. Three jagged entrances opened at the far end. Shadow headed through the one on the left, leading everyone into a room built of smoked glass and distorted mirrors. Josh gaped.

In the center of the room was a massive stockpile of weapons, most yanked off wall displays in the Castle or pulled from the mail-clad hands of the rusting suits of armor that lined the hallways. Other pieces of the arsenal seemed to have come from Timescape. Josh saw African spears, broadswords, wooden clubs, and maces—none of them real, most hollow or made of rubber. But they still looked dangerous, and many were tough enough to do some serious damage.

Josh looked at Shadow. "People could really get hurt," he said. "What else can we use? Our fists?"

Each of the Ghoulies grabbed a weapon and some kind of shield. Josh reached for a double-balled flail—a thick stick with two spiked orbs attached to one end with chains. The toy spikes were about as sharp as gumdrops, but Josh hoped that just the sight of the thing would keep attackers at a distance. Shadow also threw him a hooded cape from a pile of costumes, so no Ghoulie would confuse him with one of the invaders.

They returned to the Catacombs, grabbing spyscopes from the storage shelf and then continuing up through the main level of the Castle and into the turrets. From there, they could view most of Nightmare Island and see across the tunneled bridge into Atlantis. Only a glimmer of light remained in the sky, turning Necropolis into a phantasmagoria of twisted shadows and gaping abscesses.

"Nightmare time," said Shadow. "Our time."

Josh wasn't so sure. In the distance, he could see what looked like a thousand spots of light—Islanders with glow sticks and flashlights and battery-powered lanterns. They were streaming over the other three connecting bridges and converging on Atlantis. They swarmed there like hornets, then headed toward Nightmare Island.

Josh watched transfixed as the sea of lights poured into the fanged entrance. When they emerged on the Nightmare side, the lights stopped moving, piling up on each other—Nasra and her soldiers had gotten their barricade up in time. But the delay was brief; there was a wild roar, then a splintering of wood and screech of metal. The deadly flood broke through, separating into three streams and surging into different areas of the Island.

"We've got to get down there," said Josh. "They're not going to be able to hold them."

"No," said Shadow. "I told you—we've got to protect the Castle. Besides, you wouldn't last two minutes down there. You don't know the traps." He reached out, turning Josh's scope toward Blandford Cemetery. "Look there."

Peering through the eyepiece, Josh could see small shapes stumbling through the graveyard like doomed victims in some twisted video game. They moved slowly, fearfully. Some were grabbed by shambling corpses and pulled into crypts. Others leaped to avoid tombstones that crashed to the ground inches from where they stood. Still others were swallowed by open graves that had been camouflaged with a thin lattice of moss-covered sticks.

Terrified shrieks floated up the hill to the Castle, and the river of lights once again slowed.

"It's working," said Shadow. Josh saw his look of grim satisfaction. Somehow, it chilled him.

Dozens more battles churned in the dark cauldron beneath them. In Dismal Swamp, Ghoulies dressed as trolls or rotting zombies snatched invaders from the walkway, locking them into the body segments of the Nightcrawler. A few tried to escape into the cypress groves, only to find themselves suddenly hanging upside down in hunting snares.

At the Midnight Circus, Milo's army wandered down the deserted midway, looking nervously from side to side. Then the old calliope let out a tortured shriek, and a moment later, painted Freaks and demon clowns jumped out from the ticket booths and concession stands, dragging the intruders into the SideShow tents, where steel cages had been hidden.

But the ocean of lights was endless, still seeping across the connecting bridge, forcing itself into the blackest comers of Nightmare Island and weaving its way up through the Howling Forest. Shadow's expression turned tense.

"They'll be here soon," he said. "Alert the others."

Josh tore down the stone steps, calling to other Ghoulies along the way. Moments later, several of them emerged along the parapets, dragging heavy buckets and steaming cauldrons. Others thronged just inside the Castle gate, weapons in hand. Josh pushed his way to the front of those defenders, to where RiffRaff was standing. They waited tensely as the invaders' lights slid across the trunks of the Howling Forest, moving closer.

The next line of defense went into action. Ghoulies perched in the branches of the Taunting Trees began hurling rocks at those below, or cut loose the giant spiderwebs that stretched between the branches. Some of the enemy collapsed under the cat's cradles of thick rope; others ran, only to be tripped by vines that had been strung between the trees. But for every attacker that fell, five more came, then a dozen. The Ghoulies were dragged from the branches, and the howling mass pushed forward.

RiffRaff began breathing faster, sweat glistening on his face.

Josh put a calming hand on his shoulder. But then, looking out at the advancing horde, seeing the utter conviction burning on each face, he felt an eruption of fury. How could they still believe Milo? How could they all be so *stupid*?

"That's right!" he yelled. "Keep coming. Maybe we can *beat* some sense into you!"

A moment later, the Castle was under siege.

The defenders went into action, tipping the black cauldrons on the parapet walls. Scalding water poured onto the first wave of attackers, who screamed and fell back, pushing frantically against those behind them. The next wave of invaders forced themselves forward, only to be met by a hail of jagged rocks raining down from the battlements and parapets. Stones cracked against skulls, cut into faces and arms, knocked dozens to the ground.

Cries from the mob grew louder, and some of the invaders began to stumble blindly back down the hill. RiffRaff raised his fist.

"We're murdering 'em!"

But the barrage of rock and water slowed as supplies dwindled, and the mob roared forward. Josh raised his flail high over his shoulder, the vicious orbs dangling behind him. It was his turn now. Time to get back at them for everything they'd done.

A cry came from the balcony above them. Shadow.

"NOW!" he called. "ATTACK THEM NOW!"

The Ghoulies howled out of the Castle entrance, and the invaders leaped toward them. Josh scanned the crowd, looking for his first target. His eyes locked on a sword-wielding pirate, who spit the moment Josh caught his eye. Josh stretched his arm backward, ready to swing the flail.

But then, just behind the pirate, Josh saw Micki, the rainbow-haired girl he'd once volunteered with. And Chelsea, just behind her. There were other kids he knew, too. Friends of his.

He shot a look upward. Shadow had moved to one of the lower balconies. He was leaning out over the battle scene, his fingers gripping the railing, his eyes wild.

He looked like Milo.

"No," whispered Josh. He shoved his way toward one of the stone griffons that guarded the Castle and clambered up onto its shoulder.

"Stop!" he shouted, facing the crowd. "This is crazy! Look at who you're fighting!"

Some of the kids nearest to him hesitated.

"It's kids you've worked next to, eaten with," gasped Josh. "Not your enemy. Not a bunch of monsters." He looked upward. "Shadow! We're turning into them! We've got to stop this before anyone else gets hurt!"

Shadow stared at him, the blood draining from his face. The melee slowed, almost imperceptibly, a few kids looking like sleepers waking from a dream. Then a tall figure detached itself from the crowd, gripping something in both hands.

"Too late," said Caleb, and a club whipped toward Josh's head.

CAPTURED

Josh struggled back to consciousness, feeling as though he were lying on shards of glass. Every inch of him throbbed, and a dull buzz filled his ears. The left side of his head pulsed and burned; he reached a hand toward his cheek.

"Don't," said someone, catching his fingers. It was Cassandra, sitting just next to him. "It's pretty bad."

Josh peered at her through swollen eyelids. "What happened?"

"We lost," she said, emotionless. "There were just too many of them. They knocked down the blockade in just a few minutes, and the Swamp and Circus didn't last long either. And there's not much left of Necropolis—just a couple of the bigger buildings."

Josh closed his eyes again.

"What happened at the Castle?"

"The same thing, from what I heard. There were a couple dozen of them to every one of us. We didn't have a chance." Josh suddenly remembered his pathetic call for peace, and grimaced. What an idiot he'd been.

Cassandra seemed to read his thoughts. "I heard what you did. At least you tried."

"Yeah. Great." Caleb's sneering face flashed in his mind. "So what happened after I got whacked?"

"What you'd expect. Milo's soldiers shoved their way into the Castle, smashing everything. Then they headed down to the Catacombs, freed the Protectors, and stormed the UnderGround. Soon there weren't enough Ghoulies left to fight. The power came back on a little while after that, and King Neptune proclaimed a great victory." Her voice was bitter.

"What about Tish and Miguel? And the O'Bannions? They ever show up?"

"No. Or if they did . . ."

Josh forced his eyes open again, just in time to see Cassandra drag a hand across her face. Her arms were a bloody mess of cuts, and her legs were scraped raw.

"You all right?" he asked.

"Yes. But a lot of others aren't. There were kids lying all over Nightmare, kids from both sides. Some looked pretty badly hurt." Her voice became almost inaudible. "I haven't even seen Styx, or Meeps, or some of the others."

Josh sifted through what he'd heard, the implications chilling him. But they couldn't stop now. They couldn't let what had happened paralyze them.

"So what do we do next?" he asked.

Her brow furrowed. "What do you mean?"

"What's the plan? Where's Shadow?"

Cassandra's expression changed. Without saying anything, she leaned over and slipped her arm beneath his back. Gently, she began to raise him off the ground. He gasped at a sharp pain near his collarbone, but soon he was sitting.

"Look."

For the first time, he registered something besides Cassandra's face. They were in a huge gray box of a room, with large rectangular openings on three sides. The floor was concrete, and the walls looked like they were made of corrugated steel. Dim utility lights glowed every few feet. Ghoulies were everywhere, most slumping in exhaustion or rigid with fear, the rest wandering along channels of exposed floor, like drugged rats in a maze.

"Where are we?" he asked.

"I don't know. None of us do. Once the fighting was over, the Goons started herding us together, like it was some kind of roundup. They made us rip off parts of our shirts and tie them around our eyes, and then they started moving us out of Nightmare. I'm not sure where we ended up. I just know that we crossed two bridges."

"What about me? I didn't walk."

"Wounded kids were loaded onto trams, and the 'enemies' were brought here and dumped on the floor like garbage. The Goons didn't care if someone was bleeding or had broken bones. I saw you get brought in and dragged you over here with me."

"Thanks."

She nodded. "You're almost lucky you're all smashed up—no one recognized you." She pointed across the room. "Look who wasn't so lucky, though."

Josh looked, and saw a girl with long raven hair huddled in a corner. Aiko.

"What do you suppose that's all about?" asked Cassandra.

Josh didn't have to guess. Moira must have found out about Aiko and Milo, then set her up, or just accused her of being part of the resistance. Milo would have had no choice but to go along.

Josh couldn't feel too bad for her—she'd known what side she was choosing.

He went back to examining their prison, trying to figure out where they were being held. The walls offered no clue. But what looked like three huge squares were cut into the floor down the center of the room. One was slightly elevated. Josh stared at them a moment, then looked above him, at the ceiling. It, too, was subdivided with what seemed to be retractable panels.

"We're in some kind of a theatre," Josh said.

"What?"

"Look. These are hydraulic platforms, like Shadow used to rise out of the reflecting pool, and that"—he pointed above him—"must be the floor of the theatre. The panels pull apart, and scenery or performers get sent up on the platforms."

Cassandra looked from the floor to the ceiling. "I think you're right."

Footsteps thudded on concrete. Moments later, more Protectors streamed into the rooms, each with a club, a pole, or a braided whip from Heart of Africa.

"Come on!" they yelled. "Everyone up."

The Ghoulies struggled miserably to their feet, huddling close to each other. The Protectors began poking and prodding them, forcing them through the entrances and surrounding rooms until they reached a large central area. Two ramps faced each other in the center, rising up through the ceiling. Dim shafts of daylight came through the openings, highlighting clouds of dust raised by the milling mass of prisoners.

Josh saw two familiar figures shuffling in from another entrance, and gasped.

"Ari! Lana!" Their heads whipped around, and they rushed toward him and Cassandra.

"God," said Lana. "What happened to you?"

"Forget me," said Josh. "What're *you* doing here?"

Lana's face crumpled. "After Neptune's last speech, a whole mob of Goons showed up at Little Wizards. Said they had to protect the kids from the Ghoulies."

"They called all the caregivers together," said Ari. "To give us 'directions.' Next thing we know, we're on a tram heading for Timescape. And then we're here."

"Zoe never showed up?" asked Josh.

Lana's brow furrowed. "Zoe? No. We never saw her."

Damn, Josh thought. Then they got her, too. "What about the kidlets? Maddie and Sam and—"

"We don't know," said Ari. "We don't know anything that happened after they took us away."

Josh went dizzy with fear for his sister, for his whole family. But he didn't get a chance even to imagine what might be happening to them. A gang of Protectors stomped into the room, forcing them all toward the center.

"Up the ramps!" shouted one of the Goons. "All of you."

The captives shuffled upward and disappeared through the openings. As the first ones reached the surface, a roar rose outside. Josh and Cassandra looked at each other, eyes wide. The sound grew louder and louder, like an oncoming train.

Then it was their turn to step on the ramp.

The first thing Josh saw was a square of sky, gray and smeared with clouds. As his head rose above ground level, he saw a huge circle of tiered seats, rising a dozen stories above them and black with jeering spectators.

They were in the Coliseum.

COLISEUM GAMES

Josh's eyes swept the stadium. Protectors were stationed all around the field, including the ones who'd been briefly held in the Catacombs. They were putting on little shows for the audience, taunting the Ghoulies nearest them and making them do tricks. Josh could see Farrel stabbing at one wounded Ghoulie with a long pole. The boy kept trying to drag himself away, but Farrel followed, snorting like a pig. A group of spectators cheered him on.

What's happening? thought Josh. What the *hell* is happening? He scanned the crowd, looking for someone, anyone, who might help them. But even the kids he knew were almost unrecognizable, their faces warped by fear and anger.

And then he spotted the Little Wizards. Dozens of kidlets, jumping up and down as their Protectors laughed, pointing to the desperate Ghoulies.

"Look!" Josh heard one of the Goons yell. "King Neptune caught the bogeymen!"

"Get 'em," a little boy cried. "Get the bogeymen!"

Josh felt sick. Then he saw Maddie. She was standing with Sam and Devon in the middle of the laughing mass of children, holding tightly onto Giz's hand. Devon held Shana. She was crying, but the rest of them were utterly still, horrified by what they saw in front of them.

Suddenly Maddie spotted him.

"Josh!" she shrieked, letting go of Giz's hand and starting to struggle down the aisle. Devon saw Josh, too, and pushed Maddie back. Then he shoved Shana into her arms and tried to force his way past the Protectors who guarded them.

"No!" shouted Josh. "Devon, go back! Take care of the kids!" Devon ignored him, but one of the Protectors grabbed him, shoving him roughly back into the crowd of kids. Devon stared down at Josh, helpless.

"Get the bogeymen!" the boy yelled again.

Now the kids around him began to chant, joined by their Protectors.

Get the bogeymen! Get the bogeymen!

Within seconds the cry spread through the stadium.

GET THE BOGEYMEN! GET THE BOGEYMEN!

On the north side, the chant suddenly died and a cheer rose from the stands. All faces turned toward the Emperor's Box. Milo had just emerged from the doorway, his trident in his right hand, Moira at his side. They were followed by Evan, Toad, and Eli. Milo smiled and waved at the crowd, which responded by whistling and stomping, applauding with hands held high over their heads.

Milo stepped up onto a speaker's platform at the edge of the box. He grinned broadly, holding the trident high in the air.

"VICTORY!"

"VICTORY!" the crowd echoed, mimicking his gesture with their fists. They continued cheering until Milo lowered his scepter.

"Today is a great day," Milo said, his voice echoing around the stadium. "Nightmare has been destroyed, and our enemies have been captured."

The crowd shouted wildly, hooting at the prisoners below.

"And now we know the mastermind behind it all, the one who planned every horrible thing that happened, maybe even back to the Riots. But know this: he'll never harm us again."

Milo pointed dramatically to the center of the stadium. The ground there separated, two of the hidden panels sliding backward. A metal box rose from the opening. A cage.

Inside was Shadow. His arms were bound, and there was a gag across his mouth. The platform rose higher in a twisted parody of his rise from the flames just a few hours before.

Josh gasped and started to struggle to his feet.

"Don't," said Cassandra, her own eyes wide with horror. "Or you'll be in there with him."

"I give you the leader of the Ghoulies, the ruler of Nightmare Island," said Milo. "Shadow."

Angry shouts rose from the mob, everyone leaning in toward the arena, shaking their fists and screaming at Shadow, at all the Ghoulies. And Josh, despite everything he'd seen, was astonished at what they'd all let themselves believe.

Something flew through the air, landing with a dull thud just a few feet from Cassandra. A chip of concrete. Another came only seconds after that, hitting a smaller Ghoulie that Josh suddenly realized was Spike. The boy screamed in pain.

The crowd cheered and applauded, then began searching the areas around them. Soon hundreds of objects were streaking toward the Ghoulies, who cowered beneath raised arms in a futile attempt to protect themselves. The Protectors backed off to the edges of the arena to avoid the hail of stones. Josh glanced at the Emperor's Box and saw Milo smiling triumphantly at Moira.

He's not going to have to do a thing, Josh thought dully. The mob's going to do it for him.

He heard dozens of the missiles striking metal and realized that Shadow's cage had become the main target. The boy stood motionless, trying not to flinch even when fragments of rock made it through the bars. Josh staggered toward the center of the field, not sure what he was going to do when he reached Shadow, only knowing that he had to do something. Cassandra was immediately at his side.

Josh reached Shadow's prison and stood on one side of it, facing the crowd, his arms stretched along the bars as though his body were impervious to rock. Cassandra stood next to him and did the same. Then dozens more Ghoulies struggled toward the cage, surrounding it completely as more rocks and shards of concrete flew toward them.

Josh felt a kick on his right shoulder. Glancing up and behind him, he saw Shadow shaking his head furiously, trying to scream them away through the gag in his mouth.

Josh looked away. A rock hit his forehead, and blood dripped into his eyes.

Suddenly there was a new sound—a blast of air horns and plastic trumpets. Josh looked toward the noise, wondering what fresh amusement Milo had planned for the crowd. The answer thundered in through three of the side entrances. A new group of warriors had arrived, all of them carrying weapons—spears and swords and clubs and staffs. Most were dressed as Roman soldiers.

The crowd went wild.

They're really going to do it, thought Josh. They're going to kill us.

The soldiers scanned the field, searching out their first victims. A group of them spotted the cage and pounded toward it, yelling a battle cry. Josh braced himself, unable to take his eyes off the heavy weapons they carried in both fists. One of them slowed as he reached Josh.

"Better late than never, right?" Startled, Josh looked up into the grinning face of Matt O'Bannion.

REVELATION

Josh's knees started to buckle, and Matt grabbed his elbow.

"I thought you were more of Milo's Goons," Josh said.

"So did they," said Matt. "That's how we got in. Here." He tossed Josh one of the swords. Tish, Greg, and Miguel appeared a few seconds later, also in Roman armor.

"God," said Tish, staring at Josh. "You look like you were hit by a truck."

"I was. Its name was Caleb." Josh squinted into dust and watched as other soldiers raced around the field, handing weapons to the least hurt of the Ghoulies, shouting for the rest to move to the center of the field. The Protectors looked at each other, vaguely aware that something was wrong.

Up in the Emperor's Box, Milo rose to his feet, eyes flicking around the field.

"They'll be on to us in a second," said Josh, looking back at Matt. "How many are with you?"

"Not enough. A couple dozen each from Timescape and Inspiration. A lot of your Ghoulie pals found us, too—the ones the Goons missed in the roundup."

"Better than nothing," said Josh, gripping his sword. "At least we'll go down fighting."

"They're coming," cried Tish, and Josh saw some of the Protectors moving in from the edges of the stadium. Cassandra grabbed a club from Greg and began hammering at the lock of Shadow's cage.

Some of the spectators jumped up, pointing and screaming.

"Stop her!" cried Milo. "And the soldiers, too! None of them are part of this!"

A half dozen Protectors picked up speed, sprinting toward the cage. Josh jumped to help Cassandra, pulling on the bars as Shadow kicked at them from the inside. Then Greg pushed Josh aside and yanked.

The heavy door screeched open and Shadow jumped down, twisting around so Cassandra could cut his bindings. He ripped the gag from his mouth and turned back to her.

"Thanks," he said softly.

"Shadow!" shouted Kyle, and tossed him a sharpened broadsword. Shadow caught it and spun around to face his enemies. Josh and Cassandra stood on either side of him, Miguel, Tish, and Greg a few yards away.

Matt jumped up on the edge of the platform. "Defenders!" he yelled. "Are you ready?"

"Ready!" they yelled. And all of them lifted their weapons.

Josh looked up at the Emperor's Box and watched Milo's expression change from shock to fury. And then it changed again—to exhilaration. He leaned onto the edge of the box, eyes wild.

"Excellent!" he cried. "Protectors, give them what they want. A real battle! A fight to the death!"

The crowd screamed its approval, and the Protectors began charging toward the wounded Ghoulies and their Defenders. There were at least three Goons to every soldier, almost all of them bigger and heavier. Josh wondered how many seconds he'd last.

"Protectors, halt!" The Goons stopped, confused, and Caleb

pushed through them, his club held firmly in both hands. He strode across the field until he was just opposite Josh.

"You two," he growled, looking at both Josh and Shadow. "I want you two for myself."

He raised his club.

Shadow jumped forward, slashing at Caleb's leg with the sword. The big kid bellowed in pain, and his hands loosened around the club. Josh grabbed it and cracked it against Caleb's knees. Caleb howled again and collapsed.

"You almost had us," said Josh, leaning over him. "Too bad you're stupid."

But the attack triggered others. The Goons hurled themselves toward the Defenders, weapons raised. Wooden swords crashed against each other, clubs and maces thudded on flesh. The Defenders began falling, one after the other, and the crowd in the Coliseum was back on its feet, filling the stadium with bloodthirsty cries.

"STOP! STOP, YOU MANIACS!"

The voice rang through the Coliseum, echoing off the curved walls. On the field, the warriors froze, and the crowds in the stands went silent, all looking for the source of the command.

A lone figure stood at the top of the southern wall, shaking with fury, a loudspeaker in one hand.

Zoe.

Josh stared, then cried out to her, his throat tight. She looked frantically into the arena, saw him, and closed her eyes in relief.

Milo looked up at her from the Emperor's Box.

"Zoe," said Milo, his voice floating across the now-silent stadium. "I've been wondering where you were."

She turned toward him. "I'll bet you have."

"Were you off hiding somewhere? Making your own little traitor's plans?"

"No. I've just been on a trip. And I brought something to show you." She looked at the crowd, raising her voice. "Something to show all of you!"

Along the top row of the Coliseum, other figures appeared, emerging from the entrance ramps that zigzagged up the inner walls of the Coliseum. First five, then ten, then more and more, climbing to the upper rim until they stood atop every section of the stadium. They said nothing—just looked down at the speechless crowd.

None of them had been seen on the Islands before.

"What is this?" said Milo. But Josh, looking at his expression, realized that he already knew.

A girl stepped up next to Zoe. She was tall and lean, her hair cropped short, her flowing shirt a riot of color. But the most striking thing about her was her voice. It was rich and deep, and it demanded attention.

"I am Amina," she said, looking out over the stadium. "Amina was also the name of an African warrior queen. I chose it for myself a year ago because I knew I'd have to fight to survive. And I have fought, and I have survived."

"My friends and I come from a colony a few miles from your Islands. We've been living there for a long time now."

No one moved.

"It's a good place," said Amina. "There's a lake nearby, a warehouse full of supplies, and plenty of places to live. And we're building all the time, because people are starting to hear about us, and new settlers are arriving every day.

"We call our home Tumaini."

"Hope," Tish murmured. "That means 'hope.' "

Zoe shot a look across the stadium.

"Not exactly monsters, are they, Milo?"

The crowd in the stands turned back to the Emperor's Box. Milo was clutching his trident like a lifeline, his face strained and desperate.

"It's a trick," he muttered.

Matt stared in disbelief. "Did he say what I think he said?"

"Yeah," said Kyle. "He did."

Zoe put her hands on her hips. "A trick, Milo? Like the Invasion? Maybe. But then how do you explain this?"

She signaled to a group just below her. Three figures detached themselves from the crowd in which they'd been hiding and stepped up to the tier where Zoe stood. They turned to face Milo.

And Josh saw Kim, Paravi, and Ryan O'Bannion.

Matt and Kyle cried out to their brother, and Miguel and Tish screamed the girls' names. A shocked babble of voices rolled across the stands, all eyes locked on the three returned Scouts.

Milo stood a little straighter, then climbed up on the speaker's podium and repeated the astonishing words.

"It's another trick!" he shouted. "The Scouts . . . they've been in on it with Shadow from the beginning. And the others, they're not from Outside. There is no colony!"

The crowd went silent.

"Protectors!" he cried. "Go after them! Bring them down to their Ghoulie friends!"

No one moved. No one except Josh.

Dropping his sword, he sprinted to the side of the stadium, breaking through a row of Protectors who no longer tried to stop him. He leaped over the low wall at the edge of the field and began pushing through the crowd toward the Emperor's Box, shoving aside anyone in his way.

"Stay back!" cried Milo.

Josh burst into the box, striding up to Milo, forcing him backward and screaming in his face.

"It's over, Milo! Everyone knows." He grabbed the boy's shoulders, slamming him against the side of the box. "It's over!"

"No!" said Milo desperately. "No, it's not."

"It is for you." Josh grabbed the trident out of Milo's hand and lifted it over his head. Then he smashed it down on the edge of the box, cracking it in two.

Milo cried out, stumbling forward. He stared at the broken scepter, shaking.

"The King is dead," said Josh, turning to face the rest of the Core. "And so are all of you."

SECOND EXODUS

Josh grasped the two sections of the broken trident and turned toward the spectators, holding the pieces high over his head. A wild cheer rose around him—from the Ghoulies in the field, from Matt and Kyle's Defenders, from scattered pockets of Islanders around the stadium.

The rest of the crowd remained silent, watching. Then, heads down, they began creeping from their seats, moving in dazed confusion toward the exits. They kept their faces turned away from those who were still in the field, too ashamed to look at them.

Josh looked once more at the Core. Moira was staring at Milo—her expression a mix of horror and disgust. Evan and Eli were backing away from both of them, and Toad had already left the box—Josh saw him scurrying toward one of the exits.

Josh no longer cared about them. He threw down the broken trident, jumped the wall of the box, and began scrambling across the stands, sprinting toward Zoe, who was leaping down the stadium tiers like a two-legged gazelle. They slammed into each other, Josh almost knocking her over. He grabbed her, kissed her, squeezed her so hard she gasped for breath.

"So this is the better idea you came up with?" he asked her finally.

"Yeah," she said. "What do you think?"

"Not bad."

"Josh! Zoe!" Sam, Maddie, and Devon were catapulting toward them. Devon was struggling to carry Shana, and Maddie was dragging Giz, who was running so fast his limp was almost invisible. A moment later, Josh and Zoe were buried in a tangle of arms and legs.

Josh hugged his sister tightly. "I'm so proud of you, Bratty. You stayed strong."

"So did you," she said. "You're a hero!"

"Zoe is, too," yelled Sam. "And she's MY SISTER!"

Giz looked at Zoe and Josh solemnly. "I knew you weren't bad guys!" he confided. "No matter what the stupid King said."

Josh laughed, then turned to look down at the stadium floor. The missing Scouts were already there, hurtling toward the center of the field. Tish and Miguel grabbed Kim and Paravi. The four of them spun around, screaming, and then melted into a tight knot, arms around each other.

Matt and Kyle barreled toward Ryan like football tackles. The three of them crashed to the ground, yelling and punching and yanking each other's hair. And then, finally, they were hugging. A few seconds of that, though, and Ryan started pounding both brothers on the head.

Josh smiled.

Shadow appeared next to him, noiseless as always. He nodded at Zoe and the rest of their family, then looked at Josh. They clasped each other's arms, unable to speak.

Shana looked at Shadow hesitantly. "Is *he* the bogeyman?"

Shadow smiled and crouched down next to her. "No, I'm not the bogeyman. I'm Seth. Nice to meet you."

Shana reserved judgment.

"You're Josh, I presume?"

It was Amina, with a few of her companions. Josh nodded.

"I've heard a lot about you." She glanced at Shadow. "You, too."

Shadow looked at Zoe, one eyebrow raised. She shrugged, smiling.

"Thanks for what you did," said Josh. "For coming with Zoe, and bringing the others. Another minute or two . . ."

"I know," said Amina. "We saw."

Josh took a deep breath.

"So," he said. "What do we do next?"

Zoe nodded at Amina and her companions. "Amina said some of the Islanders can go with them, to their colony."

"Some?"

"Our village can't hold everyone from your Islands," said Amina. "It's big, but not big enough. We'll take in who we can, though, and give the rest food and as many weapons as we can spare."

"But—"

"Don't worry. We've sent messengers to some of the other colonies, telling them that more settlers are on the way."

"Wait," said Josh. "What other colonies?"

Zoe looked triumphant. "There are a lot of them, Amina said. Set up anyplace people can feel safe—gated neighborhoods, malls, anyplace with walls."

"We need the walls to protect ourselves," said Amina, answering Josh's question before he could ask it. "From the thieves and wolf packs and crazies."

Now Shadow looked surprised. "I didn't know there were wolves around here."

"Just human ones," said Amina. "Gangs that go around attacking the smaller colonies. They live in one for a while, use up all the supplies, and then move on to the next."

So Outside has its monsters, too, thought Josh. He thought about Maddie and the other kidlets, wondering what kind of a world he'd be taking them into. Then he looked back at Amina.

"Who decides?" he asked finally. "I mean, who decides which people go to Tumaini?"

Amina looked at him, and then at Zoe and Shadow. "I think you do. You and your friends."

Before another week passed, the second exodus began. Amina's group led the way, having stayed on the Islands to help organize the departure. Everyone who was leaving wore an overstuffed backpack and carried several bags of blankets and clothes, or pushed strollers full of essential supplies.

In one group were those chosen to go to Tumaini. Although Josh and the O'Bannions had been tempted to reward only those who had supported the resistance, Tish argued that they had to think beyond that, to consider those who'd be less likely to survive on their own. They also needed to choose kids who had skills to offer, and who could contribute to their new home.

Several other groups would stop briefly at Tumaini, then continue on to other colonies. These groups, too, were carefully selected to include a mix of kids from all the Islands, and a diverse set of talents and abilities. It was a little odd to see Timescapers and Brainiacs walking alongside pierced, tatooed Ghoulies, but the combination would make for stronger communities.

A final group, more ambitious and adventurous, had decided to head out on their own to establish a new colony. Not surprisingly, the O'Bannion Boys were the ones behind the idea, and Greg had immediately signed on. The four of them invited some of their pals from Timescape, as well as a few of the geniuses from Inspiration Island.

Paravi joined up, too, which surprised no one—she and Ryan O'Bannion had returned from the Outside as more than fellow Scouts. Then Miguel volunteered, his experience as a hero making him eager for new adventures, new adversaries to overcome. And since Miguel was going, Kim figured she might as well go, too. A new colony would need someone good at inventing.

The last to approach them was Aiko, who asked the brothers if they would please take her with them. She could show them how to bring along some of the movable hydroponic systems, she said, and teach them how to maintain them.

The O'Bannions looked at one another.

"Why not?" said Ryan. "Everyone deserves a second chance."

"Not everyone," said Matt.

"Well, most people, anyhow."

Kyle shook his head. "Yeah? Well, what about—"

"Shut up," said Ryan, "and keep loading the tools." He looked at Aiko. "You're in." She smiled gratefully.

Zoe, Josh, and Tish stood with their kidlets on the beach, watching the first of the Islanders file toward the monorail tracks.

"You guys really okay with Tumaini?" Josh asked. "There's still time to change our minds, go with one of the other groups."

"Amina said they don't have teachers," said Tish. "And with Ari and Lana bringing all the Little Wizards there, I think they're going to need some. So I'm good."

"Me, too," said Zoe. "Besides, what I really want to do is find where the glow came from. It wasn't from any of the colonies Amina knows about, and that's where I want to end up. So wherever we stay now is probably just temporary."

Josh shook his head. Zoe was never going to take the easy route to anything.

Now Shadow and Cassandra arrived. Cassandra was wearing

jeans and a windbreaker—the only thing unusual about her now was her long white hair. Shadow, though, still looked every bit the Ghoulie leader, solemn and somewhat sinister. Josh was surprised.

"I thought you were going to be Seth again."

"Changed my mind."

"Why?"

Cassandra smiled. "I prefer him this way."

Josh returned the smile. "So what did you two decide? Where you headed?"

"Nowhere," said Shadow.

"And everywhere," added Cassandra.

Zoe shook her head. "Why can't you guys ever talk like normal people?"

Shadow actually laughed. "Habit. But what we mean is, the two of us decided we weren't comfortable choosing one place. So we'll move from colony to colony, watching and listening. Seeing what people have done. It should be very interesting."

"So maybe we'll still see you?" asked Josh.

"You will. I'll make sure of it."

Josh nodded. And then, suddenly, he felt the old, prickling sensation that told him he was being watched.

He looked back at the Coral Palace, now faded and pock-marked, its fragile spires crumbled and revealing the wirework beneath. It was the one structure that wasn't empty. Josh saw flickers of movement inside and peered at the Palace more closely. And then he saw them.

Silhouetted in the windows, peering from behind doorways and turrets, were the ones who weren't leaving, who had not been invited to join any of the new colonies. They had wanted the Islands to be their world, and now they would be. Or they could venture Outside alone, with no help from anyone else.

A single figure emerged from the inner rooms. Milo walked out onto Neptune's balcony, the top of the broken trident grasped tightly in one hand. He moved to the edge of the platform, gazing out over the ruined buildings, the dead gardens, the broken streets. And then he looked down at the empty courtyard, raised his scepter, and began to speak.

Watching him, Josh realized that, at least in his mind, Milo was still who he wanted to be. Who perhaps now he always would be.

King of the Isles of Wonder.